A Deadly Vineyard Holiday

G·K
Hall
&Cº

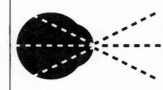

This Large Print Book carries the
Seal of Approval of N.A.V.H.

A Deadly Vineyard Holiday

A Martha's Vineyard Mystery

Philip R. Craig

G.K. Hall & Co.
Thorndike, Maine

Published in 1997 by arrangement with Scribner, an imprint of Simon & Schuster, Inc.

G.K. Hall Large Print Core Collection.

The text of this Large Print edition is unabridged.
Other aspects of the book may vary from the original edition.

Set in 16 pt. Plantin by Minnie B. Raven.

Printed in the United States on permanent paper.

Library of Congress Cataloging in Publication Data

Craig, Philip R., 1933–
    A deadly vineyard holiday : a Martha's Vineyard mystery /
Philip R. Craig.
        p.   cm.
    ISBN 0-7838-8278-5 (lg. print : hc : alk. paper)
    1. Large type books.   I. Title.
[PS3553.R23D42   1997b]
813'.54—dc21   97-18108

For my daughter-in-law,
Gail Gardner Craig,
who has walked the golden sands
and breathed the sea-clean air.

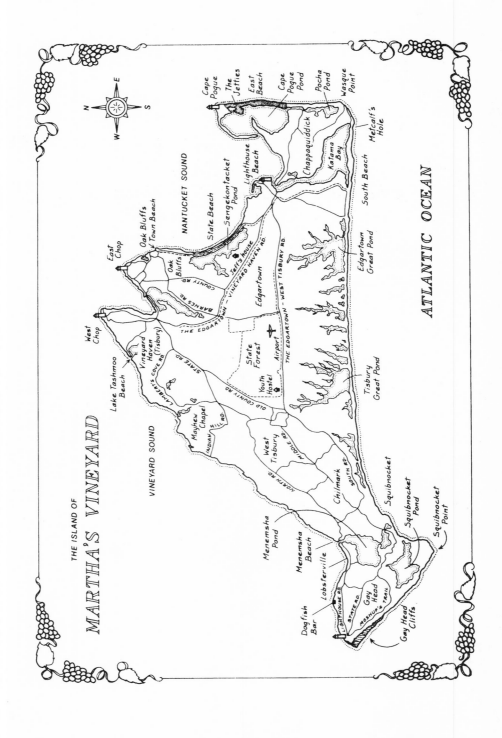

THE ISLAND OF
MARTHA'S VINEYARD

". . . Three things that all ways threaten a
    man's peace
And one before the end shall overthrow his
    mind:
Either illness or age or the edge of vengence
Shall draw out the breath of the doom-
    shadowed."

— Lines 69–72,
"The Seafarer"

1

It was almost five o'clock when I saw the girl coming down the beach from the west. The sun wasn't up yet, but the sky was brightening, and there was enough light for me to see my treble-hooked redheaded Roberts hit the water out beyond the breakers. I had been there since a bit after three, and had four pretty good fish for my efforts. As the girl came up, I hooked another.

She stood by my old Land Cruiser and watched as I brought the fish in, and when I carried it up to the truck, I got my first real look at her. She seemed no different from a lot of other teenage girls on Martha's Vineyard in August. She was wearing a T-shirt and shorts, and was carrying a pair of pink sneakers in her hand. A sweatshirt was tied around her neck. I wondered what she was doing out on the beach alone at that hour of the morning.

"That's a nice fish," she said. "What kind is it?"

I got the lure out of the fish's mouth, and added it to the other four in the fishbox. "Blue-fish. They don't have any business being here

9

this time of year, but they're here anyway, so I'm getting them while I can. You a fisherperson?"

She shook her head. "I've gone crabbing with a net."

"Bluefish give you a real tussle," I said. "They're fun to catch."

"It looks like it. What are you going to do with all the ones you've got here?"

"I'll take one home for Zee and me, and sell the rest."

"Are they good to eat?"

"They are, indeed. You've never had bluefish? How have you managed to live on Martha's Vineyard and not eat bluefish at least once?"

She shrugged and gave a small smile. "I don't live here. I'm just visiting." She glanced west along the beach, then turned back and reached out a hand toward the fishbox. "Can I touch one?"

"That last fish is still alive, so don't let him get hold of your fingers. Bluefish have teeth like little razors."

She touched the fish and it flopped and thrashed. She jerked her hand back and laughed. "It must be fun to catch a fish like that one!"

There was an odd combination of sophistication and innocence about the girl, and, being just about old enough to be her father, I tried to imagine what it would be like to watch other people fish and not know how to do it myself. But I had been fishing as long as I could remember, thanks to my own father, who had gotten a rod into my hands before I could read.

"You want to give it a try?" I asked.

Her eyes widened. "Yes!"

I got my spare rod off the roof rack and put a Ballistic Missile on the leader.

"This is a good casting plug," I said. "And the bluefish love it."

We went down to the water, and I showed her how to throw the bail on her reel, to hook the line on her trigger finger, to take the rod straight back, and to bring it straight forward, releasing the line at about a 45-degree angle to the horizon.

Then I made a couple of casts, showing her how it was done, and gave her the rod.

"Don't try to cast too far, at first. Just concentrate on throwing straight out. And don't worry about making mistakes. Everybody makes them."

"Okay." She threw the bail, hooked the line with her finger, and took the rod back. Her first cast went into the surf right at her feet.

"You didn't release the line in time," I said, as I walked back to the truck for my own rod.

She nodded, and reeled in and made another cast. Straight up into the air. She looked around. "Where did it go, where did it go?" It landed beside her. She jumped.

"You released too soon," I said, coming back to the water. "Try again. Be patient." I made my cast, and my Roberts went far out, where I wanted it to go.

Beside me, the girl made her third cast, and

this time it went out into the breakers. She reeled in, looking intent, and cast again.

We fished there for perhaps fifteen minutes, and I got a sixth fish. She watched as I brought the fish in about halfway, her eyes bright.

"You want to bring him the rest of the way?" I asked. "They're out beyond your cast, so you probably won't hook one of your own this morning, but we'll trade rods, if you want, so you'll know what it's like to try to land one."

"Yes! But what if I lose him?"

"Then you can talk about the one that got away. Don't worry about it. Everybody loses fish."

"But he's your fish."

"He isn't anybody's fish until you land him. Here." I took her rod and gave her mine. The fish almost pulled her into the water, but she hung on with both hands. "Keep the line tight, or he'll throw the lure. Get the butt of the rod between your legs, and do like you saw me do. Haul back on the rod, then reel down and haul back again. When you get him to the beach, back up and pull him ashore."

She did that, and slowly the fish came in, swirling and fighting. I stood and watched her. Her face was flushed, and her teeth were hard together, but there was a wild joy in her expression. She got the fish to the shore and backed up fast, pulling it, flopping, twisting, up and away from the water.

"I got him! I got him!"

"You got him. Now let me get him."

I hooked my hand into the fish's gills and carried it, thrashing and still fighting, to the truck, where I got the lure out of its mouth and dumped it in the fishbox.

"Congratulations," I said. "You just landed yourself your first bluefish."

Her face was full of excitement. "I'm so tired! I thought I'd never be able to land him! I'm so happy he wasn't bigger, or I might not have been able to get him in!"

"Your surf-casting muscles just aren't in shape yet. You do this for a couple of weeks, and you'll be able to land a whale."

She grinned. "This one seemed like a whale. How much does he weigh?"

I got out the scales, and hung the still flopping fish on the hook. "Eight pounds, more or less."

"Wow!"

Then she looked past me, toward the west, and the joy went out of her face. She leaned her rod against the Land Cruiser. "I've got to go," she said, starting east. "How far is it to Edgartown?"

"About four miles," I said, turning to look where she had looked. Half a mile away, a Jeep was coming along the beach, its headlights still on in spite of the brightening morning. I watched it approach, wondering what it was about that Jeep that had swept the happiness from the girl's face.

When I turned back, she was gone.

I put the fish back in the fishbox, put the girl's

rod on the roof rack, then walked back down to the water. When the Jeep pulled up and stopped, I was making a cast. When I glanced behind me, two men were out of the Jeep, looking inside my truck, and a man and a woman were walking down toward me. They were all wearing informal clothes, but somehow they seemed to be wearing suits. A bit of wind lifted a shirttail, and I saw a hip holster. I reeled in the Roberts. No bluefish took it.

"Excuse me," said the man who had come down to the water. "Have you been here long?" He was powerfully built and looked to be a very fit fifty or so.

"Long enough to catch those fish your friends are looking at."

"How long is that?" asked the woman.

I looked at her. There was anxiety in her eyes, and suspicion in her voice.

I felt pushed, and irritation fluttered somewhere in my soul. But I remembered the hip holster, so I said, "I got here about three hours ago."

Beyond her, the two men at the Land Cruiser were looking under it and opening a door to look inside. I decided to ignore the hip holster, even though I suspected that where there was one, there were probably more.

"You're just here to fish?" asked the man.

"Yeah. Excuse me." I caught the swinging lure, put the rod on my shoulder, and walked up to the truck. The men there paused and looked at me with hard eyes. The anxiety I'd seen in the woman's face was in theirs too.

"I don't think you'll find anything in there worth stealing," I said, pushing the open door shut.

Neither of the men seemed impressed by my snappy dialogue.

"You see anybody come by here?" asked the closer of the two.

"I've fished this beach for thirty years," I said. "I've seen a lot of people come by here in that time. Right now I see you. And a minute ago I saw you in my truck."

Behind me, the man and the woman came up. Four people with pistols, and me with a fishing rod.

"You're in trouble, mister," said the closest man. "Don't give me any more lip. Just answer my question."

I felt my temper taking over. "You have a badge or something, or are you just a hoodlum with a gun and a loud mouth?"

His hand went to his back and came out with a pair of cuffs. "That does it," he said. "You're dead meat."

I let go of the Roberts that I'd been holding against my rod, and its treble hook swung by his nose. He ducked back.

"Now, let's hold everything," said the man behind me. "Ted, put those cuffs away. Mister, grab that plug before somebody gets hooked with it. Here, take a look at this."

15

He held out his ID. I hooked the Roberts behind a guide and took the card: WALTER POMERLIEU, SECRET SERVICE. I gave it back.

He nodded. "Yeah. All of us."

I pointed a thumb over my shoulder toward Ted. "Even him?"

Pomerlieu nodded. "Even him. You know who we are now. Who are you?"

"His name's Jackson," said Ted. "It's on his registration."

I glanced at him. "Don't jump to conclusions, Ted," I said. "Maybe I stole this truck."

Ted's eyes narrowed, and he stepped forward.

"Stop," said Pomerlieu. Ted stopped.

"It's good to know that Ted can read," I said to Pomerlieu. "Otherwise I'd be seriously worried about our national security. I'm J. W. Jackson, and nobody, not even me, would steal this truck. What's going on?"

"We're looking for a girl," said Pomerlieu. "Teenager. You see her come by this way?"

"Hell, Walt, he may be one of them that took her!" said the woman. "What's he doing here all alone on the beach? If he's just a fisherman, why aren't there other fishermen here, too?"

"Yeah," said Ted. "What's this guy really doing here? Pretty coincidental, isn't it? The girl's gone and this guy's here. I think we should take him in. He may be able to tell us a lot."

"You're a pretty pair," I said. I dug out my wallet and gave my license to Pomerlieu. "There. That's me, and that's where I live. You want to

16

check me out, call the chief of police in Edgartown. Who's the girl?" I knew who the girl had
to be, because there couldn't be any other girl
on Martha's Vineyard who'd have four Secret
Service agents looking for her. But I thought I'd
ask, just to see what they would say.

"Never mind who the girl is," said Ted. "Just
tell us if you've seen her."

Pomerlieu handed my license back. "We will
check you out," he said. "It's our job. Now do
tell me, please, if the girl came by while you were
here. It's important."

I thought he was right. "Yeah," I said, "she
came by. She hung around awhile, then asked
me how far it was to Edgartown, and headed east
along the beach. I got the idea that it was seeing
your Jeep that sent her on her way."

Everyone looked east. There was no one in
sight.

The woman wore a worried, angry face. "If she
didn't go until she saw our Jeep, that means she
was here just a few minutes ago. If she went that
way, where is she?" She turned to me. "If you're
lying . . ."

"What? Will my pants catch on fire? She
started that way, and the next time I looked, she
was out of sight."

The woman came close. "If you know anything
you haven't told us, you'd better tell us now."

"I know one thing," I said. "I don't care for
you or your friend Ted very much, and I'm
beginning to understand why the girl decided to

17

take off. Living with either one of you two all the time would drive anybody away!"

"All of you! Stop it!" said Pomerlieu. "East, you say."

"That's what I said."

"Come on," he said to the others. "We'll go east."

Ted hesitated, then got into the Jeep. He waved a finger at me. "I'll find you again, if I need to."

"I'm in the book. I'm not hard to find."

The woman was looking at me as they drove away.

The fish were probably gone, but my nerves needed to settle. I wondered why it was that some people rubbed each other wrong from day one. The woman, Ted, and I seemed to be like flint and steel. Sparks just naturally flew when we were together.

I went down to the water and made a couple of dozen casts. No fish took my lure, but the tension went out of me, and I felt better. I don't like to be angry.

I put the rod on the roof rack and drove east into the rising sun, following the tracks of Pomerlieu's Jeep. When I got to the Herring Creek parking lot, I shifted into two-wheel drive and headed north, past the airport. I didn't see the girl or the Jeep, and wasn't sure I wanted to.

The market wasn't open yet, so I drove through the almost empty streets of Edgartown and on north to Ocean Heights, where I turned down our long, sandy driveway and followed it into our yard.

When I opened the back of the truck to get at the fish, the tarp in front of the fishbox moved. As I reached for the tarp, I knew what I'd find: trouble, in the shape of a teenage girl.

I pulled the tarp away and looked at her. She brushed at her eyes and hair. Then the president's daughter smiled at me, and climbed out of the truck.

2

The first time the president of the United States vacationed on Martha's Vineyard, the island sank six inches into the sea from the combined weight of Secret Service agents and media people.

The *Vineyard Gazette,* normally fairly disinterested in the rich and famous who abound on the island, brought out a special edition, the Boston and Cape Cod papers were full of presidential stories, and both local and national television news programs were replete with scenes from the Vineyard. Hotel rooms on the island and even over on Cape Cod became unavailable to ordinary folk, as they filled with reporters, photographers, and government agents. The presidential car, a dull-colored, bulletproof Suburban, arrived, along with the dozens of other vehicles that were needed to form the caravan that went wherever the great man went, and to ferry security and other political personnel back and forth.

Groupies of both political parties gathered at the airport to greet the airplane that brought the president and his family to Edgartown, and later worked hard to be where he and his wife or their daughter might show up, in public or private places. Among the social elite, much maneuvering took place as dinners, cocktail parties, and other such functions were arranged.

All in all, if you listened to the news, or watched it, or read the newspapers and magazines, you would have thought that the Vineyard had been turned quite upside down by the president's two weeks on the island, and that most island lives had been altered dramatically by his presence.

In fact, had it not been for the media coverage, most people on the Vineyard wouldn't have been aware that the president was even there. He and his family stayed in a house down a long drive that was well protected by Secret Service agents, and his appearances in public places were generally unannounced, so that even if some people wished to see him, touch him, talk to him, they wouldn't have been in the right spot to do it.

And most people, at least the people I knew, didn't want to do that anyway. Their general attitude was that the guy and his family needed a vacation, and that the best thing to do was let them have one by staying out of their lives.

That was again our plan when the First Family made a second vacation visit to the Vineyard. But life is what happens when you plan something else, and now chance had intervened, and I had a problem.

"Hi," said the girl, dusting herself off and looking around. "Is this your house?"

"It is. What were you doing in my truck? I thought you were walking to Edgartown."

"Well," she said, "I saw how close the Jeep was, and I knew they'd probably catch up with me if I went on down the beach, so I ducked up behind a sand dune till they were gone. Then while you were fishing, I snuck into the truck. I figured since they'd looked there once, they wouldn't look there again. How far is it to Edgartown from here?"

"About as far as the last time you asked me," I said, putting my mouth in gear while I tried to get my brain started. "Since you're here, you want to give me a hand? There's a freezer on the porch there, and I need more ice to keep these fish cool till I can get them to the market. There's a bucket by the freezer. Bring a bucket of ice and we'll put it over the fish."

"Sure."

She went up through the screen door onto the porch, and I did some fast thinking.

When she came back with the ice, I dumped it into the fishbox and looked at my watch. "Breakfast time. You hungry?"

She looked hungry but wary. "I'd better be going. Which way is town?"

"Up the driveway and take a left. I'm J. W. Jackson. What do people call you?"

She lied. "I'm Mary Jones."

"No, you're not," I said. "You're Cricket Callahan, but if you want me to call you Mary Jones, it's okay with me. Whatever I call you, let me

22

tell you something: If you plan on going into town and having nobody recognize you, especially this time of the morning, and more especially with God only knows how many Secret Service agents and cops in a panic to find you, you'd better plan again."

She looked angry, but not surprised by my comment. "That's the trouble," she said. "I can never get away from them. It's like being in a zoo!"

I remembered the one interesting article I'd read about her family's first visit to the island. It was a compilation of remarks from island kids her age who'd been asked what they thought about her vacationing here. Every one of the kids had felt sorry for her because she could never be free from prying cameras and security.

"You're away from them now," I said. "But you can't just run off like this. Your parents will be worried sick." To say nothing of Walt Pomerlieu, Ted, and company. I could imagine the thoughts, fears, and actions that must already be ruining their day.

"My parents aren't even awake yet," said the girl, still angry but wavering.

"Don't bet on that," I said. "How old are you?"

"I'm sixteen. What difference does it make?"

"It means you're old enough to understand the situation we're in. I'll give you the bad part first: You're the daughter of the president of the United States, and as far as everybody up at that house where you're staying is concerned, you've disappeared. Since you've been gone quite awhile, I'm pretty sure somebody's screwed his courage to the sticking point and told your folks by now. And because you're missing, a lot of people there are going to suspect the worst. And at least four of those people are probably thinking that I have something to do with your disappearance. And they're right, thanks to this ride you just took in my truck. So I imagine I'll be having visitors before long, and when they get here, they're going to be relieved to find out you haven't been kidnapped or killed by some loony or loonies, but they're also going to be pretty pissed off, and some of them will be sure that somehow or other I was involved with your taking off in the first place. You have not done me any favors by coming home with me this way."

She brushed her hair away from her brow. "I never thought of that. I'm sorry. I'll wait, and when they get here, I'll tell them what happened. I'm really sorry." She pushed some remaining bit of her childhood away from her, and its loss bothered me.

"On the bright side," I said, "they aren't here yet. You have a little time to yourself, and I plan on mixing up some blueberry pancakes for breakfast. You a pancake eater?"

"I'm not hungry."

"You ever make pancakes?"

"No."

"It's time you learned. You can help in the

kitchen. Come on in. The smell of breakfast cooking will wake Zee up, and she'll eat with us."

"Who's Zee?"

"Zee is my wife. Last night she worked until midnight, so she missed this morning's fishing expedition. But she'll get up for your blueberry pancakes."

We went inside, and she paused in the living room and looked around. Her eyes fell on the coffee table.

"What's this?"

"That's a padlock in a vise, and those things are lock picks. I'm still trying to learn how to use them. I play around with them sometimes when I'm sitting on the couch. It beats watching TV."

"Are you a locksmith?"

"No, but I've always wanted to know how to pick locks. I can pick some now, but I still don't have the magic touch."

She picked up our copy of *Pistoleer* and looked at the cover. Zee, 380 Beretta in her hand, smiled back at her. Zee, who had come in fourth in the women's division of a pistol competition she and Manny Fonseca, her instructor, had attended, had come in first in the looks department and had made the cover. Sexism at its best.

The girl put down the magazine, and we went into the kitchen, where I got out the pancake makings.

"I don't know," said the girl. "I've never done this before."

"You never landed a bluefish before this morning, either, but you managed that. You can do this, too. It's good to know how to cook. It makes you more self-sufficient. Besides, you can cook the stuff you really like to eat whenever you want to."

I gave her the mixing bowl, and she went to work while I got the coffee started and set the table for three. Before I was through, Zee came out of the bedroom, wrapping her robe around herself, looking like Aurora. She smiled brightly at me and then a little less brightly at the girl.

"Good morning. I smell breakfast."

She came to me and gave me a first-of-the-day kiss. Then she looked again at the girl. Then she looked yet again, then lifted her eyes to mine. Hers were wide.

"She tells me her name is Mary Jones," I said. "We met on the beach, and she followed me home. Now she's trying her hand at pancakes. You can join us as a member of the experimental eating group."

The girl took a breath. "I'm not really Mary Jones," she said. "I'm somebody else."

"You're Cricket," said Zee. "I've seen your picture."

Cricket Callahan nodded. "I'm Cricket."

"She stepped out of her house for some fresh air," I said. "Before she goes home, we decided we'd eat. Cricket, this is my wife, Zee."

Cricket gave Zee a good look. "Oh," she said. "You're the model. You're on the cover of that magazine in there. Or are you a movie star or something?"

"I'm not a model or a movie star," said Zee. "I'm a nurse up at the Vineyard hospital."

"She just looks like a movie star," I said to Cricket. "Now, while you two tend to the vittles, I'm going to make a phone call to let your folks know where you are and that you're okay. By that time, we'll be ready to put on the feed bag."

"Okay," said the girl with a sigh. "I guess that's what you have to do. But I wish you didn't."

I went into the living room and phoned the chief of the Edgartown police at his home. His wife, Annie, answered and told me he'd gotten a call early and was at the station.

Terrific. I could imagine what the call was about. I phoned the station. The chief was busy. I told the officer to interrupt him, especially if he was talking with some Secret Service people.

She said, "Wait a minute," and went away. Not much later, the chief was on the phone.

"What?"

"Cricket Callahan is cooking blueberry pancakes at my place with Zee and me." I told him how it had come about. "She's fine, and in no danger whatsoever," I said. "Tell whoever comes to get her to be quiet about it. I don't want a Normandy invasion down here. Get in touch with an agent named Walter Pomerlieu. He seems to have his head screwed on straighter than some other feds I've met."

"He's right here," said the chief. "I'll give him

your message. Don't let the girl leave."

"I don't keep prisoners or slaves," I said. "I won't tie her to a tree, but I think she'll still be here when her keepers show up. Tell Pomerlieu we plan to finish breakfast before he takes her home."

I rang off and got back to the kitchen in time for my first stack of pancakes. I smeared them with butter and maple syrup and took a bite. Cricket, the breakfast chef, watched, her head slightly tipped to one side. Zee looked at both of us.

I chewed, swallowed, took a sip of coffee, and nodded. "Good."

Cricket smiled. Then she looked at Zee. "You want some?"

"Does a wolf bay at the moon?" Zee sat down and slipped two pancakes from the tray onto her plate.

Cricket poured batter into the frying pan and added more cakes to the tray as they came out of the pan. Then, while she ate, I cooked. Between her and Zee, the pancakes disappeared rapidly. When the last cake was on the tray, I heard a car coming down the driveway. I put the cake on Cricket's plate. "Eat it up. That'll be your father's people, come to take you home to your folks."

"I don't want to go home," said Cricket. "I like it here, where there aren't any people watching everything I do."

Zee put a hand on her arm. "You can come

back anytime you want to."

Cricket looked at me as I got up. "Maybe we can go fishing again?"

"Why not?" I said. "You seem to have the makings of an island girl: You can land a bluefish and cook up a damned good pancake. That's more than a lot of people can manage."

I went outside as the chief's cruiser and a second car pulled into the yard and stopped. Out of the backseat popped Ted and the woman I'd seen on the beach that morning. Out of the front seat, more slowly, climbed Pomerlieu and the chief.

Ted and the woman flashed their eyes all around them, taking in the house, the shed, the yard, and the gardens with sweeping glances. Then they looked at me. They were not smiling.

"I think you all know each other," said the chief.

I gestured toward the woman. "I've met Ted, but not his pal, there."

"Agent Joan Lonergan," said the woman, ignoring my sass. "Is Cricket here?"

"Inside, polishing off the last pancake. Go on in. You'll find my wife there, too. Her name's Zee."

Pomerlieu nodded and Joan Lonergan went into the house. Then Pomerlieu came closer to me and said, "I know you told the chief, but now tell me. How did she end up here? You said she walked away down the beach."

"And no lies this time," said Ted.

I looked at Ted, then back at Pomerlieu. "We have a leash law in Edgartown," I said. "Dogs aren't supposed to run loose. Curb yours."

Ted made a noise that actually did sound like one a dog might make.

"Back off, Ted," said Pomerlieu. "And you, Mr. Jackson, I suggest that you try not to make enemies if you don't have to. Ted, here, had the duty when the girl slipped out. He takes his job seriously, and he has a suspicious mind, which goes with his work. He's a little tense right now."

"He can relax," I said. "The girl's fine. Nobody lured her away. She just has a case of cabin fever." I told him the story I'd told the chief. "I think she just wants to be able to live like an ordinary girl," I said, "instead of like a piece of public property."

"I don't blame her for that," said Pomerlieu, "but the fact is that she's not just an ordinary girl. She's the daughter of the president of the United States, and there are people loose out there who would like nothing better than to get their hands on her."

The driver of the second car got out and looked at Pomerlieu. Pomerlieu nodded and two women got out of the car. I had never seen the younger woman, but I recognized the older one. It was Cricket's mother, Myra Callahan. Both of them were dressed in their Vineyard vacation clothes, and both looked simultaneously worried and relieved. As well they might, I thought, anticipating how I might someday feel if my teenage daughter took off during the night and was found the next day with two strangers in an old hunting camp in the woods.

Followed by the younger woman, Myra Callahan came to us. She had a firm stride. "You must be Mr. Jackson. I'm Myra Callahan." She put out her hand and smiled a smile I imagined she must have smiled thousands of times during her husband's political career. The smile didn't reach her sharp lawyer's eyes.

I shook the hand. It was the first White House hand that had ever taken mine. "Your daughter's inside having breakfast with my wife," I said.

But when I turned, I saw that I was wrong. Joan Lonergan, Cricket, and Zee had come out onto the porch. Myra Callahan's hard eyes grew softer. She went past me.

"Cricket, you had us all worried." Then, "You must be Mrs. Jackson. I'm Myra Callahan. I'm afraid my daughter has taken advantage of your hospitality."

"Not a bit," said Zee, holding her robe together with one hand and shaking hands with the other. "Cricket's earned her keep by catching fish and cooking breakfast."

I thought of what Pomerlieu had just said, and felt sorry for all of the Callahans. Fame alone can make you someone's target. Fortunately, most criminals, including would-be assassins and kidnappers, aren't too bright. If a lot of the wacky people out there were as smart as they are venomous and mad, more well-known people would be damaged or dead.

"Sorry, Mom," said Cricket. "I shouldn't have let you worry. I just wasn't thinking."

Her mother sighed. "I know it's hard for you, dear. Well, no damage done."

"Where's Dad?"

"Your father decided to make his morning run as usual, so all of the reporters would be watching him instead of me when I came here. We weren't sure Mr. and Mrs. Jackson would want the media on their doorstep."

"You can be sure we don't," said Zee. "Thanks."

Myra Callahan was looking around. At the old hunting camp that was our house; at the balcony on top of the screened porch; at the flowers along the fences, in the window boxes and hanging pots, in the half barrels, and in front of the house; at the vegetable garden; at the shed out back and the corral, which housed my wheelbarrow, trash cans, and other gear too bulky to be put inside; and at Sengekontacket Pond and Nantucket Sound out to the east, beyond the garden.

"This is nice," she said unexpectedly. "My dad used to take us up to a lake when we were kids. We stayed in a place like this. We didn't have electricity or running water. There was a hand pump in the kitchen and kerosene lamps and an outhouse in back. It was wonderful."

"This place was like that when my dad bought it," I said. "He put in electricity and running water. We even have two showers, one inside for wintertime, and one outside for the rest of the year. Come in, if you'd like."

"I'd love to."

Zee stepped aside, and Myra Callahan went into the house. Cricket had a surprised look on her face. "Gosh, Mom, you never told me about that cabin."

"I think I should have. This brings it all back."

In the living room, Myra Callahan looked at the fishing rods hanging from the ceiling, at the Norwegian wood-burning stove I'd installed beside the fireplace, at the lock and lock picks on the coffee table, at the gun cabinet, at the two best decoys my father had carved, and at the pictures amid the books and maps and charts and other mementos that lined the walls.

"My gosh, it really is an old hunting camp."

She picked up the copy of *Pistoleer* and looked at Zee's picture, then at Zee herself.

"You shoot?"

Zee waved an airy hand. "It was my first competition. I came in fourth."

"First in the eyes of the cameraman, though. And I can see why."

"Thank you," said Zee, who had come to accept that people believed her to be beautiful, but who could never understand why. I sometimes wondered who she saw in her mirror.

We went into the kitchen, and Myra Callahan looked at the pots hanging from the ceiling and at the magnet-held cartoons and messages on the refrigerator. A couple of the cartoons were about

33

her husband. She grinned when she saw them.

"I'm afraid the dishes aren't done yet," said Zee. "We just finished breakfast. Cricket made the pancakes. She can cook for us anytime."

"The stove uses bottled gas," I said. "We like gas for cooking, and if the electricity goes off during a storm, we still have the stove. We've got a portable generator, too, to run the water pump and the freezer and the refrigerators, if need be."

"*Refrigerators* plural? There's only one in here."

"There's another one out on the porch beside the freezer. A little one just for beer."

"Just for beer?"

"And soft drinks."

We showed her the spare bedroom, where we kept the rest of the decoys my father had carved.

"For guests," said Zee, gesturing at the twin beds.

"Or children," said Myra Callahan.

Zee gave her a quick glance, and we went up onto the balcony and looked out over the garden and Sengekontacket Pond to Nantucket Sound. It was too early in the day for the August people to be over there on the barrier beach between the pond and the sound, but there were already some sailboats moving across the far water in front of the soft morning wind, heading who knew where.

"Isn't it beautiful?" said Cricket. "It's so quiet. I wish we were in a place like this."

Her mother nodded almost dreamily. "I know what you mean. I'd forgotten how wonderful it was to be at the cabin. I think I had more fun there than . . ." She came back to the present. "But I'm afraid it's not possible, dear. Besides, in only a few days you have to be back in Washington to start school."

I looked at Zee and saw in her face a sympathy for the girl that I felt myself. I looked at Cricket. "As a matter of fact, you're welcome here anytime," I said. "Of course, you'd have to earn your keep. Go fishing, wash your share of the dishes, help weed the garden, and stuff like that. We even know some kids your age you could hang out with in your spare time."

Cricket's eyes widened. "Really?"

"Really," said Zee, nodding.

"Mom?" Cricket clutched her mother's arm.

"Well, I don't think . . ." Myra Callahan paused and looked at Zee and me and I thought I saw both love and fear in her eyes. Love of her daughter, fear of what? Of the crazies who stalk the famous?

"No one would even know she was here," I said. "We could say . . . we could say she's a relative from out west. I have a sister out there, near Santa Fe, in case anybody bothered to check up."

It didn't take much to convince Cricket. "Come on, Mom! Say yes! It'd be great! I won't have to have Walter Pomerlieu and Ted and Joan and Karen and all the rest of them hanging around all the time. I can go do what other kids do!"

"Well . . ."

"It'll only be for a few days, Mom!"

"Isn't that the tone they call a teenager's favorite whine?" I asked her mother, but looked at Cricket, who immediately studied me to see if she could read my face.

She could, and rolled her eyes. "All right, I'm sorry. No more whining. But, please, Mom. Let me stay here!"

"I'll have to talk with your father. And Walt Pomerlieu isn't going to like it."

"Walter Pomerlieu doesn't like me to do anything. He'd like me to live in a gilded cage!"

"It's his job to take care of you."

"I know. But if I was here, he wouldn't have to!"

"Cricket," I said. "This decision isn't going to be made here or now. Your parents and Walt Pomerlieu don't know anything about Zee or me. They aren't going to let you come here or go anywhere else until they're sure that it's safe."

"But you're not dangerous, Mr. Jackson."

"What makes you so sure? Besides, your parents and the Secret Service people don't know that. They need time to check us out. It's their job. You have to let them do it. Afterward, if things work out, we'd love to have you stay here for a while if you still want to."

"I'll still want to!"

Walt Pomerlieu came up onto the balcony.

"We should probably be going, Mrs. Callahan. The president will be finishing his run about now, and he'll be anxious to see you two."

At the cars, Myra Callahan again shook hands with Zee and me. "I can't thank you enough for your kindness to Cricket. I'll be in touch soon."

As she and the others climbed into the cars, the chief spoke quietly in my ear. "Something else maybe you should know. They tell me that at least one of the wackos who threaten the president is right here on the island. Maybe more than one." He got into the driver's seat.

I looked at Ted. Perhaps in his place, knowing what he knew, what he lived with every day, I'd act like he acted.

Sitting between him and Joan Lonergan, the president's daughter leaned across and opened a window.

"Thanks for everything!"

"You can fish with me anytime," I said, stepping back.

"And you can always have a job as cook," called Zee, smiling.

The car turned around and drove away, and Cricket Callahan waved good-bye. Ted and Joan did not.

"Well," said Zee, taking my arm. "The day has gotten off to an interesting start."

True. Of course, "May you have an interesting life" is an ancient curse, and though we couldn't know it that morning, we were already involved with a murderer. On the other hand, maybe if I had been paying more attention to the survey of mythology that was currently one of our bathroom books, I might have guessed that the Moerae were still at work, even though ancient Greece had long since crumbled into dust.

3

Two days later, we found out Cricket might actually accept our invitation when our breakfast was interrupted by a phone call from Walt Pomerlieu telling us that we'd soon have visitors. Soon was the word, since he was calling from a car that came down our driveway and unloaded several people in our yard before we even finished our coffee.

One of the people was Joan Lonergan. She came up to our door with Pomerlieu, while the others spread out around the place, looking things over. With her was someone we already knew: Jake Spitz, of the FBI.

"What are you doing here?" I asked, shaking his hand.

Spitz smiled at me, then at Zee. "We're everywhere. I heard that you two got married. Congratulations."

"You know each other," Pomerlieu observed.

"I was up here on a job a while back," said Spitz. "We ran into each other then."

Pomerlieu thought that over, then put the thought aside. "We'd like to take a look inside," he said. Joan Lonergan nodded agreement.

Zee, coffee cup in hand, shrugged and waved

the two of them in.

"That's the spare bedroom," I said.

They went in and stayed awhile.

Spitz looked after them. "What would we do without the old-boy network?" he said. "The intelligence crowd is almost incestuous. Everybody knows everybody else, and half of them are related to each other."

"Including those two?"

"Including Walt Pomerlieu, at least. I don't know about Joan. She and Ted Harris only joined this outfit a year ago. But Walt is old New England blood with almost as old intelligence-security ties. I think his dad was OSS."

"How about you? Are you an old boy?"

He grinned. "There are exceptions."

We watched agents inspecting the grounds, peering here and there, looking in the shed out back, eyeballing the gear in my corral, and wandering into the surrounding woods.

When Pomerlieu and Lonergan came out of the house, Pomerlieu was saying, "The agent will take the bed nearest the door."

"Right," said Lonergan. She looked at me. "You have a gun case in there. You a hunter?"

"Sometimes. I don't seem to do as much as I used to."

"What about those lock picks?"

"I got those in a yard sale up-island. I can even open a lock or two."

"You interested in housebreaking, Mr. Jackson?"

"Do you think there's still time for me to have a successful vocation in that field?" I asked. "Or am I too old to begin a new career?"

Zee rolled her eyes, and Pomerlieu shook his head, but Lonergan was not amused. "There's a gun magazine in there with your picture on it, Mrs. Jackson. You're a competitive pistol shooter?"

"My first competition," said Zee, waving a finger at the magazine. "I came in fourth."

"You keep a weapon here in the house?"

"Indeed I do." Zee looked at me. "How many firearms do we have in here, Jeff?"

I ticked them off on my fingers: "One thirty-aught-six rifle, three shotguns, my old thirty-eight S and W revolver, and your Beretta three-eighty. That's six, all told, if I can still count."

"You do a lot of shooting," said Pomerlieu.

"I don't like all these guns being here," said Lonergan.

"You were a policeman," said Pomerlieu to me. It wasn't a question.

"Quite a while back."

"I understand you were shot and still carry the bullet."

"Yes. They decided it was better to leave it there than to try to get it out. You're pretty well informed."

He nodded and looked at Zee. "And you're a nurse at the hospital here."

"I am."

41

"You look around here some more," he said to Joan Lonergan. "Let me know if you have any other concerns." He glanced at a man taking a look at my Land Cruiser. "These agents are surveying the area to ascertain the security situation here. We have to know as much as we can about the grounds, possible approaches to the house, and that sort of thing."

"Come up onto the balcony, then," said Zee. "You get a good view from there." She watched Joan go into the kitchen, and frowned slightly. Then she sipped her cooling coffee. I wondered if she was thinking about the breakfast dishes, which were still on the kitchen table.

We went up to the balcony and looked out over the yard and gardens, over Sengekontacket Pond to the roadway on the far barrier beach, and over that to Nantucket Sound and the distant haze that hid Cape Cod.

"We eat up here sometimes," said Zee. "And we have cocktails here, too." She pointed down toward the pond. "The Rod and Gun Club is just the other side of those trees. That's where I do my target shooting. People shoot down there off and on all week long. Skeet and targets. I know you're worried about guns, so you should know that they go with this territory. After you've been here awhile, you don't pay much attention to the gunfire down there."

"Is there a path between here and there?"

"No. You can make it through the trees and oak brush, but there's no trail."

"How much land do you have here?"

"About fifteen acres," I said. "But there's no fence around it, so it's hard to know where our land stops and the next guy's starts."

"Who's the next guy?"

"Felix Neck is one of them."

"The wildlife sanctuary? I've heard of it." He looked around at the trees flowing away from the house. Then he looked carefully at the pond and the far barrier beach. I thought I knew what he was considering.

"It's a very long shot, even for a first-class sniper," I said. "Besides, there are hundreds of people over there on the beach and in the water all day long, and he'd have a hard time not being seen."

He glanced at me. "You a sniper when you were in Nam?"

"No."

"We'll check out that area over there, of course, but from here I'd say that we have people who can probably get in there, take their shots, and get out again without ever being seen by anybody. And if we have people like that, somebody else might have them, too."

"Terrific," said Zee.

"Not to worry." Pomerlieu smiled. "I'm paid to have an active imagination. I fret about airplanes, submarines, and all sorts of unlikely possibilities. It goes with the job, but I'm really a family man, myself. You want to see my wife and kids?"

43

"You bet," said Zee, who was of late deeply interested in such pictures.

Pomerlieu was already pulling out his wallet and displaying a photo of a comfortable-looking woman and two teenage boys. Mom and sons were smiling, showing large teeth in equine faces. "Maggie and the boys are visiting her sister here, while I'm up here on the job. That's Dan and that's Milt." He was obviously proud of his crew.

"You're a lucky man," said Zee enviously.

"I am, and that's a fact," agreed Pomerlieu. "Your family is the most important thing in your life."

Zee took my arm. "You're right about that."

An hour later, he and his people all went away.

"What do you think?" asked Zee. "Did we pass or flunk?"

"I don't think Joan Lonergan has much confidence in us. My burglar tools and our shooting irons did not please her."

"She's probably just mad because I get to live with you, and she doesn't."

"I was too modest to suggest that myself."

The Callahans' decision came faster than I expected. A phone call from a happy-sounding Cricket said she was coming right after lunch.

"I thought her father was famous for not making quick judgments," I said to Zee.

"Spoken like a man who has never been hounded by a teenage daughter," said Zee. "When I think of the things I put my father through . . ." She frowned. "If Cricket plans to

44

do anything out in public while she's with us, we've got to do something about the way she looks so people won't know who she is. I wonder . . ."

"Dora's Dooz," said my mouth, acting on its own.

"Dora's Dooz?" Zee gave me a quick and none-too-kindly look. "You mean La Belle Dora, the hairdresser, your old flame? What about her?"

Sometimes our brains are somewhere else, but our mouths are always right here. Still, I felt unjustly accused.

"I didn't know you when I dated Dora. Anyway, that was a long time ago and we're both married now. To different people, I might add."

"I know that. What about her Dooz?"

Dora LaBell and I had enjoyed a busy few months together during the time I'd first come down to the island to forget about my life on the Boston PD and the marriage that my police career had helped to dismember. After our heady time as a couple, both of us had gone on to other people, and Dora had opened Dora's Dooz, a beauty salon within which I had never stepped, but which, according to other women I'd come to know, was the right place to go if you wanted to become a new you.

Dora had married Mahmud ibn Qasim, better known as Big Mike. Big Mike was a sociable guy who loved to talk. You never told him anything unless you wanted it to become public knowledge. His ancestors had once lived in the land of the five seas, but he now ran Mike's Electric in Vineyard Haven. Big Mike's name was an irony since he was barely as tall as his short wife, but he was fiercely proud and protective of her, making up with passion what he lacked in stature, and he was rumored to carry a Persian dagger in his boot. Both he and Dora were, as some wag noted, small but big enough.

"Dora's Dooz," I now said. "Dora has magic hands. . . ."

"How would you know?"

Ancient memory, in fact. But I said, "Hundreds, even thousands, maybe millions of women have told me so. Just because you never have to go to a beauty parlor doesn't mean that other women don't. They all say that Dora can make you over so your best friends barely recognize you. You've heard that yourself. Admit it."

"Well . . ."

"And Dora's just the opposite of Mike. She never gossips. At least, she never did when I was seeing her. She probably hears amazing things from her customers, but she never passes anything along. She keeps her mouth shut. You've heard that, too, haven't you?"

"Well, yes . . ."

I put my hands on her shoulders. "So, let's ask Dora to come up here as soon as Cricket gets here, and have her redo Cricket. Make her into a new girl. What do you think? Dora will never tell, and Cricket will be able to go places just like a normal person can."

Zee brooded, then took a deep breath and let it out. "Okay. But I'm not going to call her. She's your friend. You call her."

"But this is woman stuff."

"You call her."

So I called the salon, told the voice on the other end who I was and that I wanted to talk to Dora, then got Dora and told her who was coming to my house and what I wanted. Dora was surprised but cool.

"Well, well. This'll be a first for me. I'll be there. But let's not tell Mike that I'm going up into the woods to your place. If he finds out what I'm doing up there, it won't be hush-hush very long."

Just after lunch, she arrived. I introduced her to Zee and was pleased to note that after they eyed each other they also smiled real smiles.

"I see why we've never met," said Dora. "You don't need any help from the likes of me."

"You should see me early in the morning. No, maybe you shouldn't."

"She doesn't need you in the early morning, either," I said. "The person who needs you is Cricket Callahan, and I think that's her right now."

Sure enough, a car was coming down our long, sandy driveway.

"I thought our guns and stuff might have made us persona non grata," said Zee. "But I was wrong."

"The guns probably don't make them happy," I said, "but maybe me having been a cop and you being a nurse compensated. Let's see now, Cricket can be my cousin visiting from out west. . . ."

"What will we do with her?" asked Zee, sounding slightly anxious.

"Treat her like we'd treat a cousin from out west," I said. "We'll invite her to do whatever we do, and let her do whatever she wants to do."

"She's too young to do whatever she wants to do, but I think she should probably do things with kids her own age. She has grown-ups around her all of the time, and she needs a change. I'm going to call Mattie Skye and see if Jill and Jen will come over."

"To meet my cousin. Good idea."

"Right. Those two are always up to something or other, and they have a lot of friends."

"My only plan is to have a clambake this weekend," I said. "So this afternoon I think I'll go see if I can nail a few quahogs."

The car pulled into the yard. It was a completely nondescript car, the very kind you'd never expect the daughter of the president of the United States to be riding in.

A young woman got out of the driver's side. I recognized her as being the person who had been with Myra Callahan two days before. She wore shorts and sandals and a shirt that was loose enough to hide a pistol at her belt. She carried a large handbag. Cricket Callahan got out of the passenger's seat. She looked happy. "We're here!" said Cricket.

"I'm Karen Lea," said the young woman, putting out her hand. It was a firm hand. "I'll be staying with Cricket."

So there would be two cousins instead of one.

"Grab your bags and take them into your room," I said. "Then stick this car over there by ours. This is Dora Qasim."

Dora took in both Cricket and Karen Lea with swift, professional glances.

"Dora is going to do some work on Cricket," I said, and told our guests the plan.

"Oh, good," said Cricket. "Then Karen and I will be able to go anywhere and nobody'll know us!"

"That's the idea," said Zee. "And while you two get settled in and Dora does her work, I'm going to make a phone call."

The women went into the house, and I went out back to the shed and collected my rake and floating wire basket. As I was putting them into the Land Cruiser, Zee came out, looking pleased.

"The twins just got their driver's licenses, and they're coming over in about an hour. Any excuse to use the family car, I suspect. Their father may not get his Jeep back all summer."

Karen Lea came out the kitchen door and looked around. I waved her over.

"Wander around all you want," I said. "Look the place over. There's one thing, though. Even after Cricket gets her new look, we have to have

49

a story we can agree about."

"What do you have in mind?"

I gave them the cousins-from-out-west idea, but Karen shook her head. "Neither one of us knows enough about out west. How about cousins from, say, Maryland or Virginia?"

"Fine. You're sisters. Two of my father's little brother's kids. My father never had a little brother, by the way, but what the hell."

"Fine. That makes me Karen Jackson," said Karen. "And you're cousin Jeff."

"You can stay Karen," I said, "but Cricket can't be Cricket if she's going to stay anonymous. She's got to be something else. Let's go see if she has any druthers."

We went into the living room, where Cricket was having mysterious things done to her hair. I explained the situation and looked at her. "This is your golden chance. You get to pick your name. Most of us never get to do that. We get stuck with some name our parents give us."

"I've been thinking about that," said Cricket. "How about Deborah? That's a good name."

"Debby for short?"

"Okay, Debby for short. Debby Jackson."

"Fine. I'm cousin Jeff, and this is your sister, Karen."

"Two daughters of friends of ours are on their way over," said Zee. "Jill and Jen Skye. After they've been here about ten minutes, you'll know more about island social life for kids your age than we could tell you in a thousand years.

50

They're good kids."

"Do they know who we are?" asked Karen sharply.

"No. But you can trust them, so it might be a good idea to tell them the truth. They'll go along with the story we've agreed to, and if they substantiate it, their friends will believe it, too."

"Their friends?" asked Karen. "Cricket is going to meet their friends?"

Zee's chin seemed to firm up a bit. "Cricket isn't, but Debby should, I think. She needs to be a normal girl for a while, and that doesn't mean sitting around here with the old folks."

Karen had a look on her face that I'd seen earlier on Joan Lonergan's.

"What are you guys going to be doing?" asked Debby Jackson.

"I am bound quahogging," I said. "I have in mind a clambake about Sunday afternoon, if that sounds good to everybody. Naturally, you're all invited."

"It sounds good to me," said Debby. "Quahogs are those hard-shelled clams, aren't they? The kind they eat raw?"

I gave an introductory clam lecture: "The littlest ones are called littlenecks, and about half the people in the world like them raw on the half shell, while the other half wouldn't eat one on a bet. The next size up are called cherrystones, and they usually get cooked, one way or another. We like them broiled on the half shell with some garlic butter, a few bread crumbs, and a bit of bacon. They call those clams Casino, and a lot of people who wouldn't eat a raw littleneck will scarf down Casinos by the peck. Then you get up to bigger quahogs that you chop up for chowders or stuff and bake in the half shell. It just so happens, by the way, that Zee and I make the best stuffed quahogs on Martha's Vineyard, so you have a treat in store."

"His modesty is one of his most appealing characteristics," said Zee.

"Can I help you catch them?" asked Debby J., smiling.

"Sure," I said. "But you don't have to if you don't want to. Maybe you shouldn't decide till the twins get here. They may have something better in mind."

Dora did some final snipping and shaping, then pulled a large pair of glasses out of her bag of stuff.

"These have clear glass, so you can wear them whenever you're in public. And I have these clip-on dark glasses that you can fit right over them. And there's this floppy hat, too."

She put the glasses on Cricket's face and the hat on her head, then held up a mirror in front of her.

Cricket stared. "Is that really me?"

I would have asked the same question. Cricket no longer looked like Cricket. "You're Debby Jackson now, for sure," I said.

"I think that will do the job," said Dora, gathering up her gear. "Well, I've got to get back to the shop."

"You're a genius," said Zee admiringly.

"I'll send you the bill," Dora said to me. She patted Cricket on the head. "You have a good time, sweetie." Then she looked at me. "Like I said, I don't think we should tell Mike about this job. If we tell him what I did up here, he'll spread it all over the island. If I don't tell him what I did up here, he'll think I came up for a little hanky-pank with you, J.W. So we won't tell him anything."

"Hanky-pank?" asked Zee, a hint of ice in her voice.

"Mike gets jealous before he thinks," said Dora, arching a brow at her. "A lot of people do that. You know what I mean?"

Zee actually pinked a bit.

"We go back to Washington on Monday," said Karen. "You can tell him then, and it won't make a bit of difference."

Dora left and Debby Jackson admired herself in her own mirror. "Nobody will recognize me!"

"We'll soon know," said Zee, having recovered from her blush.

And not too much later we heard a car coming down our driveway. John Skye's Jeep Wagoneer pulled into the yard and stopped, and out jumped the twins.

"Hi, Zee. Hi, J.W.," said the first one.

"Hi, Jill," I said. "How are you and your evil twin?"

"I'm glad you've finally learned which one of us is which," she replied. "But Jen is the good twin, not the evil one."

"She's only saying that because she's Jen, not Jill," said the other twin. "I'm Jill, and I'm the good twin."

"I knew that all the time," I said. "I was just pretending to be confused. Jill and Jen, these are my long-lost cousins from Virginia, Karen and Deborah, better known as Karen and Debby."

There was a chorus of *hi*'s, and an exchange of smiles and quick examinations.

I said, "Since Karen and Debby are new on the island, and you two are old hands, I thought maybe we should put you together, so you Yankees can show these rebs what there is to do. Of course, if you all decide you can't stand one another, you can go your separate ways, and no hard feelings."

"We don't know each other well enough yet to hate each other," said a twin. "You look familiar," she said to Debby J.

"I have one of those faces that always reminds people of somebody else," said Debby. "Sometimes it's really annoying. Now, which twin are you? It doesn't make any difference, but I'm not like cousin Jeff. I can tell you apart. I just have to have a different name for each face."

"Can you really tell us apart?" The twin grinned. "That's great! Usually, only Mom and Dad can do that. Okay, I'm Jill and she's Jen. She's the evil one."

"Congratulations on getting your driver's licenses," said Zee. "Wheels are power."

"Yes!" The twins shot fists into the air. Their smiles were bright.

"Dad's let us have the Jeep for the afternoon," said Jill or Jen, "and we're headed for East Beach, over on Chappy, where there aren't so many people. It'll be great!" She looked at Karen and Debby. "You want to come?"

"A moral dilemma," I said to Debby. "Shall it be the beach or the quahog flats?" She hesitated. "I vote that you head for the beach," I said. "You can come clamming tomorrow, when I go after steamers."

"You can take the bedspread we use for a beach blanket out of the Land Cruiser," said Zee. "I'll put some colas in a cooler and get you a couple of towels. Put your bathing suit on, Debby. You, too, Karen. Hurry up, now!"

Debby hurried, but Karen hesitated before going after her. Soon they came out, wearing beach robes and carrying bags full of whatever it is that women always seem to need, whether they're going to the beach or to a royal ball.

"I don't know about this," whispered Karen Lea as she passed by.

"You'll be fine," I said, giving her a cousinish pat on the shoulder. "See you later."

The Wagoneer drove away, and Zee and I watched it go. "I feel like their mother," said Zee. "Good grief!" She laughed, but her laugh sounded wistful.

"How does it feel?"

"Not too bad. But I think I should get to be a mother of my own babies first, and then my own little kids, before I'm mother to teenagers." She looked up at me with her great, dark eyes.

"We can work on that," I said. "In the meantime, you want to come quahogging down at Eel Pond?"

She sighed and nodded. "Sure, but I have to be home in time to go to work at four."

"A wife with a steady job is too valuable an asset for me to run risks with her," I said. "I'll have you back in plenty of time."

I put another basket and rake into the Land Cruiser, and we drove out to the pavement and turned toward Edgartown. There was a car parked beside the bike path a hundred feet or so up the road in the direction of Vineyard Haven. I thought there was someone in the driver's seat.

The car was still there when we came back with our quahogs an hour and a half later.

I pulled into the driveway and stopped and looked at the car.

"What is it?" asked Zee.

"I'm not sure," I said.

As I got out of the Land Cruiser and crossed the highway, I thought I saw the driver taking my picture. Then, as I walked along the bike path toward the car, its driver started the motor, made a U-turn, and drove away.

I thought the car had a Massachusetts plate, but I couldn't make out the number.

I walked back to the truck.

"What was that all about?" asked Zee.

"I don't know," I said. "Probably nothing."

But I didn't think it was nothing.

4

"Maybe it was just a car," said Zee when we got to the house.

I felt a frown on my face. "Maybe, but maybe not. It was parked there when we came out, and it was still there when we came back. It didn't leave till I went toward it."

"I didn't notice it when we went out," she said. "But why would somebody be out there, watching our driveway?"

I could think of four possibilities about the car and driver. The one I liked best was that the car had nothing to do with us at all. It was just happenstance that it was there when it was there and left when it left. I could also live with the idea that the car contained a watchful backup Secret Service agent in addition to Karen Lea, but one who, for some reason, didn't want to be identified as such.

The third possibility was that the car contained a writer, or a photographer, or some such real or would-be media type who had gotten on to the fact that Debby J. was or might be staying at our place. If that story ever got out, Debby's privacy would disappear, along with the security that went with it.

And finally, the notion I liked least, it could be that the car might have contained one of the bad guys I'd heard mentioned, who, like the hypothetical media type, had learned, somehow, that Debby was with us.

In case either of the last two possibilities proved true, Pomerlieu's people should be alerted.

I offered these thoughts to Zee, who nodded, frowning. "You're right. We should call Walt Pomerlieu. But how could anyone have learned that Cricket —"

"Debby."

"Sorry. How could anyone know that Debby is here, and not out at the compound with her folks?"

I said, "I'm not a spook or a spy or anything like that, but I imagine there are several ways. I can think of a couple."

"Like what?"

"Well, they say that there's a place at the end of the president's driveway for media types. A tent or a portable office or something like that. Maybe one of those sharp-eyed characters stationed there writes down the license plate numbers of all the cars that go in or out, then puts tracers on them to find out who they belong to. Or maybe he sees Karen and Cricket — I mean Debby — drive out and just follows them. Maybe it's as simple as that. He sees them drive into our place and decides to check things out by parking outside and keeping track of who comes and goes."

"Do people really do things like that?"

"So I understand. There's big money in scoops about celebrities. And there's another possibility."

"What?"

"Somebody on the inside, who knows Debby is here, told somebody on the outside."

"Who would do that? Isn't that a violation of ethics, or illegal, or something?"

"People do unethical and illegal things all the time."

"But you're saying that somebody right there in the compound, somebody they trust, might deliberately give out information that could put Cricket — sorry, *Debby* — in danger!" She then thought the next thought. "And Karen and us, too!"

"I never said the person did it deliberately. Maybe, if he did it at all, it was just one of those mistakes we make with our mouths. We let something slip accidentally, and the slip gets passed on till it gets to the very ears we don't want to hear it."

Zee pointed to the telephone. "Slip or no slip, you'd better call Walt Pomerlieu right now." She bit her lip. "I wish the girls were home."

"The girls are all right, unless there really is somebody after Debby, and that somebody not only noticed that Debby and Karen were in John Skye's Jeep when it left here, but just happened

60

to have an ORV and followed them clear out to East Beach. Pretty unlikely, I think." But I wished they were home, too. I curled my fingers around the back of Zee's neck and ran them through her hair. "We're getting parental."

"Yeah. And we aren't even parents yet." She put her hand on mine and sighed. She had been getting broody even before we were married, and the condition hadn't gone away. She patted my hand. "Make that call."

Pomerlieu wasn't there. Even he was off duty sometimes, apparently. I got Joan Lonergan instead. I told her about the car, and said, "That wouldn't have been one of yours, would it? Because if you've got somebody else out there keeping an eye on things, I'd like to know about it."

"It's not one of us," she said, thinly disguised concern in her voice. "Let me talk with Karen."

I told her where Karen and Cricket were, and who they were with. I also told her that Cricket was now Debby, and that she and Karen were cousins of mine.

"You mean you let them go off to the beach by themselves? Jesus Christ!"

"They'll be fine," I said. "Nobody knows they're there. Debby will have a good time, and there won't be a single newshound or security agent to spoil it, providing Karen keeps her pistol and her radio transmitter in her purse and doesn't get too uptight."

"You don't know what you're talking about,"

said Joan Lonergan angrily. "Nobody was supposed to know the girl was at your house, but apparently somebody does. So they may know where she is now, too! I'm going to contact Karen. I'll talk to you later. We may have to end this business right away!"

The phone buzzed in my ear. I looked at it, trying to see Lonergan's face, then hung up. Lonergan knew something I didn't know, and I wondered what it was. Especially since it frightened her, and she didn't seem to be the type who frightened easily, even though she got emotionally involved in her work, as did Ted, and, like Ted, saw dangers everywhere. If Ted and Joan were edgy and suspicious, I figured there had to be a reason.

"What did he say?" asked Zee.

"Not he, she. Pomerlieu was out, so I talked to Joan Lonergan. The guy in the car wasn't one of their guys. She's calling Karen."

"Karen has a radio with her? Of course she does. In her bag. Let's try the CB. Maybe the girls have their receiver on."

I went out to the Land Cruiser and flipped on the CB radio. There wasn't much chance that Jill and Jen had the CB turned on in John's Wagoneer, but it was worth a try.

But they didn't answer my calls, so I went back into the house. Zee was wandering around, uncharacteristically distracted.

"You'd better get ready for work."

She glanced at her watch. "Oh, my gosh!" She

started for the bedroom, then stopped. "I'm worried."

"Don't be," I said, worried myself. "Everything's going to be okay."

She went to get showered and into her uniform. Not much later, looking crisp and cool, but still with a slight frown, she kissed me and drove up the driveway, on her way to the hospital in Oak Bluffs.

About ten minutes later the phone rang. It was Zee. "That car's back there again! Right where it was before! I'll bet he came back as soon as he saw us go down our driveway! I think you should call the police!"

I wondered what the police would say to the driver. *Hey, buddy, what are you doing here? The neighbors are complaining.*

I got my lock picks, then went out to the Land Cruiser and got my binoculars, then walked up the driveway until I was pretty close to the pavement. There I took a right and cut through the woods, paralleling the highway, for a couple of hundred yards. When I figured I'd gone far enough, I made a left turn and walked out to the road. Sure enough, I was behind the dark-windowed car, which was again parked beside the bike path, facing toward Edgartown.

Using the binoculars, I had no trouble reading the license plate.

Apparently, the driver wasn't looking in his rearview mirror much. I crossed to the bike path and walked down to the car. The bike path was typically busy with walkers, bikers, and Roller-bladers, so I was just another such, and no cause for alarm.

When I got to the car, I suddenly knelt, dropping out of sight of anyone who might have been watching me from inside. Nothing happened. I glanced up and down the bike path. No one was close. I got out my key ring, pushed a key against the valve, and slowly let the air out of the right rear tire. Then I got up, put a smile on my face, and leaned over and tapped on the passenger-side window.

The driver looked at me. I widened my smile and tapped again.

"What do you want?" he asked.

"You know you have a flat tire?"

There was a pause. "Flat tire?"

"You've got a flat tire," I said, raising my voice and gesturing toward the back of his car. "You must have run over a bottle or something."

There was another pause. Then the driver-side door opened and a slightly overweight middle-aged man got out. He had thinning hair with a bit of gray in it and looked rumpled. He closed his door so it wouldn't get taken off by passing traffic and walked around the back of the car. He looked at the tire.

"What the hell? Will you look at that! Gawd damn!"

"Flatter than a punctured state zoologist," I agreed.

"Gawd damn!" He scratched his head. "Now

what am I supposed to do?"

"Change it," I said. "Put on the spare."

He looked at me and frowned slightly, as if trying to place me. Then he seemed to recognize me, and stepped back. "You ever changed a tire? I haven't. I don't even know if I've got one. Gawd damn!" He took another step back and eyed me warily.

I looked at the flat tire. It stayed flat.

I gestured toward my driveway. "My house is down there. You could call a garage."

He looked at the driveway. "Naw, I don't want to go down there." He looked up the road toward Vineyard Haven and saw the driveway, fronted by a stone-carved sign, for the wildlife sanctuary.

"What's that place?"

"That's the Felix Neck wildlife sanctuary."

"They'll have a phone. I'll try there." He looked at the tire. "Gawd damn!"

"Well, good luck," I said, and walked toward my own drive. I turned and waved and saw him lock his car. He waved disconsolately back and started off the other way. When he disappeared into the driveway to Felix Neck, I threw a U and went back.

I am a poor picker of locks, but the driveway into the Felix Neck sanctuary is a long one, so I knew I had plenty of time. I needed it, too, what with interruptions from passing cars and cyclists, but finally I got the passenger-side door open. Inside, I shut the door and had a look at things.

According to the registration in the glove compartment, where it lived amid a collection of unused film, the owner of the car was Burt Phillips. Burt's car contained photographic gear along with empty styrofoam coffee cups, pizza packaging, sandwich wrappings, and a half-empty pint bottle of bourbon. There was also a rumpled copy of the *National Planet,* an incredibly popular paper that specializes in outlandish stories, doctored photographs, and inflamed headlines. In it I found a tale of a deceased celebrity who had returned as a ghost and fathered the child of a woman who now hoped to get a portion of the celebrity's estate. The byline was Burt's.

Burt didn't seem to have a cellular phone, which indicated that he wasn't quite up-to-date as far as modern technology goes, but his camera was tucked down under the front seat. There were some pictures of me and of Zee's Jeep and maybe of John Skye's Wagoneer, too, on that film, and I had no intention of photos of me or mine appearing in the *National Planet,* so I rewound the film and took it out, then reloaded the camera from Burt's glove compartment supply. Then I got out of the car, locked the door, and went home. Maybe between the missing film and the flat tire, Burt would decide snooping on me wasn't worth it.

At the house, I called Zee and told her about Burt Phillips so she wouldn't worry. Then I made another phone call to Walt Pomerlieu. Walt was still not available, according to the voice on the far end of the line. I left a message telling what I'd learned about the car and driver.

It wasn't good news, but it could have been worse. It could have been a killer out there, instead of a stringer for a popular rag.

Some better news arrived a bit later in the form of John Skye's Wagoneer and its four occupants.

The three younger ones were happy and salty. Karen Lea pretended to be, but was not, so I knew Lonergan had gotten through to her.

Debby and the twins were considering plans for the evening, apparently. The idea leading the race seemed to be pizza at Giordano's, followed by a funky film at the theater across the street.

Debby suddenly remembered she was my cousin as well as my guest, and looked at me and Karen, then back at the twins.

"I'll call you guys later. Okay? Maybe cousin Jeff has some other plans."

"J.W., you should let her come with us," said Jill or Jen. "You really should."

"You don't even know if you have wheels tonight," I said. "Go home and find out if John will loan you his car again before you decide what you're going to do. We'll have Debby call you after she washes off some of the sand and salt she's collected."

"Rats," said one twin to her sister. "I never thought of not having the car tonight. Daddy said we could go to the beach, but he never said anything about tonight."

"We'll have to butter him up," said the other twin.

"We can probably butter up Dad," said the first twin, "but Mom might not want us driving at night, and it's a lot harder to butter her."

They looked at Debby and Karen. "We have to work on our parents. You work on J.W. We'll talk later. Today was fun!"

They drove away.

I showed Debby and Karen where the outdoor shower was, and Debby and her towel went in. Karen and I walked off a few yards.

"Joan Lonergan called me," she said. "She doesn't like this car business, and neither do I. The car is back, by the way. I saw it when we came in, although I didn't see the driver. I don't like this situation at all."

I told her about my adventures with the car and driver. "It could be worse," I said. "Burt Phillips isn't a hired gun or some wacko; he's a two-bit stringer for a scandal sheet."

"Yeah? Well, what's he doing out there, watching who comes and goes here?"

I gave her the theories I'd given Zee earlier.

She stared around the yard and looked into the trees. The sound of the shower could be heard clearly.

"Save some hot water for the rest of us," I yelled.

"I will!" came Debby's shout.

"And what makes you so damned sure that this Phillips guy is what he seems to be?" asked

Karen. "What makes you think it's not just a cover, in case he gets questioned by the cops? It would be a pretty good one, wouldn't it? Old Burt Phillips isn't a hit man. Oh, no. He's just a seedy, middle-aged stringer trying to make a buck by breaking a story for the *National Planet*. Car full of crap, including, conveniently, a paper that IDs him as just what he wants you to think he is. You don't think you got suckered, do you? Is that just slightly possible?"

It did seem just slightly possible, now that she mentioned it.

Debby appeared, wrapped in her towel.

"I love your shower," she said, grinning as she trotted into the house.

"Everybody loves my shower," I called after her. I turned to Karen. "Your turn. You'll love it, too."

She looked around again, as if trying to see right through the surrounding forest, as if wishing it were glass, so nothing would be hidden from her. Then, a frown on her face, she walked to the shower.

I went into the house and started supper: The bluefish that either Debby or I had hauled in on Monday would now be transformed into stuffed bluefish, always delish. I got the fish fillets out of the fridge and mixed up some store-bought stuffing laced with some extra peppers and hot sauce. I put the stuffing between the two fillets, put the whole thing in a roasting pan, and slapped it into the oven. An army marches on its stomach, they say, and the Secret Service apparently believed we were in a war. I wasn't quite so sure, but in case we were, I wanted us to be able to move if need be.

The phone rang just about then. The masculine voice on the other end had a familiar foreign ring to it. It was an angry voice.

"What the hell was my wife doing at your house this afternoon, eh? What business did she have with you? Why did you call her to you? You tell me right now!"

"Big Mike? Is that you?"

"Yes! What are you doing, calling my wife to your house? You tell me!"

"She was just here on business, Mike."

But Mike's voice only got hotter. "Business, eh? What business is there between you and her, you seducer of women!"

Seducer of women? "Calm down, Mike. Ask Dora, if you don't believe me."

"She will tell me nothing! If not for Helen, I would never have learned of this . . . this seduction!"

Helen. So that's who had first taken my call at the salon. Dora might be tight-lipped, but Helen obviously wasn't.

"Nobody seduced anybody, Mike. My wife was here all the time."

"Don't call me Mike! And don't tell me about your wife! And don't see my wife again!"

He slammed his phone down and I looked at mine. Good grief, just what I needed: a mad

70

Mike Qasim. And until Monday, which was five days away, neither I nor Dora could tell him why she had really been here, because Mike couldn't keep a secret in a bushel basket.

Mad Mike and his Persian dagger.

What next, O Lord?

5

Debby J. wiped her lips and looked appreciatively at the scant remains of supper left on her plate. "Good," she said. Then she looked less appreciatively at Karen Lea. "I don't see why I shouldn't be able to go to the movies with Jill and Jen. I want to go."

She seemed a little petulant.

"Because," said Karen patiently, "there's a man out there watching this place and we don't know who he is."

"Mr. Jackson says he's a writer for the *National Planet*. Besides, he couldn't have seen me in the car when we went out because I was sitting on the far side, and there wasn't even anybody in his car when we came back."

Karen ate the last of her bluefish. "The point is that we don't know who he is. He might be some guy just pretending to be a writer."

"He's not even out there anymore," said Debby, with just a touch of the little whine that teenagers get in their voices when they feel unduly constrained. "So there's no reason why I shouldn't be able to go. No one will recognize me. I was with the twins all afternoon, and even when I took my glasses off to go swimming, they didn't know who I was. You saw that yourself."

Karen finished her glass of wine. "You've already had supper, so you won't be having pizza, in any case. Besides, we don't even know if the twins' parents will let them have the car. As a matter of fact, I'm sure that if they'd gotten it, they would have called by now. They're still probably trying to talk their parents into it."

"We don't need their car," said Debby. "We can use your car, Karen. Nobody was watching when we drove it in, so even if that guy is out there again, he won't know who's in the car if we keep the windows up. We can drive over and pick up the twins and all go to the movies together. Come on, Karen, say we can go!"

I decided I was on both sides of the issue. "Look," I said. "Here's what we'll do. I'll go up and see if Burt Phillips is there. If he is, we'll have to think some more, but if he's gone, you two can go to the movies. How's that?"

"That's good," said Debby, for whom any step in the direction she wanted to go was okay.

"What do you say?" I asked Karen. "If he's gone, there's no reason for you two not to go up to the flicks, is there?"

She looked at her charge. "What if you're recognized, Cricket? What then? You'll have to go back to the compound."

Debby shrugged. "That could happen anytime, anyplace. But with my hair this way, and these glasses, why should it? Nobody will be looking

73

for me there at the movies. Come on, Karen!"

I stood up. "You two rinse the dishes and stack them in the sink. I'll wash them when I get back."

I walked up the driveway, ducked into the woods, and from behind a tree looked at Burt Phillips's car. It was right where it had been before. I walked farther through the woods and looked again. The back tire was still flat.

I crossed the road to the car. I tapped on the driver-side window.

Nothing.

I went around to the other side, got out my picks, and went to work on the door. When I got it open, I looked inside. Nobody home. Everything looked the same as it had when last I'd been there. Burt had not come back to his car.

I locked the door again and walked back down my driveway.

"The car is there, but Burt isn't," I said to my make-believe cousins. "I don't see any reason why the two of you shouldn't go. Give the twins a call, and tell them you'll pick them up at their place."

"Oh, good!" Debby J. clapped her hands and looked at Karen. "Please, Karen! Be a good sister!"

"I'm not your sister," said Karen, "I'm your bodyguard."

Debby J. came over and very ceremoniously gave her a hug and a kiss. "You're a sister to me, Karen, dear. A nice, sweet big sister who wants her little sister, Deborah, to have a fun night at the movies, just like all the other girls are doing."

"I think you have a future in politics yourself," said Karen, giving in. "All right, all right, let's call the twins."

"Yes!" Debby pumped a fist into the air and headed for the phone.

After Debby made her call and headed for the bathroom to ready herself for her big night out, Karen phoned Walt Pomerlieu to tell him of the evening's plans. Walt was back on the job.

"He's not too happy," she said when she hung up. "But he says it's okay. He has two sons about Cricket's age, you know, so he knows how kids that age feel about things. If I know Walt, he'll have somebody or -bodies there at the theater, just in case. But Cricket doesn't need to know that. He's going to call again late tonight to make sure Cricket's bedded down for the night."

"You should practice calling her Debby," I said, and gave directions to John Skye's farm. After Debby emerged from the bathroom, Karen went in. When she came out, the two of them left in Karen's nondescript car. I wondered if I should build a second bathroom. If Zee and I ever had any daughters, I'd need at least one more, that was for sure.

Through the early-evening air I could hear sirens from the direction of Edgartown. It was a common sound during the summer, and usually had to do with yet another moped or bicycle accident, or with a heart attack victim. Much of

75

a police officer's work has nothing to do with crime.

I listened as the sirens came along the Edgartown–Vineyard Haven Road, then I went inside to get at the dishes. The sirens stopped somewhere not far to the north, and I thought that probably Karen and Debby had met the cruiser and ambulance coming out as they headed into town before taking West Tisbury Road to the farm.

As I washed the dishes, I thought about Burt Phillips. It seemed strange that he'd neither managed to get help nor even come back to his car. Burt hadn't seemed like the type to wait around in the woods or down at the Felix Neck buildings when he could be sipping whiskey in his car and listening to the radio and maybe, just maybe, getting an exclusive picture of the president's daughter that would earn him some good bucks.

When I had the dishes stacked in the drainer, I went out and climbed into the Land Cruiser. At the end of the driveway, I turned right and drove by Burt's still silent car, then took another right onto the long sandy road that leads to Felix Neck.

I didn't get far. There were police cruisers a couple of hundred yards in from the highway, and a uniformed Edgartown cop was waving me down. The cop was Janie Lewis. I got out.

"What's going on, Janie?"

"Some bird-watcher walked over there to get a better look at that osprey nest and found a

76

body," said Janie, gesturing with her thumb. She was trying to be cool, but was obviously pretty excited. "Looks like a homicide!"

That explained the sirens.

"Homicide?" Homicides occur on Martha's Vineyard, but they're not common.

"Yeah! Guy got his neck broken. He's out there in the woods with a broken neck. Can you imagine that?"

"Who is it?"

"Nobody's told me. Male. Forty, maybe fifty. That's all I know."

I had a sudden certainty. "There's a chance I might know the guy," I said. "Can I go back there?"

Janie hesitated. She wasn't sure. I saw Tony D'Agostine come through the trees and pointed him out to Janie. She waved him over.

"J.W. here says he may know the guy."

"Oh, yeah?" said Tony. "Come on back and take a look."

We walked back through the woods until we came to the body. I looked down at Burt Phillips. His head was at an odd angle, and his eyes were wide open. I told Tony who he was and that the car out on the road belonged to him.

"Okay," said Tony. "That squares with the ID we found on him. How do you know him? He's not a local guy."

I decided I'd walk carefully through these waters. "I met him up at his car," I said. "He had a flat and decided to come down here to phone for somebody to fix it."

Tony looked down at the body. "How come he didn't go down to your place? That's a lot closer."

"I offered, but he said he'd come here."

"Looks like he made the wrong choice," said Tony. "We'll want a statement from you. What are you doing down here, anyway?"

"His car's still out there. When I was driving by just now I saw it and wondered what had become of him, so I thought I'd come down and maybe catch up with him. I never figured anything like this." I looked around. "How do you read what happened here?"

"Beats me," said Tony. "Our detectives are waiting for the medical examiner, and the state cops are on their way. Right now we're just keeping the site clean for them. You say this guy came down this way to make a phone call?"

"That's what he said."

Tony shook his head. "He didn't break his neck falling down. He had help. What did he do for a living? You know?"

"I think he worked for a newspaper, or something like that."

"Reporter?"

"I don't know. I only talked with him for a minute."

I looked again at poor Burt. No more stakeouts for him. No more cold pizza and cold coffee, no more bourbon by the pint, no more pictures snapped with his telephoto lens, no more bylines in the *National Planet*. No more Burt. I felt a little sick.

"I'll come down to the station and leave a statement," I said, and walked away, trying to think.

At home again, I phoned Walt Pomerlieu. I seemed to be talking to Pomerlieu a lot these days. He came on the line, and I told him the latest news about Burt Phillips and what I'd told Tony D'Agostine. Then I said, "I don't know if the Edgartown police know about cousin Debby staying here with us, so I didn't mention that angle. But I've got to give them a statement about what I know, and when I do I may have to tell them. It would make things simpler for me if you told them first."

"The chief knows," said Pomerlieu. "I don't know which of his people he told. I'll get out to that scene myself right now. I have to presume there's a tie-in between this killing and your houseguest."

"Well," I said, "for what it's worth, I got the impression that Burt didn't even know what Felix Neck was, so I don't think he went down there to meet somebody. I'd guess that whoever he met was somebody he didn't expect to meet. Maybe somebody he knew or maybe somebody else who didn't want to be seen and ID'd."

"Like who?"

"That's the question. Burt was a guy who wrote stories and took pictures for the *National Planet*, and probably some other no-brain sheets like that. I'd guess he'd been at it quite a while. So maybe it was somebody he'd run into before on one of his surveillance jobs. He worked in sleazeland, and some of the people who live there aren't sweet customers."

"We'll have to look into his background. Right now, I've got to go." He rang off, and the phone buzzed like a bee.

The sky was darkening. I thought of Debby J. and Karen up in Oak Bluffs, and was glad they were there, enjoying themselves. They'd know of the murder soon enough.

I went up onto the balcony and looked northwest toward the site of Burt's last breath. The oak forest swayed in the late-evening wind, but its sighs told me no secrets of life and death.

I could just see the pole that held the osprey's nest that had attracted the attention of the birder who had found Burt's body. It wasn't much more than a quarter of a mile from my house, as the crow flies.

I went down and got some spools of dark thread. I walked a hundred feet up the driveway, tied one end of the thread to a tree, about three feet off the ground, then circumnavigated the house, about fifty yards out, tying the thread to trees and scrub oak until I was back at the driveway again. Maybe a deer would break the thread, but not much else than a human would. Smaller creatures would pass under it. I'd check the parameter in the morning.

Then, in the very last of the daylight, I walked

northwest through my woods until I came more or less to the end of my property. There was no fence there, but I knew I was about to cross over onto Felix Neck land. Not far away was the Christmas tree I'd scouted last year and would cut in December.

Through the trees ahead and to my left I could see lights, where the police were still at the scene of Burt Phillips's death. To my right, outlined against the sky, was the pole holding the osprey's nest. I looked at my watch. It had taken me about ten minutes to reach this spot, and I was familiar with my woods. Someone who didn't know them would need more time to make the trip. I wondered how much.

I turned and walked back to the house through the gathering darkness. I felt jumpy, and thought I heard strange noises under the trees. Ghoulies and ghosties and long-legged beasties and things that go bump in the night. They made me shiver.

6

Karen and Debby got home a little after ten, nattering at each other just like real sisters. When they came through the door, my hands were working on picking a new lock, having mastered the old one, and I was playing the Three Tenors' first tape, which is a doozy, and which normally makes me think that if I could be Pavarotti singing "Nessun Dorma" just once, I could die content, knowing that I had done a great thing. But tonight my mind was full of Burt Phillips, and not even the combined tenors could push him aside.

"No," Karen was saying. "We're supposed to spend the night right here."

"But I don't see why we can't stay there," said Debby. "They invited us. Their parents said it was okay. It would be fun! Why can't we?"

Karen took a deep breath. "Because we can't." She looked at me for help.

"What's going on?" I asked.

Karen opened her mouth, but Debby spoke first, her words coming fast as bullets. "Jill and Jen have invited us to spend the night at their house, and their folks said it would be okay. It'll be fun, and I want to go. Say it's okay!"

"Well . . . ," I said.

"It's not okay," said Karen. "I can't take the chance."

"Well . . . ," I said.

"I'm going to call Mom," said Debby. "If she says it's okay, it's okay, isn't it?"

"Well . . . ," I said.

"I'm going to call her right now," said Debby, and she went to the phone.

I looked at Karen's frowning face. "How were things in Oak Bluffs?"

Things in O.B. had been fine. No one in the ticket line had guessed that the girl with the big glasses was the daughter of the president of the United States, and the movie had been a summer comedy with some good laughs. Afterward, they'd all had ice cream up on Circuit Avenue.

For Debby, it had been a blast, and even nay-saying Karen had had a good time. Except for this notion of overnighting with the twins at the Skyes' house. John and Mattie Skye had said it would be fine, but Karen had never imagined that Debby would get so stuck on the idea.

"And tomorrow," Debby was saying into the phone, "Jeff is taking all of us clamming. We're going to have a clambake on Sunday! Maybe you can come!"

I felt my eyes widen. The president having clams at our house? The parking logistics alone made that unlikely. During his first trip to the island I had once caught a glimpse of the caravan taking the great man to play golf at Farm Neck, and I doubted if we could fit all of the necessary cars into our yard. There had been at least a dozen vehicles in that parade: a police car in front, another in back, and, in between, cars full of, I supposed, Secret Service agents, a car full of media types, complete with TV and movie gear, the big armored brown Suburban that presumably bore the golfer himself, more cars full of agents or other personnel, an ambulance, and a couple more cars containing other people of some kind or other. I didn't have room to park such a convoy.

On the other hand, if Debby's folks wanted to come, it would be all right with me. I'd just have to spend a little more time on the clam flats. I knew I couldn't dig enough to feed their entourage, though. Those minions would have to bring their own grub or eat downtown afterward.

I realized that Debby was talking to me. I looked up and met her inquiring eyes. Her hand was over the speaker on the phone.

"Sorry. What did you say?"

"I said is it all right if my mom and dad come for clams?"

Good grief; she'd been serious. My mouth moved and said, "Sure."

"Sure," she said into the phone. Then, to me: "What time?"

My mouth moved again. "Five-thirty." My traditional hour for clambakes.

"Five-thirty. It'll be fun. Do try! And thanks!

Bye." She turned to me. "She says they'll try to come!" Then she looked at Karen. "And she says we could spend the night with Jill and Jen. If . . ."

She paused, and Karen looked at her with narrowed eyes. "If what?"

Debby came across to me. "If cousin Jeff says it's okay. Mom says it's okay if you say it's okay, cousin Jeff. So, say it's okay. Please!" She clasped her hands in a parody of prayer.

I had to smile.

"No," said Karen, shaking her head. "I can't take the risk."

"You're just my bodyguard," cried Debby. "You're not my boss!"

I pointed a forefinger at Debby. "You stay here." Then I hooked the same finger at Karen and said, "Let's go outside and have a chat."

Out in the yard, we paused, and Karen said, "What's this all about?"

I looked at her dark form and could almost see the anger in her. Then I told her about Burt Phillips.

When I was through, she said, "And Walt Pomerlieu thinks it might have something to do with Cricket being here at this house?"

"He said he'd have to presume that."

"Me, too," said Karen, turning and looking out into the darkness. "We won't tell Debby about this. There's no point in alarming her."

"That's up to you. In any case, I think it might be smart if you change your mind about spending the night at John and Mattie Skye's place. If you go right now, nobody will know where Debby is, and she should be perfectly safe. Tomorrow, when it's daylight again, we may be able to see things more clearly."

She hesitated. "How well do you know the Skyes?"

"Well enough to send Debby to them, and then some."

"I don't like any of this. I should call Walt."

"He's calling here later tonight. I'll give him the news. Meanwhile, the fewer people who know about this, the better. The president and his wife know where she is."

"The president and his wife don't know much about security." She stared into the dark forest. "I gave up cigarettes a couple of years ago. I wish I had one right now."

I was feeling jumpy and impatient. "Why don't you tell me what's going on."

"I don't know what you mean."

"Sure you do," I said. "You and Walt Pomerlieu and Ted and Joan are all nervous as cats in a dog pound. It's probably normal for people in your line of work to be on the lookout for trouble, but you're all way beyond that stage. There's something specific that's bothering you, and since I've got Debby here, and since this Burt Phillips stuff has you all turned inside out, I think I should know what's got you spooked. What is it?"

She shook her head. "Nothing you need worry

about. All you have to do here is be the good host. Leave the rest of it to us." She sounded as chippy as I felt.

"I'll tell you what I think," I said. "I think that there's a very particular threat against the president or his family, and I think it's tied to this island. I think you think that somebody right here on the Vineyard is plotting something bad, and I don't think you've got a handle on it yet."

"You're imagining things," said Karen.

"I'm not imagining that Burt's got himself murdered, and that the trees up where it happened are probably full of federal agents. What's going on?"

"I think you'd better talk to Walt about this."

"You mean there is something to talk about?"

"You talk to Walt. If we're going to spend the night with the Skyes, we'd better get going." When she stepped into the screened porch, Debby met her and got the good news.

"Oh, thank you, cousin Jeff!" said Debby, smiling.

"Thank Karen, not me."

"Oh, thank you, dear sister, without whom I could not survive!" She gave Karen a kiss.

"Pack your bag," Karen smiled, "and we'll hit the road."

When they were both in the car, I leaned against the driver's door.

"Does the president really come to places like this for clambakes?"

Karen spread her hands. "He likes to eat, and

he's impulsive about where and when he does it. It drives security crazy, but that's the way he is."

"So he might really come?"

"He has a tight schedule, so he may not be able to make it. But then again, he's supposedly on vacation, so he might. He's the president of the United States, remember. He doesn't have to eat broccoli if he doesn't want to, and if he decides to accept your invitation to have clams here, I don't know who's going to tell him he can't, especially since he has to head back to Washington the next day."

"He'll come," said Debby. "When do we go clamming tomorrow?"

"Early afternoon. Low tide. Make sure you bring the twins. I need their muscle."

I stepped back, and Karen drove away.

About a half hour past midnight, Zee came home. She was surprised to find me still up, and said so.

We sat on the porch and I told her about Burt Phillips and what had happened since his death.

"I'm glad Debby's up at John and Mattie's place," said Zee. "But maybe we'd better send her back to her parents tomorrow. I don't like all this stuff. If somebody's after her, she'll be safer there than here."

I'd been thinking about that very issue, and surely so had Walt Pomerlieu, Jake Spitz, and the rest of the security people. But Cricket was still here, supposedly, instead of at the compound. It was a curiosity.

"Besides," said Zee, putting a hand on my thigh, "I don't like us being in the line of fire, if there is a line of fire. I don't want us to be two of those innocent civilians who get shot by mistake."

"Maybe we're not in as much danger as we think we are," I said.

"How could that be? There are dozens of agents there, and only Karen here."

"Yeah, but how many people know that Debby's here and not there? I'll bet that only a handful of people know where she is, and that that's her security. If nobody knows where she is, she's safer than if they do."

"And that's why you let her go stay with the twins. But who are they hiding her from? And what about Burt Phillips? He must have had some reason for watching our place. Did he know she was here? And if he knew, who else knows? And who killed him? And why? I don't like any of it. I really think she should probably go back to the compound. I don't want to be responsible for her safety."

"I don't know who killed Burt Phillips or why, but I can think of one reason why Walt Pomerlieu might think Debby's safer here than at the compound."

"You mean a traitor."

"One person's traitor is another person's hero," I said. "All I'm saying is that what with this Burt Phillips business and all, common sense says to send Debby back to the compound. But that hasn't happened, and the only reason I can think of for that decision is that Walt thinks there's somebody there who's a threat to her."

"But who'd want to hurt Cricket?"

Zee, ever the healer, had a hard time imagining evil intent. I had less trouble.

"On the bright side of things," I said, "the president and his wife may be coming for clams on Sunday. Debby invited them, and I said it was okay."

"You did! My gosh! I have to wash my hair!" Her hands flew up to her head, and she stared into space the way she does when she's thinking. "We'll have to clean the house, and mow the lawn, and do the flower beds so they don't look so scraggly. I should call Manny Fonseca and cancel tomorrow morning's shooting down at the club, so I'll have time to get this place looking good. And —"

I stopped her with a kiss.

"It's one o'clock in the morning," I said. "You don't want to call Manny Fonseca now. In fact, you don't want to call him at all. You should go take your shooting lesson as scheduled. I'll do the lawn and the flower beds, and we'll have plenty of time to get the house in shape the next day. Relax."

"Relax? Fat chance! I won't be able to sleep all night."

But she seemed less somber than when we'd been talking about Burt Phillips, and while I stayed up, waiting for Walt Pomerlieu's call, she

90

went to bed, where, in spite of her protests that it would not be possible, she quickly fell asleep.

The call came at two o'clock, and I swept up the receiver before the first ring was done.

"This is Pomerlieu. Hope I didn't wake up the house. Is everything all right?"

I told him that Karen and Debby were staying at John and Mattie Skye's house.

"What!"

"Mrs. Callahan okayed it. I guess the twins and Debby really hit it off."

"I should have been told!"

"They'll be quite safe. John and Mattie are old friends."

I heard a muttered curse. Then, "I'll have to post some people over there. I should have been notified."

There was an odd quality to his voice. A sort of fury I'd not heard in him before. It made me glad once again that I wasn't a Secret Service agent.

Afterward, in bed, I lay listening to the night sounds of the forest: the sigh of the wind, the groans of branches rubbing on branches, and the noises of creatures who come forth when darkness falls over the earth.

7

In the morning, early, I took two pounds of frozen scallops out of the freezer and put them in a pan of warm water to thaw, then went out and followed my dew-beaded thread through the woods and around the yard. It was unbroken. A bit of good news I was glad to have.

Back in the house, I crushed Ritz crackers until I had two cups' worth, melted a cup of butter, and mixed the crushed crackers, the butter, and the scallops all together in a baking dish. Later the Ritz Scallops could be cooked for twenty-five minutes in a 375-degree oven and would be delish, to say nothing of fattening. Meanwhile I put the dish into the fridge.

Zee and I breakfasted on the porch, eating bagels, cream cheese, red onion, and smoked bluefish, preceded by juice and accompanied by coffee. A good way to start any day, but not the only good way.

"I think that when this is over, we won't invite any other guests for a while," said Zee, licking her lips and eyeing me.

"My very thought." We downed the last of our bagels with the last of our coffee and were rising and reaching for each other when Karen's car came down the driveway.

"Rats, and rats again!" hissed Zee, as we untangled.

"Good morning," said Karen, as they got out of the car.

It was indeed a pretty morning, although it didn't seem quite as promising as it had a few moments before.

"You're up early," I said.

"We came for breakfast," said Debby. "Is there any left?"

"Plenty," said Zee. "We're done, but you two are next in line."

We cleared the table and laid out two new settings and more food and drink. Karen and Debby dug in.

"Yum," said Debby.

"One of God's great breakfasts," I agreed.

"How are things?" asked Karen casually.

I told them about my thread around the perimeter of the yard. Karen seemed pleased if not happy. I wondered if she'd ever be happy while she kept the job she had.

"When are you meeting Manny?" I asked Zee.

"Eight o'clock. We'll only be there a couple of hours at the most. That'll give him time to do some work afterward down at the shop."

"Who's Manny?" asked Karen, swallowing some coffee.

"Manny Fonseca, my shooting instructor," said Zee.

Shooting. Something else for Karen to worry about. She got up from the table, went into the living room, and came out again with our copy of *Pistoleer*. She looked at Zee's smiling face on the cover, then opened the magazine to the story inside. "This Manny Fonseca?" she asked, pointing at his name.

"That's him," I said. "The Portagee gunslinger himself. Although nowadays he's more of a Wampanoag than a white eyes."

Karen frowned some more. "What do you mean?"

I told her how Manny had always dreamed of himself as a frontier type taming the West until he discovered, to his surprise, that he had enough Wampanoag blood in him to officially qualify as a member of the tribe, and how, thereafter, he identified with the losers in the Indian wars.

"How long have you known this guy?" she asked, apparently wondering if Manny was psychologically stable.

"Longer than I've known you," I said, suddenly a bit tired of her ingrained suspicion of everyone and everything.

And as I felt that impatience, it occurred to me that I'd often been a bit testy of late, that small things that usually wouldn't bother me did so now. One reason I'd left the Boston PD was because that same sort of irascibility had started to become the norm for me, and I'd decided I didn't want it to be. Now it was here again. Not good, Kemosabe. I wondered if the tension or worry plucking at my nerves was only the result of Debby being here or had to do with something else.

Zee cocked her head to one side and looked at Karen's frowning face. She put a hand on her arm. "You can trust Manny with your life," she said. "So can Debby. He's a gun hawk, but he's a good man." She glanced at her watch. "I'd better get ready." She went inside and came out with the nylon bag that contained her shooting gear. "Anybody want to come and watch?"

"I do," said Debby, putting down the bagel she was preparing to smear with cream cheese, but doing so with a still-hungry look on her face.

"I'm leaving in about ten minutes," said Zee.

Karen opened her mouth to register disapproval. I might have done the same in her place, but I wasn't in her place, so before she could speak I said to Zee, "Maybe we'll come down later, after Deb and Karen finish breakfast. You'll be there for a while, so there's no hurry."

I looked at Karen. "The world keeps right on turning, whether we stay home or go out. Personally, I don't like to live in a cage, even though some people think they're safer inside of one. I think it's better to step outside and join the dance."

"You'd better abandon your plans to become a poet," said Zee. "Your metaphors are out of control."

I lifted my chin and lowered my eyelids. "I had the cosmic dance in mind."

"Oh," she said, "that dance."

"Dig in," I said to Debby. "When you've eaten, we'll go down to the club and you can watch my wife blow holes in targets. It's noisy but it can be fun."

"Great. This is good food!" Debby repossessed her bagel.

Karen said, "I don't think Debby should be anyplace where there's going to be shooting. It's too dangerous."

"I'm going to phone your boss right now," I said. "You can talk to him about it when I'm through."

"While you talk, I'm on my way," said Zee. "See you down there, I hope." She gave me a kiss and left, and I went into the house to make my call.

Walt Pomerlieu was there, and I told him that Karen and Debby were home again, safe and sound. He said that was good. Then I told him I wanted to know what was really going on. He said he knew how I felt, but that it was one of those need-to-know situations and that I didn't need to know.

"The high priest syndrome," I said. "Only the initiated can be trusted with the secrets of the faith. I'm always leery when people tell me I don't need to know something."

"That probably explains the lock picks," he said. "You don't like locked doors."

Good grief. Now my lock picks had symbolic psychological significance. But Pomerlieu was right. I don't like locked doors, and almost never lock any of my own, with the exception of the one on my gun case. And even there, the key is lying on top of the case so I won't lose it.

"Well," I said, "if you won't tell me what I want to know, let me tell you what I think." I gave him the same theories I'd given to Karen the night before.

He listened, and when I was through, he said, "Ah."

"That's it? Just *ah?*"

"That's it."

"Do you still have people in the woods north of us?"

"Yes. And they'll stay there. There are others south of you and somebody watching your driveway. Cricket doesn't need to know that, of course. We want her to feel as free as she can. Do you know her plans for the day?"

"Part of them, at least. She's going down to the Rod and Gun Club to watch my wife take a pistol-shooting lesson this morning, and this afternoon we're going clamming. Karen isn't happy about the target-shooting part and wants to talk with you about it."

He thought for a moment. "Are all of you going down to the range?"

"I'm not sure. I have a call to make, and I should mow the lawn in case the president actually decides to come for clams."

Again a pause. Then, "I'll want somebody at the pistol range in addition to Karen."

"I'd like to know who your agent is, so I don't have to wonder about any strangers."

He allowed himself a grim-sounding chuckle. "I'll send somebody you know."

I went out onto the porch, and Karen went into the house. Debby was scarfing down the last of the bagels and their accompaniments. The sound of gunshots came from the direction of the club.

"Excellent food," Debby said. "I can hear the shooting. Is that Zee?"

"Yes. The louder shots are Manny's and the others are Zee's. He's probably shooting a forty-five, and she's shooting her three-eighty."

"I can tell the difference." She nodded toward the living room and lowered her voice. "Am I going to get to go? I can tell that Karen doesn't like the idea."

"I think so," I said. "She's in there talking it over with Walt Pomerlieu. It's her job to worry about you, you know, and you should be glad she's so good at it."

"I know. Say, do you think I can shoot, too?"

"We'll let Manny Fonseca decide that, but he loves shooting, so I imagine it'll be fine with him. He may even give you a lesson."

"All right!"

Karen came out, and we both looked at her. She put on a small, reluctant smile. "We'll go," she said.

"Excellent!" Debby wiped her lips, got up, and gave her a hug.

"I have to make another call," I said, and went inside. If Walt Pomerlieu wouldn't tell me anything, maybe there was another way. I phoned Jake Spitz and told him what I wanted.

"It's a security matter," said Spitz. "Eyes only and all that. Sorry." He paused while I uttered a few popular words that are theoretically unacceptable in proper society, then said, "What's Joe Begay up to these days?"

It was my turn to pause. "You know Joe Begay?"

"I know a lot of people."

"And I should talk with Joe?"

"I just asked what he was up to these days. I gotta go."

He hung up, and I looked at the phone.

Joe Begay had been my sergeant in Vietnam on the unfortunate day when a Vietcong mortar crew got our patrol in its sights and unloaded on us. He had taken a hit in the head that had temporarily blinded him, and I had instantly become a seventeen-year-old kid with a lot of metal in his legs. But with me providing the eyes and Joe providing the legs, we'd gotten our surviving people out of there, and had called in an air strike that finally silenced the mortar. I hadn't been over there long enough to know what was going on when my million-dollar wounds brought me home again.

And now, twenty-some years later, Joe Begay was living in Gay Head, married to Toni, of the Gay Head Vanderbeck clan. They'd met out in

Santa Fe, where she'd gone to buy Indian arts and crafts for her Gay Head shop, and he had shown her the Navajo and Hopi worlds of his parents, then had come east to meet her Wampanoag family.

Joe now owned a conch boat and fished out of Menemsha, but for the two decades after he'd recovered his sight and gotten out of the hospital, he had done jobs for many organizations. His gift for languages and his powerful body and mind had taken him into many unadvertised situations and put him in contact with a remarkable variety of people during those years. He'd made a lot of money, had a lot of contacts, but now was not inclined to discuss his past.

But Toni had never liked knowing so little about him, and over time bits and pieces of his history had come into view until it was finally clear that Joe Begay had been more than just a sort of middleman or rep for international corporations, as he had first suggested to Toni. Nor was it certain that he was as retired as he claimed, for from time to time he still went off on "business trips" to Washington and elsewhere that sometimes kept him from his conch boat for days at a time. He claimed, possibly quite honestly, that he needed to do some consultant work outside in order to support his fishing habit, which often provided thin earnings, particularly since he paid his crewman, Jimmy Souza, very well indeed.

Jimmy Souza was a guy trying to stay off the booze that had cost him his own boat. Jimmy knew more about conch fishing than most, and it was his knowledge that kept Joe Begay's boat in business. Jimmy struggled to stay sober, and his reward for this and for his wisdom and hard work was a salary above and beyond that of most crewmen, one which kept Joe's own income from the boat on the shallow side. Thus, Joe's occasional business trips. Or so he said. I never asked for any other explanation.

There was a joke between Joe and me that each had saved the other's life. That the joke was rooted somewhat in truth was one reason, perhaps, that we'd become friends, another being the friendship between Toni and Zee, which had blossomed from the moment they'd met.

I had never asked Joe about his off-island business or contacts, but if Jake Spitz thought I should talk with Joe about what was going on with regard to Debby, I was surely going to take his advice.

Twenty minutes after Debby finished her breakfast, a car came down our driveway and parked. Ted got out, looking no better-humored than usual.

"I don't like this," he said. "So let's get it over with." He looked at me. "Are you coming along?"

Lawn mowing no longer seemed to be a priority.

"Sure," I said.

We all got into the Land Cruiser and drove to the club.

The Martha's Vineyard Rod and Gun Club is located on a point of land sticking out into Sengekontacket Pond. There's a locked gate, the combination of which is available to club members, a clubhouse, a skeet range, and a pistol range. In the waters around the edge of the point, there are good quahogs to be found, and more than once I've been out there when the skeet shooters were at work, and have had shot fall into the water all about me, like metallic rain. When that happens I tend to abandon shellfishing for the day.

Today, the gate was open, and we drove right through and parked beside Manny Fonseca's truck and Zee's little Jeep.

Manny and Zee were down at the table by the twenty-five-yard mark, shooting at paper targets that were placed in front of the tall earth embankment that was the backstop for the bullets. You had to be pretty wild to miss that backstop, but occasionally it probably happened. Neither Zee nor Manny had that problem.

I opened the glove compartment and got out earplugs for all. Ted, who was quickly out of the car and looking all around, declined his. He wanted to hear as well as possible. When he finished his survey, we walked down to the pistol range. Manny waved, and Zee, seeing his wave, turned and waved as well.

"We're working up to doing some combat shooting," said Manny, after introductions were made all around. He was wearing the black belt that held his holster, extra clips, and various pouches containing bullets and God knew what else. Behind him, on the table, was his nylon weapons bag. Several guns and boxes of bullets lay there, and I knew that before the day's shooting was over, Manny would use every weapon he had with him. He dearly loved to shoot and was incredibly good at it.

"So these girls are your cousins, eh?" said Manny. "I didn't know you had any kinfolk beside your sister out there in New Mexico."

"They're just up for a few days to breathe some Yankee air," I said. "Then we'll ship them back to Virginia."

"And this young fella? He kin, too?"

"Nope. Ted's just down vacationing for a week or so. Wanted to see the club, so we brought him along today."

Grim Ted curled up the sides of his mouth and created his best effort at a smile. Manny's eyes flicked over him, and did not miss the slight bulge of Ted's pistol holstered beneath his summer shirt.

"You do any shooting yourself, Ted?" asked Manny, completing the reloading of his clip, and slapping the clip back into his .45.

Ted thought a moment, then said, "Oh, a little now and then."

I instantly realized that Manny and Ted had reached some sort of unspoken understanding. Manny knew that Ted was a shooter, and Ted knew that Manny knew. And Manny knew that

Ted didn't just happen to be there, and Ted knew that he knew it. And knowing that Ted didn't just happen to be there, Manny also knew that Karen and Debby were not ordinary, run-of-the-mill cousins of mine, but something more, because Ted was there because of them. What Manny didn't know was how much more.

"Well," said Manny to Zee. "Let's get at it. I'll go first. Two shots right-handed in each of those three targets, left to right. Okay?"

"Okay," said Zee, fitting her hearing protectors over her ears.

Shooting with his right hand, Manny put two shots into each of the bull's-eyes of the three targets. Zee did the same. Then they did it with their left hands, then with both hands.

Then they changed weapons, using those on the table, and with these Manny still shot bull's-eyes, but Zee was less precise.

"Just practice," said Manny. "That's all. You know that three-eighty real well, but you haven't used these others much yet. When you get used to them, you'll do just as good."

"The grip on that forty-five is too big for me," said Zee. "That forty-caliber, too. My hands aren't as big as yours."

Manny nodded. "Yeah, you're right. There's guns those calibers that'll fit a small hand, but unless you really like a slug that size, it's probably better for you to use something smaller, like that three-eighty of yours or one of these nine-millimeters. Let's move up now, and see how you do from fifteen yards."

They did that, and the paper targets were blown into tatters.

When they were done, Manny looked at me. "Want to take a few shots?"

"Not now. But how about letting Debby here pop a few caps?"

He looked at the president's daughter, then at Ted, then back at the girl. "Why not? You ever shoot before? No? Well, then, we'll start you out with a twenty-two. Come on."

Debby followed him to the table, where he gave her his opening lecture on gun safety. He then took a small revolver from the table, emptied it, and showed her how it worked. He had her dry-fire it, using the two-handed grip, then had her help him put up new targets. Then he showed her how to load the gun and put her at the fifteen-yard mark.

"Okay," he said. "Now, slow and easy, single action like I showed you. Cock the hammer." She thumbed it back. "Line up the sights on the bull's-eye and squeeze it off."

The gun went off and a hole appeared in the upper left corner of the target.

"Again," said Manny. "Same as before. Line up the sights on the bull's-eye and squeeze the trigger. Don't yank it."

She shot the cylinder empty and got one into an inner circle.

"Not bad," said Manny. "We'll do it again." He showed her how to reload, and she fired another six shots, getting most of the bullets inside the outer circle this time.

She shot up a box of bullets, first shooting single action, then double, and noting correctly how much more difficult it was to hit anything when shooting double action.

When she was done, she was delighted. "It's fun! How'd I do?"

"You did okay," said Manny. He handed her the bullet-punctured target. "Here. Take that back to Virginia and show it to your daddy."

"I will!"

Manny looked at Ted. "You want to try your hand, Ted?"

Ted almost smiled. "Another time."

Manny looked at Karen. "You?"

"No," said Karen.

"Well, I guess we're done, then," said Manny. He put his hand on Zee's shoulder. "Friday morning?"

"That'll be fine," said Zee.

Back at the house, Ted looked meditatively at Debby. "That guy can shoot some," he said. "And he's a good teacher. You try to remember everything he told you."

He got into his car and drove away. I looked at my watch. Four hours till low tide. Plenty of time to try to find Joe Begay.

"I'm going up to Gay Head," I said. "Anybody want to come along?"

Everybody decided to go, so we all got into Zee's Jeep, a much more comfortable machine than my trusty but rusty Land Cruiser, and headed west, with Debby full of talk about the shooting lesson. We hadn't gone too far before I was pretty sure that a car about a quarter of a mile back was following us.

8

I took a left at the blinkers and drove along Barnes Road. Sure enough, the car made the turn, too, staying a quarter of a mile or so behind. Not too close, but close enough. When I took a right on West Tisbury Road, the car followed along.

I turned into the airport entrance.

"Why does it say 'The County of Dukes County Airport' and not just 'Dukes County Airport'?" asked Debby.

"It's a long story," I said.

"I thought we were going to Gay Head," said Zee.

"We are," I said, "but I want to see if that guy behind me is actually tailing us, or whether I'm just paranoid."

My passengers turned and looked back as the car turned into the airport entrance road.

"That blue car," I said. "Anybody recognize it?"

"How long has it been following us?" asked Karen.

"Since we left home. Maybe he's just a guy trying to catch a plane."

"And maybe I'm the queen of Siam," said Karen.

I drove up to the terminal and took a left around to the temporary parking spots, where folks load and unload their cars while waiting for airplanes to come or go. I kept driving around the circle and came back to the entrance road just as the blue car should have been coming by.

It wasn't.

It could have been in any one of several places beside or off the entrance road: at the auto repair shop, at the Steamship Authority office, where you can sometimes actually get tickets to or from the island on the day you want to travel, at the Laundromat, or at one or another of the businesses that are out there.

The car turned out to be at the auto repair shop, which is at the end of a short side road near the air terminal. I didn't actually see it there, but I did see it reappear behind us after we passed the side road on our way out.

I took a right and headed for West Tisbury. The blue car stayed well back, but followed along.

"Good guy? Bad guy? Nosy writer looking for a scoop?" I listed the possibilities to my passengers.

"Can you lose him?" asked Karen.

"Probably, if he stays that far back," I said. "But do you want to lose him? Wouldn't it be better to find out who he is?"

"Better, maybe, but not necessarily safer, and

that's what I've got to think about first. Lose him."

There are some winding roads up in West Tisbury, and unless you're close you can lose contact with a car in front of you. I drove along at a sedate pace until I was almost to the millpond, then hit the gas and sped out of our shadow's sight just long enough to hang a sharp left on New Lane and disappear.

The shadow, probably coming past the youth hostel by this time, had several choices to consider. We were gone, but gone where? Along Old Country Road to the right? Along New Lane to the left? Past the millpond and its swans, then right toward North Tisbury? Past the millpond and then left, going by Alley's Store and on toward Chilmark?

And if north, then what should he do at the Scotchman's Lane intersection? Go left? Go right? Go straight ahead to the North Road intersection? Then what? Left on North Road, or straight on State Road?

And if he turned south, should he go straight on South Road? Or had we taken a right on Music Street, another onto the panhandle, and gone straight on? Or had we gone left onto Middle Road and headed on up-island?

Or had we turned into one of the many private drives that leave the paved roads?

Shadow had problems. I wondered if he knew that Music Street, so named, they say, for the piano purchased by some culturally inclined guy who lived there long ago, had previously been known as Cow Turd Lane? I doubted it, because I didn't think Shadow was too familiar with the island; otherwise he'd have gotten closer to us when we came to West Tisbury village, so he'd know which turn we took.

Down New Lane a little way, I pulled into a driveway, turned around, and parked. If Shadow happened to pass by, I wanted to be facing him.

"We'll wait awhile," I said, "and give this guy a chance to give up on us before we go on." I offered my passengers my theory about Shadow's relative ignorance of the island and its roads.

"You know anything about surveillance?" asked Karen.

"Not much," I admitted.

"Well, for one thing, there may be more than one car involved. The first guy goes away for a while, and another car takes over. You notice any other cars sort of staying with us in front or behind?"

"No. But that doesn't mean there wasn't another one. I was watching the blue one. Is that one of your outfit's cars, by the way?"

"No, it's not," said Karen. "If you wanted to intercept somebody headed up-island, where would you do it? Beetlebung Corner, right? All the up-island roads converge there. You don't have to trail anybody all the way from Edgartown. All you have to do is go ahead to Beetlebung Corner and wait for them to come by."

"You're smarter than the average bear," I said,

turning to look back at her. "How did you, a mere off-islander, come up with that bit of wisdom?"

"I have a map," said Karen. "And I studied it, just like I was told to do at one of our earliest briefings. We all have maps."

"You almost make one have confidence in one's government," I said. "Well, you're right, unless whoever you're tailing stops somewhere this side of Beetlebung Corner. In which case, you'll wait a long time up there. But we aren't stopping this side, so if Shadow is waiting for us, he'll find us. My plan is to give him time to give up and go home and then we'll go on."

"And while you're waiting," said Karen, opening her ever-present handbag and taking out her radio, "I'll make a call and find out if that car is one of ours that nobody's told me about."

She got out of the car, crossed the road, and made her call. Ever the secretive Secret Service person.

I looked at Debby. "How you doing, kid? Pain in the you-know-where, isn't it?"

"To tell you the truth," said Debby, "I like it better this way than the way it usually is. Usually, I don't get to move around at all unless there's security everywhere. It's like living in a glass cage. I don't ever want to be a movie star or a politician, I can tell you. My dad likes his job enough to put up with it, and I can do it, too, as long as I have to, because of his career. But as soon as I can, I'm going to get out of the light. Right

112

now, here with you and Zee, it's better because nobody, not even the person in that car, probably really knows I'm here. They may think it, but they don't know for sure. So it's like being free, in a way."

"You're not scared, then?" asked Zee.

"After a while," said Debby, quite calmly, "you stop being scared. As long as I can remember, I've known there are some sick people out there who might try to do something; but it doesn't do any good to be scared about it. You just have to put them out of your mind and be careful at the same time."

Zee looked at her, then nodded. "Yes. That's what you've got to do. You're a brave cousin, Debby Jackson."

"Not always," said Debby.

Karen came back, not looking happy. "Definitely not one of ours," she said, getting in. "I think we should go back."

I'd been considering that possibility. "We were picked up at my place," I said. "If I was Shadow and if I'd lost us like I hope he has, I'd go back and wait until we came home. We do have to go there eventually, but in the meantime, I think we can go on up to Gay Head."

She looked disapproving but said nothing.

I went on. "Shadow has just been trailing us, but he hasn't tried to close. If he'd given any sign of getting close enough to do us some damage, I'd think differently. But he hasn't. He just seems to want to know where we are. And

113

now he's lost us altogether."

"Maybe," said Karen.

"Yeah, maybe," said Zee. "But if he's ahead of us, we should see him at least as soon as he sees us. And if he's gone back down-island, he really has lost us. I think Jeff's right, but you're the Secret Service agent, so you decide."

Karen gave a rueful smile. "Maybe I should go into some other line of business. All right, we'll go on. What's so damned important up in Gay Head, anyway?"

"I want to see a friend. While I'm doing that, the rest of you might take a walk under the cliffs or something like that. Do you good."

"Yes!" said Debby, with a real grin this time. "I've been at the top of the cliffs, but not at the bottom. The last time I was up there, you could see naked people down there! We could all take off our clothes!"

"Cricket Callahan!" Karen looked as if she was trying to appear more shocked than she really was.

"I think they're sort of frowning on naked people down there these days," I said. "But I could be wrong. You can give me a report when you get back."

I looked at my watch. It seemed as good a time as any to go, so I did. No blue car was in sight when we got out to the Edgartown–West Tisbury Road. I took a left and drove past the police station and the old millpond, whose swans were right where they were supposed to be. At the fork, I went left again, past Alley's Store and the field of dancing statues, then cut right onto Music Street, and left onto Middle Road, where the long-horned cattle lived behind their stone fence. Middle Road, narrow and winding, is one of the prettiest on the island, and I liked to take it when I went up-island.

No blue car appeared behind us as we entered Chilmark, and I was content that Shadow either had gone home or was waiting for us up at Beetlebung Corner.

I played tour guide, and pointed out stone fences and farms to my passengers.

"Damn," said Karen, suddenly, as we were ending a rare straight stretch of road.

I looked in the rearview mirror and saw the blue car coming over a hill behind us, at the beginning of the straight stretch.

Hmmmmmm.

Shadow, as if as surprised at seeing us as we were at seeing him, fell back out of sight as we rounded another of the road's many turnings.

"Where the hell did he come from?" asked Karen. "There was nobody there when we came out of West Tisbury."

"Luck's a chance, but trouble's sure," I misquoted. "Now we know where he is, at least. And he's not coming any closer."

"But how'd he find us?"

An interesting question. "If all he wants is to know where we're going," I said, "it's okay with me. I don't expect to be there long, anyway. So we'll just drive on."

We got to Beetlebung Corner and went on past Chilmark Center to Gay Head. Shadow stayed out of sight, but I didn't think he'd gone away.

Joe Begay's house isn't hard to find if you know where to look, which I do. The surprise was that he and Toni were both actually there, and not working. I introduced my cousins.

"Mom's looking after the shop, and Jimmy Souza's running the boat today," explained Toni, who looked a proper seven months pregnant and had that slightly tired glow that some women wear as they get closer to their birthing days. "Joe and I are just loafing."

"I didn't know you had cousins in Virginia," said Joe, his dark eyes ironic in his craggy bronze face.

"Their first time on the island," I said. "I thought maybe Toni could take them on a walk under the cliffs while you and I have a beer or two."

Joe's private stock was Ipswich Ale, an excellent brew put together up north of Boston and brought down to Joe by a friend. It was always nice to have an Ipswich Ale.

Joe looked at Toni. "How's that sound to you?"

"It sounds good," said Toni. "I can use the exercise, and I won't have to stay here and listen to man talk." She kissed him and Zee kissed me, and the women and the girl walked away down

116

the path behind the house, toward the faint sound of surf, which was carried to us on the southwest wind.

Ipswich Ale came only in half-gallon bottles. Joe got one out of the fridge and brought two glasses. We sat down on the porch. He poured and we both drank. Delish!

"Man talk, eh?" said Begay. "Cousin Deborah, eh?"

"And her sister, Karen," I said.

"If you say so." He poured us more beer. "What can I do for you?"

"Listen," I said. He was good at that, and I told him everything, including Jake Spitz's recommendation that I speak to him.

"Jake Spitz, eh? So you know Jake, and you want to know what's going on. You get yourself into some weird situations, kid. Cricket Callahan as a houseguest. Well, I swan."

I nodded. "If the girl is in danger, why are they letting her stay with me instead of, say, taking her back to Washington or at least back to the compound, where they have plenty of security? It doesn't make sense, and nobody will tell me what's going on."

"What makes Jake think I can help you?"

"Maybe you can't," I said, looking at the amber fluid in my glass. "But maybe you can."

He got up. "Let's have a look at your wife's car."

I followed him out into the yard and watched him as he looked under the hood, then got down on his back and had a look at things underneath. Finally he gave a grunt, reached up behind the rear bumper, and brought down a small object. He rolled to his feet, looked at it, and handed it to me.

"There's the reason Shadow was able to stay with you. This gadget lets him home in on you wherever you go. Let's take a ride."

We got into his big four-by-four and drove out of the driveway. The blue car wasn't in sight. We turned down Lighthouse Road and headed for Lobsterville Beach, one of the best fishing spots on Martha's Vineyard. In the old days, happy fishermen could park alongside the road and walk the short distance to the fish-filled water, but now the road is lined with NO PARKING signs, and there is only a parking lot at the far end of the beach. Gay Head's government at work again, but what can you expect from a town that has only pay toilets?

At the lot, Begay paused and attached the device to one of the cars parked there. Then we turned around and drove back, passing a blue car as it came along the road. I looked in the driver-side window, but could see nothing. A pox on tinted glass.

"We'll let your shadow trail that other car for a while," said Begay. "Meanwhile, I'll make a couple of calls."

I sat on the porch and drank more beer while he made his calls. When he finally came out of the house, I could hear the sounds of the returning women's voices coming from the path behind the house.

Begay gave me an enigmatic look. "You are in a can of worms," he said.

"Are these the famous man-eating worms from outer space?"

"The very ones," he said. "The ones with teeth."

9

L et's take a stroll," said Joe Begay. "This time I'll talk and you'll listen."

We walked down the path that led to the sea, and met the women.

"Ships that pass in the night," said Zee.

"We left you some beer," said Joe to Toni. "We won't be long."

"And they say women like to talk," said Debby J. "Hah!"

"Truly manly men have truly manly things to discuss," I said. "After all, we have to run the world."

I dodged Zee's feigned kick, and Joe and I went on toward the beach.

"Here's what I heard," said Joe. "You know anything about intelligence agencies?"

"Only what I read about in the papers."

"Well, there are a lot of agencies in the business, and they all need money from the government to stay afloat, but at the same time they all like to avoid being noticed. So they hide themselves lots of times under covers that sound good to the Washington people who hold the purse strings.

"You remember a couple of years back when the National Reconnaissance Office got a lot of attention it didn't want? The NRO handles spy satellites, but most normal people never heard of them, even though they've got the biggest intelligence budget in the country, one that's twice as big as the CIA's. You'll recall that Congress gave them three hundred million dollars to build a new headquarters and didn't even know they'd done it."

"And even while it was going up, everybody thought it was a Rockwell International building."

"That's the one. You'd think that it would be hard for Congress to fund a three-hundred-million-dollar project and not know it, but some say the NRO has an annual budget of six and a half billion dollars — that's *billion,* with a *b* — and in a budget that size, a third of a billion can get lost pretty fast. And the NRO isn't the only spy outfit that gobbles up a lot of tax dollars. Probably nobody really knows how much we spend on intelligence, but some of the smart guesses are that all told we spend pretty near thirty billion a year."

"Good grief! That's more than I make!"

"Our tax dollars at work."

We came out on the beach. There was a mist out over the water that hid the farther shores, but Cuttyhunk was in sight, and we could see fishing boats working the tides. To our left, the clay cliffs of Gay Head climbed out of the mild surf. We walked that way. Begay's hands were thrust in his pockets, and he was looking at seabirds as he talked.

"There's the National Security Council, and the CIA, and the Defense Airborne Reconnaissance Office — that's another outfit that most people never heard of. And the Defense Intelligence Agency, and the Central Imagery Office — I always liked that name, and they're cheap, too; only a couple hundred million a year. And there are the military intelligence agencies, one at least for every service branch, and there are others.

"And all of them like secrets and have black budgets to keep people, including oversight agencies, from looking at them too closely. Some of the stuff they do is so stupid that they don't want anyone to know about it, and other stuff is so sensitive that they don't trust Congress with it, and not entirely without cause, since Congress has never kept a secret in its life."

A fish hawk skimmed over the scrubby brush and we watched it disappear over a dune.

Begay went on. "One of the things these outfits don't want people to know about is how cozy they get with contractors. A whole lot of money exchanges hands, to say the least, and there are tremendous cost overruns that Congress doesn't know anything about."

"I shouldn't be surprised, then, when Rockwell International's name is on the new NRO building."

"That's the idea. Rockwell International hasn't lost any money contracting for Uncle Sam.

"Another thing they'd like to keep pretty quiet is some of their fieldwork, the black stuff and some of the gray stuff. Some of it doesn't work, and some of the rest can be pretty rough."

He stopped talking and walked on in silence. I looked ahead at the rising cliffs and wondered if he was remembering or thinking about something that had taken place during the twenty years after he'd left the army and before he met Toni. He glanced at me, seemed to become aware of his own silence, and went on:

"Anyway, these agencies not only keep busy doing their work and hiding their books, they also keep an eye on each other as best they can, so nobody will get an economic or political jump on them. And they watch other agencies, too. Not officially, maybe, but they do it. They keep an eye on the Secret Service, the FBI, the DEA, and other departments that have to do with crime or security. Part of it's probably just habit, but more of it's out of self-defense. They don't want anybody to know anything they don't. Washington's a political town, so you can't entirely blame them for watching their asses. If they don't, nobody will.

"To get to the point: The first guy I talked with just now used to work for the Department of Defense and has a lot of contacts. Now he's a civilian again. He does research for some foundation, teaches, and gives lectures. He says that even now, after years inside the Beltway, he still stumbles across secret outfits and facilities that he never knew about when he was on the government payroll.

"He told me he's heard about a threat to Cricket Callahan. Not the run-of-the-mill sort of threat that the president and his family get all the time." He glanced at me again. "And you'd be surprised how many and how routine the threats are. Most of them end up being nothing, but they all have to be checked out. This one, though, was different. Worse. But he didn't know the details, so he gave me a name to call. I called it.

"The second person I called is a woman I've worked with, so I think I got the truth, but maybe not. You never know. She knows a lot of people in a lot of places, and what she told me was this, more or less:

"During Joe Callahan's first months in office, while he was still new at the job, he apparently inherited and reapproved covert action abroad that was supposed to clear the way for the election of a government sympathetic to us. But something went wrong. Not only did a small group of innocent civilians get killed or maimed by a bomb intended for the bad guys, but those bad guys came into power as a result. A bungled job all the way around. Of course, our own people didn't actually do the deed, but they were overseeing the job, using local assets, which is the preferred way of doing things since it puts a

screen between our agencies and the conse-
quences of their work.

"In this case, though, after the bad guys got in
power they also got their hands on a couple of
the local assets who did the work, and the assets
told them everything they knew, which wasn't
much, since you never tell anybody more than
they absolutely need to know. I think you've run
into that sort of thinking in just the last day or
two, haven't you?"

"Indeed."

"So these assets didn't know much, but one of
them did know who contacted him for the job,
and he gave up that name before his first finger-
nail was gone. One thing led to another, and
pretty soon there's the latest American Satan
story spread all over the Middle East, complete
with pictures of the victims of the explosion,
including a particularly bad one of a teenage girl
whose face now looks like hamburger. There's
another picture to go with it, showing what she
looked like before. A beautiful girl. Mangled.
You may have seen the pictures in the news-
magazines."

"I did." And now I could see them again. I
tried to push them away. They didn't want to
go. I pushed harder, and looked at the rising clay
cliffs and then out to sea, trying to let nature
clean my memory of the post-bomb picture of
the girl whose face no longer had eyes, a nose,
or skin.

I must have made some sort of sound, for

Begay looked at me for a moment.

"Yeah," he said, walking on, "it was pretty bad, all right. Jesus, the things we do."

Ahead of us, there were young people taking an illegal mud bath between sorties by beach cops, who were supposed to prevent such things, the idea being that such use of the colored clay that had washed off the cliffs would somehow destroy the cliffs themselves. I tried to figure how long it would take the mud bathers to wear away the towering cliffs. Quite a while, I guessed. Meanwhile, the bathers were having what seemed to be a quietly good time. I wished them well.

"Anyway," said Joe Begay, "these letters that started to come in about Cricket Callahan include the pictures of that girl. They say, as I understand it, that Cricket's going to look like the girl looked after the bomb. Every time a letter comes, the pictures come, too. The letters say that Joe Callahan ordered the action, and that it's only fair and just that his daughter pay the same price as the other girl paid. Of course, there's a good chance that the president never really knew what he'd okayed. The agency that supposedly did the job probably clothed the mission in the sort of jargon that later lets everybody claim they knew nothing about the details. It's part of the Washington waltz."

My forehead felt tight. "Does Cricket know about this?"

"She probably knows there's been a threat of some sort, but she doesn't know the details."

"Well, that's one good thing, at least. Have they got a line on whoever's sending the letters?"

Begay stopped and looked at the mud bathers. "What do they get out of that?" he asked.

"Ask your wife," I said. "If she's anything like mine, she spreads something like that over her face every now and then and lets it dry. Something to do with making her skin better. Ask Zee, or ask Toni, but don't ask me."

"These people are all face, I guess," said Begay. "Let's go back."

We turned and retraced our steps, the cliffs now to our right and the lapping waves to our left. Overhead, the seabirds circled and called beneath an arching blue sky.

"They've been trying to trace the letters, of course," said Joe Begay. "One thing about them is that they've been mailed to Cricket from wherever she's staying. Of course, she never actually gets them. Her staff opens all her mail, and you can bet that Cricket never sees these or a lot of others. The point is that when she's in Washington, they're mailed from Washington. When she travels with her parents, they're sent from wherever they stay. Early this spring, when the president and his family were in England, a letter was sent from London. That's how it works."

"And now one's been mailed from Martha's Vineyard," I said.

"Two, actually," said Begay.

"Counting their first trip?"

He nodded. "It was mailed to them here and

127

was posted from Edgartown. Just about a year ago, a week after the Callahans got here."

I thought for a while, then said, "It sounds to me like whoever's sending the letters has a lot of resources. Your normal would-be assassin or blackmailer doesn't have any way to get to a local mailbox everywhere that Cricket travels."

Begay nodded. "Thus the theory that whoever it is is part of the president's retinue, or at least has an inside contact who's cooperating by mailing the letters wherever Cricket goes."

I thought some more and saw what looked like a bit more light. "That's why Cricket is still with Zee and me, and not back in Washington or at the compound. Because in either of those places she's exposed to more suspects than she is when she's with us. At our place, the only possible suspect is —"

"Right you are. Cousin Karen. No other member of the Callahan staff or the Secret Service is around. Only Karen Lea."

Only Karen Lea. "But that wasn't Karen who was tailing us," I said.

"No, it wasn't. It might have been another agent, though, somebody Walt Pomerlieu sent to keep tabs on things, Karen included."

"It wasn't an agent. We checked."

He smiled at me. It was an ironic, grim little smile. "Did you?"

"Yes." Then the lightbulb went on in my brain. "No. Karen told us that it wasn't another agent. But —"

"That's right," said Begay. "But if she's one of the bad guys, and if she wanted to get free of surveillance, one of the best ways to do it is to give you the idea that your shadow is a bad guy, and get you to shake him, as, in fact, you did, with my help."

I ran possibilities through my head. They did not produce happy thoughts. "The trouble is that you can't trust anybody. It could be Karen, or it could even be Walt Pomerlieu, or it could be somebody I don't even know about. It could be anybody."

"Too bad Louis Renault isn't here to round up the usual suspects," said Begay dryly. "Still, I think we can eliminate the president and his wife, and for the moment, let's eliminate you and Zee. And if you really feel daring, you can eliminate Toni and me."

"All right, I'll eliminate all of the above."

"And you can eliminate everybody you personally know on the island. None of them are in on this."

"Are you sure?"

"I'm sure enough not to waste any time worrying about them. But that's not to say that nobody outside the compound is involved. A second part of the current thinking is that some disgruntled spook or ex-spook may be in on it. My lady in Washington says the details in the letters show a pretty esoteric knowledge of what went wrong over there. And as you may know, there are so many spooks and ex-spooks on this island that some people call it Spook Haven."

I hadn't heard that one before.

"A bunch of the old boys have retired here," he went on. "In any case, whoever is doing this has a serious grudge and also has at least one person close to the president."

"Why haven't they been able to nail him?"

"It's an imperfect world," said Joe Begay, as we approached the house. "I'd say they may be close. I think that's why the girl is with you. So they can close the trap with her out of the way, and so she won't get hurt in case something goes wrong." He gave me another of those small smiles. "Don't look so skeptical. It's working so far. The girl is still fine."

"Terrific."

"You still got that old thirty-eight of yours?"

"Yeah. At home in the gun case."

"You might load it up and stick it in your pocket. The president is only gonna be on the island for another few days. If anything is going to happen here, it'll happen before he goes. And you know the old NRA saying: 'It's better to have it and not need it than to need it and not have it.' "

"Yeah, yeah." Manny Fonseca loved the NRA and that quotation in particular. But I don't like the organization's idiot fringe, and I really hate it when they're right.

10

There was a cheerful babble of baby talk going on when we came into the house. There seems to be nothing women enjoy more than talking about babies. Their own, if possible, but anyone's will do. I have heard grandmothers and great-grandmothers eagerly exchange detailed stories of their long-ago pregnancies and deliveries as though they had just happened yesterday. And the younger women and girls are all ears and, if they are young moms, eager to discuss their own babies and the labors involved in producing them.

"This talk is a female hormone thing," said Joe Begay, making sure his voice was just loud enough to be heard by the women. "Sort of like guys talking about the National Football League. You'll have to get used to it now that you're married. Oh, hi, ladies."

"It's nothing at all like the National Football League," said Toni, raising her chin a bit. "You just don't understand. Testosterone has clogged the arteries to men's brains."

Zee gave her a wide smile. "That explains a lot about Jeff that I never understood before.

You're so smart."

Toni patted her belly. "Having babies makes you wise and strong."

Zee had envy in her face. It was still there when she looked at me. "Have you finished with your manly conversation? National Football League talk or whatever it was?"

"Our Super Bowl predictions are all made, and the bookies have our money," I said. "Time for our gang to head back down-island, if we're going to go clamming."

"What about our shadow?" asked Karen. "He'll keep following us."

"No, he won't," said Joe Begay, and he told her about the bug and where we'd put it. "With any luck at all, Shadow is hanging out in some driveway over in Lobsterville, waiting for you to come out of the parking lot there. You should be home before he figures it all out."

"When we get there," said Karen, "we'll check the other cars. If this one was bugged, the others probably are, too."

My very thought.

We said our good-byes and drove back down to Edgartown, passing the famous Chilmark gravestone of a once-renowned comedian who OD'ed himself to death at the height of his fame. His grave, a sacred site to his admirers, who honor his memory by adorning his stone with roaches, bottles, and beer cans, was once located farther into the cemetery. But the legions of his pilgrim fans wore such a wide trail to the holy sepulcher that the entire cemetery was in danger of being seriously damaged, so the Chilmarkians did the smart thing and moved the stone right next to the road, so it's the first one you see when you go in.

"Just like Jim Morrison's grave in Paris," said Debby J., who thus revealed that she knew more about Paris than I did.

"Of course," said Zee, "some people say that the grave is still right where it used to be, and only the stone was moved."

"It's not what's true, it's what people think is true," said Debby.

"More evidence that you have a future in politics," said Zee, with a smile.

"No," said Debby firmly. "When I grow up I want a job that doesn't attract any attention."

"You can become a professional clammer," I said. "I'll teach you the art this afternoon."

"Good."

"Or you can be a nurse or a schoolteacher or a cop," said Karen. "Nobody ever pays any attention to them."

"There are endless possibilities," said Debby. "Is this a great country, or what?"

Not a bad kid, for a president's daughter.

When I got to John Skye's farm, I turned in.

"*Qué pasa?*" asked Zee.

"I thought I'd invite John and Mattie and the twins to the big clambake. Debby and her sister here can use some company closer to their own age."

"Oh, good!" exclaimed Debby.

"I also thought some of the Skye gang might want to go clamming with us this afternoon."

"Good again!" cried Debby.

We pulled into the yard, where, not so long ago, Zee and I had gotten married under a summer sun. We got out of the Jeep as Mattie Skye came out of the house. Seeing Debby and Karen, she pointed toward the barn.

"Jen and Jill are in there, working on some tack," she said.

Debby and Karen went toward the barn.

"You're all invited to a clambake Sunday," I said to Mattie. "There'll be some other people there, too." I told her when.

Debby, Karen, and the Skye twins came out of the barn. "We've been invited to go clamming," said one of the twins. "Can we take the Wagoneer?"

Mattie gave a look of appeal to the sky.

"We really do have to go clamming with them," said the other twin. "Because there are four of us Skyes, and we can't expect J.W. and Zee and Karen and Debby to get clams for all of us, too. We have to go and help out."

"And we'll need the Wagoneer to do it," said her sister.

"Well," said Mattie, with a sigh, "I guess it's all right. John is going to be busy in the library, working on that book of his, and I'm not going anywhere. But you girls have to start saving your money so you can buy a car of your own. You

134

can't expect to use the Jeep every time you feel like."

"Spoken like a classic mom," said a daughter, giving her a fast hug. "Where are the keys?"

"You and Debby can ride with us," said her sister to Karen. "We'll all go to Zee's house first, so you can get your baskets. Then we'll go . . ." She looked at me. "Where?"

"Eel Pond," I said.

"Excellent!"

As we approached our driveway, I did a good deal of looking here and there, along the highway and in the trees on either side, but saw no Secret Service agents, villains, or any other kind of human beings, not even the normal joggers and bikers. Ditto for the driveway itself. I pulled into the yard and did another fast survey. Nobody was in sight.

I went through the house and out the back door, then followed my thread around through the trees. It was unbroken. I came back into the yard as John Skye's Wagoneer came down the driveway. By the time the Wagoneer had unloaded its passengers, I was underneath the Land Cruiser, looking for a bug. I looked everywhere I could think of, but found nothing. Karen was searching her car, and I went to help out. Just as I got there, she found it. It looked like the one Joe Begay had found on Zee's Jeep.

Karen ran a hand through her hair. "Just my car and Zee's. Why not yours?"

"Maybe Shadow never got a chance to bug it."

135

I thought maybe I should know, but I didn't. Neither did she.

"Strange," she said. She looked at the bug. "Maybe our people can trace this."

Maybe they could. I looked at my watch. "Maybe this isn't important anymore, but if we want to go clamming, we've got a low tide to catch."

She gave a little snort. "The world doesn't stop turning, does it?"

"No."

"Let's go clamming, then."

I got into my bathing suit and the pink Papa's Pizza T-shirt that I wear when I go clamming, donned the cap with my shellfishing permit pinned to it, and went out to my shed and dug out four clamming baskets, two metal ones and two made out of plastic milk cartons. All had Styrofoam flotation laced to them, and lines you could use to tie them to yourself so the tide wouldn't carry them off. I got out a clamming fork, a clam rake, and my combination toilet plunger and quahog rake: plunger on one end of the long handle, rake on the other. And I found a half-dozen pairs of rubber gloves.

Some people like to dig clams with a clamming fork or clam rake, and others like to suck them up out of the mud with a toilet plunger and then gather them up with a quahog rake. Zee and I prefer to crawl around on our hands and knees and dig them up by hand, in sort of a mini–strip-mining operation, wearing rubber gloves to save wear and tear on our fingers.

With all the gear I had collected, along with whatever the twins had brought from home, I figured we had enough stuff to accommodate whatever clamming style our gang would prefer. I tossed everything into the back of the Land Cruiser, added two five-gallon buckets, and when the women and the girls came out of the house in their bathing suits, we were ready to go. Over her suit, Karen wore a loose-fitting shirt. The better to hide her pistol, I suspected. She also carried her huge shoulder bag, which contained who knew what in addition to her radio.

Eel Pond, on the northeastern side of Edgartown, is a rich depository for several kinds of shellfish: quahogs, soft-shell clams, and mussels. It is fished all summer long, but never seems to suffer too much from such use. In fact, its mussels are barely harvested at all, although they are perhaps the sweetest and best-tasting of all the shellfish. Unlike many of our fellow islanders, Zee and I are enthusiastic mussel collectors and eaters.

Today, however, soft-shell clams were our intended prey, so we drove down to the town landing on the pond, unloaded our gear, and walked off to the right, over the slippery mud and through the grass and sea lavender, toward the place where a little island rises out of the water at low tide. We waded across the pond to the neck of land on the far side and came to our favorite shellfishing spot.

Zee and I donned our gloves and went down on our knees. Karen and Debby, new at the job, paired off with the twins, with the clam rake, clamming fork, and plunger.

East, beyond the beach grass on the spit of land beside which we were digging, and south toward the Edgartown lighthouse, Little Beach was filled with August people vacationing with all their might, as well they should, considering the prices they were paying for the privilege. We could hear laughter and voices floating on the wind, and could see the tops of sails outside of the lighthouse, moving in and out of Edgartown Harbor. In the opposite direction, near the landing, where we'd parked our cars, small sail- and powerboats were moored, including two eighteen-foot catboats much like our own *Shirley J.* There were other shellfishers working the shallows on the far side of the little island and enjoying the warm summer sun on their backs.

Eden. Before the birth of Cain.

By mid-August, Eel Pond had been seriously shellfished, and the clams that had been so abundant in June were now harder to find. Which meant that today it would take us maybe two hours, instead of one, to get our mess. No problem, though, since what could we be doing that was more enjoyable than what we were already doing?

The girls were laughing over their clamming efforts, and Karen was trying to, but it was clear that she was also seriously and constantly looking everywhere around us: toward the houses to the west, the people and boats to the north, the beach to the east and south, back to the landing, where people occasionally came or went, carrying clamming baskets. She was ever the bodyguard, and never got far from the shoulder bag she'd laid on the beach grass by the edge of the water.

"What a life she leads," said Zee quietly, reading my mind, as she does more and more. "I don't think I could stand a job that made me see everything as potentially threatening. Do you think there's some vacation island somewhere where Secret Service people can go and relax without their radios and guns?"

"They probably have a bar they go to in Washington," I said. "Cops have bars like that, where they drink with other cops and know that whoever they're with understands them."

"Did you go to that kind of a bar when you were a cop?"

"Sometimes. I imagine that doctors and nurses have their own watering holes, too."

She nodded. "Booze and drugs are two of our problems. We take stuff to keep us going, then other stuff to bring us down so we can get some rest. I wonder if it's the same for the Secret Service people. I mean, how does Karen ever get any sleep? She looks twice at every shadow and twitches at every sound."

I had just excavated a clam graveyard full of dead, mud-filled shells, but had now discovered a nearby suburb of their living relatives, and was capturing them at a goodly clip. There was life in the sea after all!

One of the nice things about clamming is that while your hands are busy doing one thing, your eyes and mind can be doing something else. Happy with my discovery of the clam suburb, I looked up at Zee and ogled her cleavage. "Did I ever tell you that you have a dynamite bod?" I asked her.

"I thought it was my mind that attracted you."

I ogled harder. "Is that where you keep your mind?"

"Apparently it's where you keep yours."

"Actually, mine roams here and there."

"I think," she said, "that Karen has her eye on something."

I sat up on my heels, turned, and looked. Two tall men wearing shorts, shirts, and dark glasses were walking along the shore toward us from the direction of the landing. They seemed to be much interested in us. I glanced at Karen and saw her moving toward her shoulder bag, eyeing the men and loosening the buttons of her shirt as she went.

I got up and walked out to where Debby and the twins were trying to plunge clams up to where they could rake them into their baskets.

"How you doing?" I asked, stepping between Debby and the oncoming men.

"We've got some," said a twin.

"I'll tell you one thing," said Debby. "I don't think anybody should complain about how much fried clams cost! It's fun catching them, though. Are we going to get enough for everybody? Or should I tell Dad and Mom to bring some, too?"

A twin looked at her. "Are your parents coming? That's great!"

Debby looked down at her plunger and worked it up and down.

"Oh, didn't I tell you?" I said. "Her folks will be in New England this weekend. They're going to try to get to the clambake."

"That's your uncle and aunt from Virginia," replied a twin. "I never knew you had any uncles and aunts."

"Ah," I said. "Every family has its secrets. My uncle and aunt probably don't talk about me, either. Anyway, Debby, we should be able to get enough today. Your dad won't have to bring any."

I was watching the two men come toward us. The shirts they wore were the loose kind, with tails long enough to come down over their belts.

Their dark glasses hid their eyes, but as they approached along the western shore, beyond the water we had crossed, their heads turned toward us, and one of them took a hand from a pocket and waved. I raised a hand. The men smiled.

"Beautiful day," one called. "What are you after?"

"Steamers," I said.

"How are you doing?"

"We're making progress."

"Good, good. Well, have a nice day."

They walked on south toward the beach.

I turned and looked at Karen. She was standing in the water next to her shoulder bag, buttoning her shirt and looking after the retreating men.

I thought Secret Service people probably had a high rate of suicide and heart attacks.

11

We worked the clam flats for two hours, until it seemed to me we had enough for invited guests and then some. For entertainment, I taught the girls the words of the Old Pioneer:

> No longer a slave to Ambition
> I laugh at the world and its shams,
> As I think of my happy condition
> Surrounded by acres of clams!

Then we collected mussels from the mud bank. Since almost no one in Edgartown harvests them, they're easy to find, so it didn't take us long to get a lot. The two men in sunglasses never showed up again, nor did any other such people.

"We'll put all these guys, clams and mussels both, into buckets of saltwater overnight," I said to Debby, as we waded back to the landing. "That'll let them spit out any sand or mud they may have collected. Then tomorrow, we'll rinse off the clams and we'll scrub the mussels clean and put the whole lot in the fridge until clambake time. You are officially drafted to be a mussel scrubber, because it's part of your island survival course."

"Actually," said a twin, "it's because scrubbing mussels takes a lot of time and is pretty boring."

"Why did I somehow guess that?" asked Debby, looking up at me as we sloshed along.

"Just for being a smart mouth," I said to the twin, "you and your good sister can show up after breakfast and help this poor little Virginia cousin of mine do the job. I know you'll be glad to help out so you can prove people are wrong when they say that teenage girls are all lazy slobs who only want to hang around malls and never want to do any real work."

"I'm the evil twin," said the twin. "I thrive on avoiding work. I'll send my moral, clean-living, good sister over while I sleep late."

We came up onto the landing ramp and I put the clams and mussels into the Land Cruiser. Then I filled the two five-gallon buckets with saltwater and put them in, too.

There were still people out on the sunny water, raking for quahogs or digging for clams. The boats continued to bob on their moorings. Debby looked around.

"It's really pretty here."

"Did you know there's an official clamming song?" I asked.

"No."

" 'My Darling Clammin' Time.' "

Zee sighed, and the others all sneered and groaned. Zee and I got into the Land Cruiser, and the others got into the Wagoneer, and we all drove back to our house.

There, I put the shellfish into the buckets of water, and Karen got her receiver into her ear and reported our return to whoever was on the far end of the communication link.

I had been thinking about the directional bugs on the cars. Karen's car and Zee's car had them, but my Land Cruiser didn't. How come? I stared down at the buckets full of saltwater and shell-fish, and it came to me.

I went into the house, changed into shorts and my T-shirt that said FRANKLY, SCALLOP, I DON'T GIVE A CLAM on the front, and found the roll of film I'd taken out of Burt Phillips's camera.

"What's that?" asked Zee. "Have you been taking pictures of something?"

I am not famous for my photography, so it was a legit question. I told her where I'd gotten the film.

"I think the police might call that theft," said Zee, frowning. "Or at least removing evidence from a crime scene."

"When I removed this, it wasn't a crime scene," I said. "Nobody was dead yet."

"It's still theft."

"Burt Phillips won't press charges. I'm going to have this developed."

Zee was still not sure she approved of my career as a film thief. "What do you expect to find?"

"I don't know. But maybe I'll find out who

put those bugs on your car and Karen's. I think that the reason those cars were bugged and the Land Cruiser wasn't is because whoever bugged the cars did it while the cars were together but the Land Cruiser was someplace else. And the only time I can think of when the cars were together and the Land Cruiser was someplace else is when Karen and Debby were off to the beach with Jill and Jen in John Skye's Wagoneer, and you and I were off quahogging with the Land Cruiser, and Karen's car and your Jeep were here in the yard."

"And Burt Phillips was up at the end of the driveway," said Zee, nodding. "He was there when we left and when we came back. So you figure he was there while we were gone, too."

It was my turn to nod. "With his trusty camera, taking pictures of whoever came in or out of the driveway. That's why I took the film in the first place. So he couldn't sell pictures of Debby J. and the rest of us to the *National Planet*. I didn't think any of us aspired to be featured in that rag."

"So you really are a noble guy after all," said Zee, "and not just a common crook." She put her arms around me. "I should have known."

Her lips were sweet, and they stayed on mine for a while. When they left, she took a deep breath and said in a small voice, "It's too bad we have company right now."

"Yes." I held her against me, resenting the layers of clothing between us.

"Oops," said Debby's voice from the doorway. "Sorry. Bye."

We looked toward her as she backed out of the room, and untangled ourselves.

"It's okay," said Zee, tucking a strand of her hair behind her ear. "We were just necking a little."

"Mom and Dad do that sometimes, too," said Debby, and my opinion of the presidential couple immediately went up a notch or two. It was good to have a president who still smooched with his lady now and then.

"I'm headed for town," I said. "You want to come along? You can hang out with Jen and Jill and your sister, Karen, and watch the tourists. It's a popular sport in the summertime. You get to see some odd sights."

"Yes," said Debby. "We'll be ready as soon as I can get dressed." She disappeared, and a moment later I heard the Wagoneer going out the driveway, taking the twins home to change into downtown clothes.

"So you figure that maybe Burt Phillips might have gotten a picture of whoever it was who went down our driveway and bugged the cars there," said Zee.

"You got it, kid."

A half-hour later, the Wagoneer returned and disgorged Jill and Jen. Karen came into the living room. She was wearing clothes that made her look barely older than Debby. "I hear we're going downtown. I'm not sure that's wise. There are a lot of media people on this island, and they've got sharp eyes."

"Remember the purloined letter," I said. "Hiding in plain sight can be a pretty good plan. The four of you look a lot like a normal teenage quartet. Your only problem is that you're all too good-looking. Guys will probably be all over you."

"That sounds good to me!" said Debby, coming into the room followed by Jill and Jen.

"We could use some men in our lives," agreed a twin.

"Good grief," said Karen. "That's all we need. Boys chasing us."

"I didn't say *boys*," said the twin. "I said *men!*"

"Let's go in Dad's Jeep," said the other twin. "It's big enough for all of us."

"I get to drive," said her sister. "It's my turn."

"Well, I've got to get ready for work," said Zee. She pulled my head down and gave me another long kiss, then headed for our bedroom to change. "Have fun downtown," she said as she went.

"I think she likes you," said a twin approvingly. I was pretty sure it was Jill, but I was never absolutely sure which twin was which.

Karen ran her tongue over her lips and looked at me.

"We'd better get going," I said.

The five of us climbed into the Wagoneer and set off. There was no one out at the end of the driveway watching. Jen, maybe, took a right and we headed into Edgartown. "The Dairy Queen is the first stop," she said.

"Oh, good!"

We crawled through the A & P traffic jam and pulled into the Dairy Queen, where, to my surprise, we found a parking space. The Dairy Queen is one of Edgartown's gold mines, along with the On Time Ferry, which runs the hundred yards between Edgartown and Chappaquiddick. Neither owner has lost any money lately.

"I'll leave you four to fatten up here," I said, "and I'll meet you downtown in, say, an hour in front of the yacht club. That'll give you time to cruise Main after you pig out here."

"Aren't you staying with us?" asked Karen.

"I have places to go, things to do, and people to see," I said. "I'm a busy man. I'll see you all later."

"Places to go, things to do, and people to see," said a mocking twin.

"The younger generation is going to the dogs," I said. "No respect for their elders."

I walked down past Cannonball Park, on along beside the graveyard, took a right on Pease's Point Way, and fetched the police station. Naturally, the chief was not there.

"Downtown someplace," said Kit Goulart, who was behind the front desk.

Kit and her husband, Joe, were about the size of a matched team of plow horses. I widened my eyes and stared at her massive bosom. "Nice badge you have there, officer."

She laughed. "You already have all the woman you can handle, buddy boy."

True.

"How's the Secret Service biz these days?" I asked.

"The president will be headed back to Washington on Monday," said Kit. "Then we'll return to normalcy, as Harding used to say."

"Any secret scuttlebutt you'd like to pass along?"

"Not a bit. Nobody ever tells me anything."

One reason Kit had lasted so long at her job was precisely because she never gossiped about her work.

"I hear that when Joe Callahan is done being president, he's going to come back to Edgartown and try to get your job."

"He's welcome to it," said Kit. "When he does that, I'll run for president. I like the retirement plan."

I walked down to the photography shop on Mayhew Lane, looking for the chief as I went, but not finding him. After dropping off the film, I peeked into the coffee shop to see if he was there, but he wasn't. I walked up Main, amazed as usual by the number of tourists who seemed to think the street was a sidewalk and paid no attention to the cars that crept among them.

I spotted the chief at the corner of Summer Street, where he stood in front of the Bickerton and Ripley Bookstore politely but firmly telling a group of bicyclists that they couldn't ride their machines on Main Street. They seemed astonished at this news, but followed the chief's fatherly but unbending command to park or push their bikes.

He watched them go off and shook his head. "As a social class, I don't think bikers can read," he said. "They don't seem to be able to understand signs. We do have a 'No Bicycles or Mopeds Allowed on Main Street' sign up there where they come in, don't we?"

"I do believe you do," I said. "My own theory is that they never lift their eyes high enough to read the signs you put up for them. They just sort of look at the ground in front of them. Maybe you should write the signs on the pavement."

"And how about all those racing types who ride in the road right beside the bicycle path? The ones with the tight pants and the little helmets and the thousand-dollar bikes and the intense looks? You know the ones I mean. They pedal faster than most people can drive, but they won't use the bike paths. What's with them, anyway?"

"Bike paths aren't good enough for them," I said. "Too slow. Too many walkers and Rollerbladers and out-of-shape bikers to get in their way. They need to speed to have healthy lifestyles. You can't expect them to mosey along like everybody else."

"Next year for sure I'm going to retire and go to Nova Scotia for the summer," said the chief.

"I'll come back here after Labor Day."

"When you start your talk about Nova Scotia, it's a sure sign that it must be getting toward the end of the summer. Just hang in there, Chief. It'll all be over in a couple of weeks."

Another pair of bicyclists came down the street and looked surprised when he stopped them and sent them walking on their way.

"I could do nothing else but this all day long," he said. "What's this about Big Mike Qasim threatening to thrash you for going after his wife? Do you know he's supposed to have one of those Middle East snickersnees in his boot? You might keep that in mind if you meet him. What'd you do to make him so mad?"

I told him about Dora fixing Cricket's hair.

He shook his head. "Terrific. And Mike being the blabbermouth that he is, nobody can tell him the truth because it'll be all over the island five minutes later. How do you get yourself into these messes? Do you practice?"

"It's a natural talent."

"I believe you. Well, you've tracked me down. What do you want?"

"Don't be snippy with me just because you're mad at these bicyclists. I'm being a good citizen and informing you of current events."

"Like what?"

I told him about the blue car that had followed us, about finding the bugs in Zee's and Karen's cars, and about what Joe Begay's contacts had said. I also told him my theory about when the cars were bugged, but I didn't tell him about the film.

He listened while people went past us into the bookstore, which is Edgartown's finest. When I was through, he said, "So you think that dead guy, Phillips, may have seen somebody go down your driveway? And that somebody may have been the one who bugged your cars?"

"We call him Shadow. Or maybe it's a her. Yeah, I think maybe Burt Phillips saw Shadow going in and coming out."

"So?"

"So it occurred to me that if Burt saw Shadow, Shadow probably saw Burt, too."

"And?"

"It further occurred to me that maybe Burt met Shadow again, later, down the road to Felix Neck, and that Shadow may have killed him."

12

The chief looked at me. "And how do you figure that?"

"I've been running it over in my mind, and it makes as much sense as anything else I can think of. Now let's suppose that Burt is just what he seems — a small-time stringer and photographer who's gotten word, someway or other, that the president's daughter is spending time down with the famous Jackson family. He posts himself and his telephoto camera —"

"How do you know he had a camera with a telephoto lens?" interrupted the chief.

"Because I saw it in his car when I talked to him. Besides, guys like that always have cameras with telephoto lenses, don't they?"

"Maybe."

"Anyway, it doesn't really make any difference whether he had a camera or not. The point is that he saw Shadow or somebody go down our driveway while all of us were gone. And either then or when the somebody came back out, after bugging the two cars he found down there —"

"And maybe the house, too," said the chief

in an offhand voice.

I stopped talking. That idea hadn't occurred to me. Good grief, I'd suffered an attack of dumbness and I hadn't even noticed it. A bug in the house seemed very possible, now that the chief had mentioned it.

I took a deep breath. "I'll check into that when I get home," I said. "Anyway, as I was saying, the somebody sees Burt and knows he's been spotted, but it's too public a place to do anything about it, what with cars and bikers and Rollerbladers and walkers going by all the time, so he decides to wait for a better time.

"He drives past Burt's car, headed toward Vineyard Haven, acting like he's going on his way. But instead he goes into the first driveway he comes to, which happens to be the one going into Felix Neck. He parks in there a ways, and acts like a bird-watcher or something when people drive in and out, but the bird he's really watching is old Burt so he can maybe trail him home, or some such thing as that, and rub him out where it's safe.

"But as things turn out, Burt comes to him. . . ."

"Serendipity," said the chief.

I gave him an admiring look. "I didn't know you knew big words like that. I thought you were just a small-town police chief who never read anything more complicated than the *Playboy* centerfold."

"Omnia vincit amor," said the chief. "Ipso

155

facto. E pluribus unum. And I can do pig latin, too."

"Mea culpa," I said, "I've greatly misjudged you."

"As you were saying . . ."

"To use your term . . . serendipity, indeed, for Shadow, if not for Burt. Burt makes his mistake when he decides not to accept my offer to use my telephone, probably because he recognizes me as the guy who walked over to talk to him earlier in the day. Since he doesn't know whether I'm friend or foe, he goes down the Felix Neck road instead, where, probably amazed at his good luck, Shadow, or whoever, meets him and breaks his neck, so Burt will never be able to ID him, then gets in his car and splits."

The chief was silent for a while, then said, "We're trying to track down people who might have driven in or out of Felix Neck and may have seen something useful to us. Some person or a car or anything. So far, no luck."

"I see Shadow as a smart guy, so I'm not surprised."

"So you think he was in there just waiting to kill Burt?"

"Maybe not just that. Maybe he figured Burt would be out there in his car for a while, so he took a walk through the woods to my place, scouting the grounds so he could get in and out again if he wanted to. And afterwards, he went back to waiting for Burt to move."

"You realize," said the chief, "that if he was

in there watching Burt, he was also watching you when you talked to Burt."

"Yeah, I realize that."

"If the guy knew who Burt was, why didn't Burt know who the guy was? How did he let himself get close enough so the guy could break his neck? Wouldn't he have been careful about not getting too close? He didn't want to get close to you, remember."

"Maybe he never saw the guy. Maybe the guy saw Burt coming along the driveway and slipped up behind him. Joe Begay says there may be spooks involved in this business, and there are some spooks who could probably break our necks right here on Main Street before we knew it was happening."

"A happy thought," said the chief, putting a hand to his neck as if to assure himself that it was still intact.

"Which brings me to another bit of news I know you'll enjoy," I said. "Cricket Callahan, aka my cousin Debby Jackson from Virginia, and Debby's sister, Karen, are here in town at this very moment, hanging out with the Skye twins while they scarf goodies from the Dairy Queen. I'm meeting them down at the parking lot in about a half hour. Just thought you'd like to know."

The chief's expression never changed, but he swept his eyes up and down the street. "Karen's the agent with her?"

"Yeah. Looks about nineteen right now. Dark

hair in a ponytail, about five five, wearing shorts and a T-shirt with another shirt over that to hide the sidearm. Carries a big shoulder bag. You'll know her when the four of them come by."

"You really think Cricket Callahan can walk through Edgartown without being recognized?" His voice told me that he didn't.

"The girls are looking for boys," I said. "I think they might find some."

"Just what I need."

"On the other hand, maybe they won't find any. Cousin Debby is wearing big glasses and has her hair shoved up under a floppy hat with a fake blue flower on it. She looks cute, but she doesn't look like the pictures I've seen of Cricket Callahan. As far as I know, not even Jill and Jen know who she really is, although you never know about those two. They may be just playing along because they like cousin Debby and don't want to wreck her Roman holiday. Besides, if anybody does spot her, I imagine my cousins will laugh and say a lot of people think she looks like Cricket, and it's worse than usual now, because the president's on the island. That might do the job."

"And it might not. What are the twins wearing?"

I told him. Up the street, a cruiser was inching our way behind a covey of bicyclists who were looking this way and that, seeing everything but the sign forbidding them to come farther.

"Okay," said the chief. "I'll have my people

keep an eye on them. It's nice to have the president vacation here, but it's also a pain in the ass. Did I tell you that one of my guys loaned the Secret Service guys his little portable TV? You know, the itsy-bitsy kind you can plug into your cigarette lighter? So now, up there in the woods at night, at least one of the guys supposedly guarding the president is really watching the late show. If it's not one damn thing, it's another."

He started up the street. When the bicyclists came by, he ignored them and waved down the cruiser. It stopped and he got into the passenger seat and reached for the radio.

Behind me, business seemed good at Bick and Rip, as buyers of beach books went in and out. Up and down Main Street the August people were looking tanned and eager to shop as they moved along the sidewalk, ducked in and out of stores, and walked blithely across the street with barely a pause for the cars. Down at the four corners, a summer cop was doing a pretty good job of keeping traffic moving and pedestrians alive.

I try to avoid going downtown in the summer, but I like it in the spring and fall, when the weather is good, the people are mostly gone, and you can actually find a parking space on Main. In those bright days you know a lot of the people you see, the air seems fresher, and the essential stores are open. There are fewer of these essential stores every year, as the T-shirt shops and stores catering to tourists gradually push them out of their high-rent buildings. When my father first brought me to Edgartown, Main Street sported two grocery stores, two drugstores, two liquor stores, a stationery store, a hardware store, and a store that sold useful clothes for the townspeople. Now there are mostly souvenir shops, galleries, jewelry shops, and tony clothing stores. The street is still as lovely as ever, but if you need something useful you have to go to Vineyard Haven to get it.

It was a refrain that had probably been sung for as long as there had been an Edgartown: *The good old days are gone, alas, alas.*

I was becoming an old codger, and I wasn't even forty yet. An ill omen for my future. What would I be like when I really was a codger?

I walked down the crowded street, looking at the colorful August people in their various shapes and sizes, their clothes and packages and bags, their cameras and maps, their swiveling heads, their thrusting necks as they stared into windows. Their faces mostly smiling, sometimes discontent; their voices filling the air with plans to meet or eat or shop or sightsee, or with reports of what they'd eaten or bought or seen. Wives giving husbands advice, husbands protesting that they didn't need it, mothers hanging on to children, fathers carrying babies, prams being pushed, young men and women eyeing each other or laughing with one another as they walked, bicycles being ridden or pushed.

A street full of life and escape, full of people

who did not guess that the daughter of the president of the United States was among them somewhere, or that Shadow and his friends were out there somewhere, too, full of venom, wishing her worse than dead.

I stood on the dock between the yacht club and the Navigator Room, and looked out at the *Shirley J.* as she swung on her stake about halfway across to the Reading Room. I had a strong impulse to go steal Zee away from the hospital, get the dinghy and row us out to the boat, and sail away for a while. Maybe over to Tarpaulin Cove or up to Cuttyhunk. We'd stay until the president and his family went back to Washington and took their troubles with them, then we'd come back and settle into our own lives.

I saw us sitting on our couch in front of the living room stove on a cool fall night. We were happy, and it was quiet. I looked again and saw a child on a rug, being watched by the cats, Oliver Underfoot and Velcro. I looked again and the scene was gone and I was back on the dock. But I had gotten a sudden insight into why I'd been so testy of late. I was a family man now, and was secretly worried that I didn't lead a sufficiently sound economic life to be one. It's all well and good to live close to the wind when you're single, but when you're a married man, it's not so well and good. I considered this revelation and had a hard time believing it. Was I actually feeling guilty because I didn't take money seriously enough? Nah. It was too far out of character.

Or was it?

I heard laughter, and turned and saw my four charges coming along Dock Street amid a group of young men. Even Karen was smiling. I looked at the male faces. They were full of good humor and desire. The younger girls were sauntering with that follow-me walk that seems to come naturally to some of them.

Summer romance. A male hand swung playfully toward Debby's blue hat, but she ducked away, laughing. I walked to meet them.

The male eyes flicked over me, assessing, evaluating. I gave them all a casual smile and looked at the young women.

"Ladies, are we ready to head for home?"

Young male eyes met young female eyes.

"We want fried clams and onion rings for supper," said a twin. Her sister nodded.

"Yes," said Debby, pointing back down Dock Street. "At the Quarterdeck. High-cholesterol food! Fried everything!"

The young men nodded and murmured in agreement. "Yeah!" said one of their voices.

I looked at my watch. It seemed early for supper, but is it ever too early for teenagers to be hungry? Then I looked at Karen, who gave a slight shrug.

"We'll get takeout and go up on top of the town dock and eat there while we watch the boats coming in," said the second twin.

"Yeah," said one of the grinning young men.

It was the only word I'd heard any of the males say, but I knew they knew more.

"You can come along with us," the first twin told me, using the same trick that party throwers employ to quiet the anticipated complaints of neighbors: You're invited to our shindig (since we know you won't want to come), and now that we've invited you, you can't call the cops because of the noise we plan to make.

I was tempted to accept, just to see the looks on their faces, but did not. I would be a drag and nothing more. I made a rapid assessment of the young men. They looked lusty and collegiate, but if any of them were killers or mutilators, I'd be more than astonished. And if the four young women kept together, however flirtatious any of them might be, I could see no danger to Debby or the rest of the foursome.

"You go have clams," I said, "and I will head up to the Newes and have a beer and sandwich. I'll meet you back here in, say, two hours. How's that?"

"Great!" There was laughter and an outburst of voices.

I waved in the general direction of the Quarterdeck. "Off you go. See you later."

"You're sure you're not coming?" asked Karen, as the others turned away and headed for Dock Street. "Your wife's at work, so you're all alone."

Her hand touched my arm.

"Come on, Karen," called one of the young

men, looking back.

"You have an admirer," I said, flicking my eyes toward the retreating group. "You'd better get going."

Her hand lingered a moment longer and her eyes looked up at mine. Then she turned and went after the others.

I watched them cross the parking lot and disappear down Dock Street. A nice-looking bunch of kids. Of course Karen only looked like a kid. She was a woman. A grown-up woman. And a good-looking one. I could still feel the touch of her hand on my arm. I brushed at the spot with my hand and walked up to the Newes From America, a bar that's good in the summer and even better when the tourists are mostly gone, since then there's room enough to breathe.

The Newes serves up good pub food and has an excellent choice of beers and ales. If you buy enough drinks there, you get to have your name on the wall. If you drink even more, you get your own bar stool. I do most of my drinking at home, so I wasn't a contender, but that early evening I climbed a couple of steps up the ladder while I ate and drank and thought about Debby and Karen and whoever it was out there who wanted to destroy Debby's face, and about the inside agent who was in on the plot, and about being financially responsible.

I felt pretty good about letting Debby go off and act like a normal teenage girl for a while. Not only was she with a group of friends, but

Karen was with her, keeping her eyes open.

Besides, there was no way Shadow and his friends could even know that Debby was downtown, so the worst thing that could happen would be to have somebody actually recognize Cricket and make a big deal out of it.

Then I remembered what the chief had said about a possible bug in our house, and I realized that Shadow might very well know exactly where Debby was. I threw some money on the table, went out the door, and ran toward the town dock.

13

They weren't on the street level of the dock, where men and boys, standing or seated beside their bait buckets, fished for whatever might or might not be in the water below. I ran up the stairs to the walkway on the top. The harbor was filled with boats, and lots of people were admiring the view, but none of them were mine.

Maybe they'd decided to take the On Time over to Chappy. I looked down at the crisscrossing ferries and across the channel to the far side. I didn't see them. I looked back toward town and didn't see them. I glanced at my watch. A half hour before our scheduled meeting time. They could be anywhere. I imagined my group of young men and women walking the tourist-filled streets of Edgartown, happy at being together, flirting and making jokes amid the crowds, but seeing only one another, not seeing a vial of acid in a gloved hand until it was too late. Then, in the chaos and confusion, as Debby screamed and scrubbed at her face and eyes, Shadow would slip away, unnoticed and full of vengeful joy.

Where would teenagers go? I trotted down the

steps and along the docks behind the Sea Food Shanty, behind Porky's tackle shop, past the dock where *Mad Max*, the big catamaran, was moored between its daily cruises. To my right, boats were coming in for the night, and beyond them boats swung at their moorings. Beside the docks, there were people standing, sitting, walking, and watching the boats. But none of them were Debby or her friends.

I cut across the parking lot and went up to North Water Street, my eyes flicking this way and that.

No one.

I walked down to the four corners and talked to the summer cop who was directing traffic. He was the right age to have noticed four pretty young women passing by. He hadn't seen them.

There was another young summer cop up the street. I described the group I was looking for. He held out a hand about chest high.

"You say one of them was a girl about yay high, with big glasses and a blue hat?"

"That's one of them."

"Well, she wasn't in a group. She was with a guy. They went up North Summer Street. I noticed her because I thought she looked like somebody I know, but I couldn't think of who it was."

"A lot of people tell her that," I said, and loped up North Summer Street.

I got to the intersection of Summer and Winter streets. There was no Debby ahead of me, or to my left, so I took a right. Maybe she was in one of the stores between Summer and North Water. I went in and out of them.

No Debby.

Why hadn't she stayed with the others? Who was the guy she was with? One of the boys I'd seen earlier, or someone else? Shadow?

I looked at my watch. It was almost time for our scheduled rendezvous. I jogged to the parking lot, trying to see everything in every direction, listening for an outcry that might spell violence, kicking myself for having been so stupid as to have allowed my charges to go off with a bunch of people I didn't know.

At the parking lot I found Jill and Jen talking to three boys. Karen stood apart, her eyes looking everywhere, her face pale. She saw me and ran to meet me.

"Did you find her?" Her voice was fearful.

"No. How did she get separated from the rest of you?"

"I don't know. One minute she and Allen were with us, and the next they were gone!"

"How long ago?"

She looked at her watch. "Not long. Fifteen minutes, maybe."

"Where?"

"Right on Main Street. After we ate, we walked along Dock Street and up Main. Window-shopping. Then she was just gone! I thought she might be with you. I've got to call this in!"

"I guess so," I said.

But Karen never made her call.

"Hi!" said Debby, and we turned to see her coming across Dock Street, leading a young man by the hand. "I hope we're not late. Allen was showing me the thrift shop. What a neat place. They have some clothes that my parents would just hate! You all should have come!" Then she looked at Karen's face. "Uh-oh."

"Your sister was worried," I said, stepping between them. I looked at the boy. "You must be Allen."

He dropped Debby's hand. "Uh, yes, sir. Allen Freeman." He waved toward the harbor. "My folks have a place over on Chappy. If we're late, it's my fault. I was telling Debby about the thrift shop and she said she'd never seen one, so —"

"No, it's not his fault," said Debby. "I was the one. I just wasn't thinking."

"You can't afford to stop thinking!" said Karen in a low voice full of anger.

"I'm really sorry," said Allen Freeman, looking understandably confused by the degree of outrage in Karen's voice.

"You're not late," I said, doing a dance step to keep casually between him and Karen, "so no harm done. It's just that it's been a long day and some of us are tired and need to go home. Right, cousins?"

"Right, cousin Jeff," said Debby, quick to try to defuse the bomb that was Karen. She turned to Allen. "Thanks. I had a lot of fun."

"Me, too," said the boy. He didn't seem to

169

know what to do with his hands, so he put them in his pockets.

The twins and their admirers came over, serenely untroubled by Debby's temporary absence. Everyone said good-bye to everyone, and Debby, Karen, and I followed the twins to the parked Wagoneer, which was out toward Starbuck Neck on North Water Street.

"What luck!" cried the driving twin. "No parking ticket!"

Luck, indeed. Edgartown's dreaded meter maids rarely miss the opportunity to ply their trade.

Karen's lips were tight together on the ride home. When the twins drove away from our house, and we were still in the yard, she shook her finger in Debby's face.

"You almost gave me a heart attack, young lady! I was just about to call Walt Pomerlieu when you showed up! Do I have to remind you that it's not safe for you to go off by yourself? What if something had happened?"

Debby seemed half chagrined and half angry. "Nothing happened! Why should something have happened? Allen was there all the time. He's nice. He wouldn't have let anything happen!"

"You don't even know Allen! You don't know anything about him!"

"I don't know anything about you, either!" shouted Debby, suddenly furious.

Karen's jaw dropped. "What are you saying? You know me. You've known me for weeks!"

"No! I don't know anything about you!" cried Debby. "I don't know anything about any of you people! You watch me and you watch my folks and you watch everybody, and you talk into your microphones and you wear those dark glasses and you're always there, but I don't know any of you! I know Allen better than I know you, Karen!" She whirled toward me. "I want to invite Allen to the clambake. Can I?"

"No, you can't," said Karen.

"I'm not asking you!" Debby almost shouted. "I'm asking J.W. Well, can I, J.W.?"

"This clambake is getting bigger every day," I said.

"Can I ask Allen? I want him to come."

"No," said Karen. "He can't come."

I think it was that last no that tipped the scales, probably because I don't like having other people tell me what to do. Zee says that it's a major component of my nature, but that she's not sure whether it's a virtue or a fault.

"Sure," I said. "You can invite him. But if he comes he'll meet your folks, and he's going to find out who you really are."

"I don't care. It won't make any difference to him."

I wondered if that was true. Allen Freeman hanging out with Debby Jackson was one thing. Allen Freeman dating Cricket Callahan might be something quite different.

"How are you going to get in touch with him?" I asked.

"You heard him," she said. "He lives on Chappaquiddick. I'll call him on the phone."

And when she said that, I thought of what the chief had said about the house.

"He probably won't be home for a while," I said to Debby. "So why don't you wait before you make your call." I crooked a finger at Karen. Her face was still angry and disapproving, but she followed me out to the Land Cruiser.

"What is it?" she asked.

"Whoever bugged the cars may have bugged the house, too. I think we should have a look. If there's a mike in there, whoever is tuned into it probably knows everything we plan to do before we do it."

The anger went right out of her face. She snapped a finger. "You're right. I've been a dope. My brain must be turning to mush!"

"Mine, too. Do you know how to find something like that, if it's there? I'm not sure I can."

She nodded. "I can do it, but there's a better way. I'll call Walt Pomerlieu on the radio and have him bring in some people with the gear to sweep the house. If it's there, they'll find it."

"Do that," I said. "Meanwhile, let's not talk over any more plans when we're in the house." I gestured toward Debby. "For instance, let's not have Debby make any phone calls until we know the house is clean."

She nodded and reached into her bag. As I walked away, she was already talking into her radio. I beckoned to Debby, who fell in beside

172

me as I walked up the driveway.

"What are you doing, cousin Jeff?"

I don't always tell people the truth, so I thought for three or four steps before deciding to do it this time.

"It's possible that our house has been bugged," I said. "It probably hasn't, but just in case it has, Karen is going to have it swept. She's calling in some agents to do it. That's why I don't want you to call Allen for a while. If there is a bug in the house, whoever is out there listening will know that he'll be coming to the clambake, and we don't want that information to get out."

She walked beside me, then said, "But if there's a bug in the house, the people who put it there already know about the clambake, so what difference would it make if they learn about Allen?"

"Maybe it doesn't. Still, the operating principle for all this security business seems to be that the fewer people who know what's going to happen, the better. But you probably know more about that than I do."

She nodded. "I hate it. I know it has to be done, but I really hate it! Someday I'm not going to need any security, and there won't be any secrets about my life. I'll be like normal people."

"Not right now, though," I said, thinking that Debby, bright and sophisticated as she was, knew little about the lives of normal people, who had no security agents surrounding them. The agents might not be there, but normal people also had secrets hidden from friends and neighbors. I knew that I, at least, had some that I kept locked within myself, and had no plans to share them. The old saw came forth from my memory: Two can keep a secret, if one of them is dead.

"Here's my security system," I said, coming to the beginning of the thread that surrounded the house. "It's high-tech stuff, I'm sure you'll agree." I told her what it was and why it was there.

"I wouldn't have thought of it," said Debby, "and I'm sorry you had to. I think I must be more bother to you than I imagined. I guess Karen's right. I should go back to the compound so you and Zee can live without all this trouble."

I glanced at her and was surprised to see a tear trickle down her cheek. The sight of that tear elicited a rush of sympathy in me, and an unexpected reaction. I put my arm around her shoulder and pulled her against me for a moment before letting her go.

"Forget that stuff, kid. I'm like Sam Spade; I don't mind a little trouble. And neither does Zee. Come on. We'll follow this thread around and see if it's still in one piece. Blow your nose and we'll run a recon."

She found a tissue, wiped her eyes, and followed me. We walked the barely visible circle of thread. For the first fifty yards it was intact. Then we came to a broken spot.

I held up a hand, and we both stopped.

Between the trees, scrub oaks, and brambles, the ground was covered with leaves, twigs and branches, and browned needles from evergreen trees.

I studied the ground, then knelt and studied it more closely.

"What is it?" whispered Debby. "Can you see any footprints?"

I brushed away a leaf and pointed at the fresh hoofprint.

"Bambi."

"A deer!" Her whisper was gone. She smiled.

I stood up and retied the broken thread. "There are hundreds of them here on the island, but most people never see them. Hunters do well during the hunting season, and some poachers do well all year round."

"Do you hunt?"

"Not as much as I used to. But I like venison when I can get it."

"I think it's cruel to hunt animals."

"We all kill something in order to stay alive. Fish, animals, plants, whatever. Only the carrion-eaters live on things they find already dead. Maybe you'd rather do that."

"Yuck!"

"Yuck it is. Come on. This deer went in this way, but he went out another way, so we're going to find another hole in this fence somewhere or other."

But the next break in the thread wasn't caused by the deer. Some person had come walking from the north, had passed through the thread, and had moved in toward the house. I touched my lips with my finger, and gestured to Debby to kneel down.

14

Shadow had come. But had he gone? I put my mouth close to Debby's ear. "Go back the way we came. Stay low and don't make any noise. When you get to the driveway, wait. I'll call you."

She nodded, her eyes wide behind her big glasses, then turned and moved swiftly back through the trees. I inwardly thanked the some-one who had taught her that it was sometimes wise not to argue.

When she was out of sight, I moved toward the house, following the disturbed leaves that marked Shadow's path, keeping low, moving slowly, looking ahead, pausing to look side to side, then moving ahead again, hoping to see before I was seen.

Hawkeye could no doubt have told to the minute when Shadow had passed here, and would have known his weight and height and maybe even the color of his eyes; but I wasn't Hawkeye, nor much of a reader of country signs. All I knew was that someone had come down through the trees from the north, had broken my thread fence, and had gone on toward my house. I went after him.

I came to a spot where I could see the shed behind the house. On its rear wall was the cutting table where I filleted my fish, and beside it the smoker I'd made of parts found in the Edgartown dump in the old days before the environmentalists seized control of it, when it was still the Big D, where you could often find just what you needed and there was an absolute money-back guarantee if you changed your mind, and you didn't need a passport and visa to get in.

Shadow had apparently paused where I was now pausing, for the leafy ground was more disturbed than usual. Like me, he had taken stock of what lay ahead of him before moving on.

Now, I took a good look all around and saw no one, then sought the sign that would show where he had gone next.

Straight ahead. I followed right up to the shed, where the trail disappeared. Shadow had apparently walked into the yard, where my limited tracking abilities failed me. Had he come and gone while we were down in Edgartown? Or was he still here? And if so, where? In the shed?

I breathed deep, eased open the door, and took a quick peek.

Not there.

In the stockade corral, where I store valuable stuff too bulky to go in the shed? I sidled over and had a look. Not there.

That left the house itself. The doors were never

locked, and I hadn't gone inside since we'd gotten home, so he could be there. I thought of the gun cabinet in the living room, and was acutely conscious of being unarmed. I went back to the shed and got a fish knife. If knives and swords were better weapons than guns, we'd still have knights in armor fighting our wars, but the knife was better than nothing. I went into the house, into the kitchen.

I heard movement in the living room and tiptoed in that direction. Karen appeared in the doorway. She looked at the knife. The little tablet of paper that we use to write shopping lists was on the table. I touched a finger to my lips, found a pencil, and wrote: *Shadow may be here in the house. Debby's safe.*

A pistol appeared in Karen's hand. One moment it wasn't there, and the next it was. Very quick.

We went through the house. Every room, every closet.

No one.

We went outside and checked the cars. No one again. We swept the surrounding woods with our eyes. No Shadow.

Karen put the pistol away. "What's going on?"

I told her.

"Where's Cricket?"

"I told her to wait up by the driveway until I called her."

"Call her, then."

"I'll walk up there and get her, just in case

Shadow is between her and us."

Both of us went. Debby was hunkered down like a fawn, behind some ferns under an oak tree. She came out into the driveway.

"Tell me what's going on."

"We don't really know," said Karen. "Somebody came down through the woods to the house and then went away again. We don't know who it was."

"But we wanted to check things out," I said. "Whoever it was is gone."

"Who do you think it was?"

"We don't know," I said. "Maybe it was just some bird-watcher who strayed from Felix Neck."

"But you don't believe that, do you?" Debby was no fool.

"You and Karen go down to the house," I said. "I'm going to see if our birder left again. If he did, I'm going to try to find out where he went. Stay inside until Walt Pomerlieu and his crew get here."

Karen looked at me. "You be careful. Are you armed?"

"I don't plan on shooting anybody," I said. "I just want to see where the guy went."

"There are probably a couple of agents up there in the woods where they found that newspaperman," said Karen. "Maybe they saw something."

"If I see them, I'll ask them."

"What newspaperman?" asked Debby.

180

"You may as well tell her about him," I said to Karen.

"Yeah." Debby looked at Karen. "Tell me about it. Nobody ever tells me anything."

The two of them went down the driveway, and I went into the woods, again following my thread fence. I came to the spot where Shadow had gone in, and I retied the thread. Then I came to the spot where Shadow had come out. Human footprints headed north toward the wildlife sanctuary. Somewhere farther along the thread I knew I'd probably find the spot where the deer had gone on south, but the deer didn't interest me. I retied the exit break and followed Shadow's trail toward Felix Neck.

The thread had been intact when I'd checked it out this morning, but after that the house had been empty most of the day, first when we'd gone to the pistol range, then when we'd gone up to Gay Head, then when we'd gone to the clam flats, and finally when Zee had left for work and the rest of us had gone downtown. Shadow could have come anytime we'd been away.

Why had he come? To harm Debby? Had he left something behind, besides the bugs we'd found on the cars? If he had, would Pomerlieu and his people find it?

Shadow didn't leave a lot of trail, but it was enough for me to follow, thanks to my seasons of deer hunting and to the heels on his shoes, which left marks where moccasins would have left none. He wasn't Hiawatha, then, nor Chingachgook, but someone else less gifted in wilderness lore and skills, and I felt I was at least his match in the forest. I moved warily, pausing to sweep the trees and brush with my eyes as far ahead as I could, then trotting along Shadow's path.

I came to the end of my land and passed over into the wildlife sanctuary. Off to my right, between some trees, I saw the pole topped by the osprey's nest that I'd seen earlier, after Burt Phillips's body had been found. Somewhere in this area, supposedly, were the Secret Service agents Karen had mentioned, guarding against the very thing that Shadow had accomplished: an approach to my house from the north. Shadow might not be Natty Bumppo, but he was apparently more of a woodsman than Walt Pomerlieu's two agents were.

I stopped in the shadow of a tall oak and followed Shadow's path with my eyes. It led to the northwest, to the long driveway that ended at the parking lot by the Felix Neck buildings. Once it got to the drive, I was pretty sure I'd lose it, because a lot of people walk around Felix Neck admiring the flora and fauna, and I, not being Lou Wetzel, either, wouldn't be able to tell Shadow's footprints from any of the others.

But maybe one of the agents, woodsman or not, had seen something. I stood and looked, turning slowly. If I was a Secret Service agent on duty in the woods, wishing I were somewhere else, probably, where would I put myself? In the shade, certainly. Would I have insect repellent, or would I be slapping mosquitoes and other bugs? Repellent, probably. Even the Secret Service probably knew there were insects in the woods, especially in woods near the wetlands along Sengekontacket Pond, and would have prepared for them.

I saw movement about two hundred yards away, across a clearing, beneath a pine tree. I looked harder and saw that it was a man stretching his arms, then doing leg thrusts to keep himself limber. His back seemed to be toward me most of the time. I walked that way. When I was about twenty-five yards away, he turned to face me, and I saw that it was Ted Harris.

He watched me come to him, his eyes no friendlier than usual.

"Birding?" he asked.

I nodded. "A flightless, featherless biped. Maybe you've seen it. It went down to my house from up this direction sometime today, and came back this way later."

His lip curled. "So now you're Daniel Boone, eh? How do you know it wasn't earlier?"

It seemed clear that Ted and I were not destined to become the best of friends. We rubbed each other wrong. "I know," I said. "The question is, what do you know? Did you see anybody go that way or come back?"

He studied me. "I report to my boss, not to you."

"You report to whoever you want to. Right

about now your boss is down at my house, sweeping it for bugs or maybe explosives my bird may have left behind before he came back up here to this sanctuary you're supposedly watching. So if you want to report to Walt Pomerlieu, he's not far away."

He looked at his watch. "I came on duty here two hours ago. Nobody but you has come past in that time."

Was it my turn to curl a lip? "How would you know? Or is it you that's Daniel Boone?"

A little smile flicked across his face. "Not all of us Secret Service types have spent our lives on the mean streets. Some of us are country hicks." He waved a hand in the direction of my house. "I watched you coming along for ten minutes, then practically had to give semaphore signals before you saw me. If anybody else came by in the last two hours, I'd have seen him."

I believed him. Almost.

"Maybe it was you who made that trail," I said.

The little smile flicked again. "That's one of the possibilities. Another is that there isn't any trail at all. Another is that you made it yourself. Or maybe the king of Siam made it."

"Oh, there's a trail," I said. "Come over and have a look. Maybe you can tell if it was the king of Siam. I don't think so, because if it was, he'd have had Anna with him, and I think this is a one-person track."

We walked back to the trail and looked at it.

"Never noticed this when I came on duty,"

said Ted. "Someday I'll probably trip over a curb and break my neck." His eyes followed the trail first to the south, then back toward the Felix Neck driveway. "One person headed north. You say this guy went down from here, then came back out?"

"I didn't back track the first trail I found," I said, "but that's what I figure." I told him everything about finding the trail except about the thread. "The trail led down from this direction and then led back."

"Smallish foot," said Ted, squatting on his heels and pointing at a print in the ground. "This guy wore shoes, not herring boxes without topses. That proves it wasn't you."

"Or you, either, Clementine, unless you can walk on your hands."

"As a matter of fact, I *can* walk on my hands. But not that far. So I guess we're both in the clear." He stood up and swept the forest with his eyes. "You're sure about it not having happened before you left this morning?"

"I'm sure."

"Why?"

"Because a snow-white dove descended from heaven, circled my head three times, then alighted on my shoulder and whispered in my ear, 'This happened after you all left the house this morning.' That's why."

He stared at me, then shrugged. "That means it happened on an earlier watch than mine. Maybe the one just before I got here."

"That's what it means," I said. "Who had that watch?"

Frank pointed a forefinger to the sky and made little circles with it. "It was probably the same dove. It told me not to tell you."

"I'll bet Walt Pomerlieu can tell me," I said.

"Ask him," said Ted. He turned and walked away, frowning.

15

By the time I walked back through the trees to our house, it was beginning to get dark. Walt Pomerlieu and a carload of agents were there. One of them was Joan Lonergan. When I came out of the woods, two of the agents stopped what they were doing and kept their eyes on me.

"I'm J. W. Jackson," I said. "I live here."

The agents kept watching. One put a hand on his hip.

Pomerlieu looked up. "Yeah, that's him," he said.

The agents nodded and went back to work. They were going over the grounds, buildings, and cars for whatever they might find. Karen Lea and Debby were fifty feet up the driveway, just watching.

"We found this in your telephone and this in your living room," said Pomerlieu. He showed me two small devices. "Everything you said in the house or on the phone could be heard."

I wasn't surprised. I had been dumb so often lately that another example of my stupidity seemed only natural.

"I'm not used to this espionage stuff" was all

I could manage as an explanation, but I could feel anger rising inside of me. Someone had actually come into my house, where nobody belonged except Zee and me and our guests, and had listened to everything we had to say. It was more than just irksome.

Pomerlieu's tone was intended to calm. "No reason for you to be hard on yourself. How could you have guessed?"

I thought for a moment. "If these bugs work twenty-four hours a day, does that mean that whoever planted them has to listen twenty-four hours a day? Because if it does, it must mean that there's a good-sized team out there, three or four people at least, taking turns at the listening post."

"It doesn't mean that," said Pomerlieu, "because they could have just taped whatever they heard and played it back later."

"So we can't guess how many people there are?"

"No," he said. "Where were you just now?"

I told him about the trail coming into the house and the one going north to the Felix Neck sanctuary, and of my meeting with Ted Harris. "He surprised me," I said. "He knows what he's doing in the woods."

"He should," said Pomerlieu. "He came to us from another agency. He was in their operations directorate for years, working mostly overseas. He switched to us when they brought him back from his last job. He does know his way around."

188

"He wouldn't tell me who had the shift before his."

Pomerlieu allowed himself a smile. "Good."

"Not from my point of view. Whoever came down here did it on that shift. I'd like to talk to the guy who was on duty."

"We'll attend to that. Don't worry."

"Don't worry? Trust your Secret Service? You jest."

The humor went out of his face. "I don't jest, Mr. Jackson. My job is to protect the family of the president of the United States, and I take that job seriously."

"You're all serious, but so far we've got somebody bugging our cars and our house, somebody following us up to Gay Head, and somebody coming down through the woods past agents of yours who never saw a thing. Who had the duty up there? Some city gink who wouldn't know a moose from a mouse? Somebody who was so busy slapping mosquitoes that he'd miss an elephant going by?"

A ripple of anger crossed Pomerlieu's face. "No elephants would get by Joan."

Joan Lonergan? "You mean Joan Lonergan was on watch up there before Ted? What does she know about the woods?"

"Probably more than you," said Pomerlieu in a cold voice. "She and Ted came to us at the same time. They were partners on their last job overseas. You could drop Joan Lonergan naked into the Amazon jungle five hundred miles from the nearest human being, and she'd walk out okay. I don't think the same could be said for you or me."

I looked at him for a moment, then said, "I'm trying to imagine Joan Lonergan naked in the Amazon jungle, but I can't quite pull it off. I keep seeing an image of Sheena. Joan doesn't have blond hair or a leopard-skin bikini, does she?"

He took a deep breath and exhaled slowly. "I don't think so."

"Neither do I, sad to say. If she's so good in the woods, why didn't she see the person who came down here on her watch?"

"That's one of the things I'll ask her," said Pomerlieu, looking across the yard to where Joan Lonergan was nosing around our outdoor shower. "When I find out, I'll let you know."

"If you think I need to."

"If I think you need to."

"What agency did they work for before they came to you?"

He put on his long-suffering face. "That's one of the things you don't need to know, Mr. Jackson."

There was a sudden gathering of agents over by the outdoor shower. We looked that way, and I saw a dusty man come out of the crawl space under the house, where Velcro and Oliver Underfoot sometimes like to go to escape the summer heat. The man brushed at cobwebs that adorned his face and showed his find to Lonergan and his other companions. Then he and Lonergan came to Pomerlieu.

"You'll want to see this, sir."

"What is it?"

The agent hesitated, glancing at me.

"It's okay," said Pomerlieu.

The agent revealed a plastic bag containing a small square box with strips of tape hanging from it. "I found it under the house," said the agent. "As near as I can figure, it was right under the bed where the girl sleeps."

"Jesus," said Pomerlieu.

"What is it?" I asked.

The agent looked at Pomerlieu, who was definitely pale but managed a shrug.

"It looks like a bomb," said Lonergan. "One of the kind you can detonate by radio. It was taped onto a floor joist."

Pomerlieu pointed across the yard. "Take it over beyond the garden and put it down. If it's what it seems to be, whoever put it there can set it off whenever he wants to. Do it."

"Yes, sir." The agent walked swiftly to the far corner of the yard and put the plastic bag on the ground, then trotted back.

"Call the bomb people," said Pomerlieu.

"Yes, sir." Lonergan walked away and lifted her wrist to her mouth.

"And go over everything again. If there was one, there may be others."

"Yes, sir." The male agent went first to his companions, who listened and then scattered,

191

two of them going back under the house itself. Then he began talking into his collar.

Pomerlieu dug out a handkerchief and wiped his face. "Good Lord, a bomb. If it had gone off . . .." He looked anguished.

"But it didn't," I said, feeling an unexpected sympathy for him. "And now it won't."

"I know, but . . ." He seemed to become aware of himself, and to pull himself together. "This is bad business," he muttered, and went into the house.

Bad business, indeed. I was shaking from fear and anger. A bomb under my house!

I watched the agents swarm over, under, through, and around my buildings, and ran different scenarios through my head. Eventually, Pomerlieu reappeared, spoke to various agents, then came over to me.

"There doesn't seem to be anything else, Mr. Jackson. I'm afraid your house has been turned a bit upside down, though. Sorry."

"Don't be. Better that than another bomb we never learned about. Listen, can you send somebody up to the hospital to check out Zee's Jeep? It may have another one of those bugs on it."

"What makes you think so? Didn't you already find the one on her car?"

"That was this morning's bug. If there's another one, whoever planted it did it this afternoon, while we were clamming. Ted went on duty about the time the girls and I drove downtown, and if we can believe him, the guy who made that trail did it before Ted got there."

"How do you know it didn't happen before you went clamming?" asked Pomerlieu.

"Because the only time her Jeep was here and people weren't was when we were clamming. If the guy who made the trail planted this bomb, he might have planted another bug at the same time."

"We'll check out her Jeep," said Pomerlieu.

"Good." I wished I knew whether the bomb and the bugs in the house had been put there this afternoon or installed earlier, when the first car bugs were installed. "You're sure you've found everything?"

He looked at Lonergan, who was coming out of the house. She gave him a nod.

He nodded back and turned to me. "I think we've found all there was to find here. Now we'll have to get to work on that trail. It's possible that you're right about the bomber having made it."

It seemed a good time to try again for information. "Do you want to tell me what you think is going on?"

He opened his mouth, then shut it again. "I understand your feelings, particularly in light of what we've found here just now. But you don't need to know. Excuse me." He stepped out into the driveway and waved Karen and Debby in.

As they walked toward us, a flatbed truck carrying a large circular container came down the driveway behind them. They stepped aside to let it pass, and it arrived and unloaded three people

I presumed to be the bomb squad. Pomerlieu spoke to them and pointed across the garden. The people backed the truck as near to the plastic bag as they could get, then began to unload gear and climb into suits that looked like they'd been designed for outer space.

"You may not tell me anything," I said to Pomerlieu as Debby and Karen came on toward us, "but it's pretty obvious that somebody has some nasty plans for cousin Debby, and that you think that person's got an agent inside the president's compound. You may have thought that Debby was going to be safer here with Zee and me than she would be out there with the presidential party, but do you still think so?"

His face was expressionless. "Go on."

Karen and Debby weren't too far away now, so I didn't have much more time.

"I've been wondering why the inside agent didn't do the job on Debby's face before now, instead of —"

Pomerlieu's big hand shot out and gripped my shoulder. "How do you know about the threat to her face? Where did you get that information?"

His grasp was strong, and his voice was hard and angry. I looked at the hand, then back at his face. "You tell me nothing, and you expect me to tell you everything. It's true, then. That story about the girl with no face, and whoever it is out there who wants to do the same to Cricket Callahan. Take your hand off of me."

He looked at the hand and took it away. I had the impression he hadn't noticed it being there. "Where did you get that information? That's confidential material! Who gave it to you?"

"How many people work for intelligence services in Washington? And how many of them know about the letters and the threats they contained? And how many of them have lovers or wives or husbands that they talk to? And how many of those people have other lovers or wives or husbands that they talk to?"

"Who told you?"

"A friend who has friends who have friends."

"What's his name?"

"I didn't say it was a he. In any case, you won't get the name from me."

Karen and Debby arrived and looked around.

"What did you find?" asked Karen, looking at the bomb squad.

Pomerlieu told her about the bugs, but not about the bomb.

Debby pointed at the truck. "What are they doing?"

"We found something we can't identify," said Pomerlieu smoothly. "When in doubt, take it out. They're removing it."

Karen frowned but, after a glance at Debby, made no comment about an operation she certainly must have recognized. Instead — deliberately, I thought — she spoke of the bugs, the lesser of two evils by far. "If they've been there long, it means that whoever installed them knew when we went downtown and could have followed us there."

I used my confident voice: "The good thing was that we went in John Skye's Wagoneer. It wasn't bugged, so they couldn't know exactly where it went unless they followed it, and they didn't have much time to get a surveillance car in place. We were probably in the clear all the time. Anyway, the house is messy but cleaned of bugs now, so you can go inside and say anything you want."

"Good! I'm calling Allen!" said Debby, and trotted into the house. Karen, frowning still more, went after her.

"Holy moly" came Debby's voice. "It looks like a hurricane hit in here!"

Pomerlieu touched my arm. "You were saying . . ."

"I was saying you won't get the name out of me. My friends have enough problems without adding you."

"I don't mean that. I mean what you were saying about the inside agent."

"It's nothing you haven't thought about yourself. It's just that the inside agent hasn't done the job himself, when, supposedly, he's had plenty of chances. I can only think of two reasons why he hasn't done it: He isn't the violent type, or he's been afraid that he'll get caught."

Pomerlieu studied my face, then nodded. "There are agents — criminals, too — who may join a violent conspiracy but who would never

196

pull a trigger or detonate a bomb. They might drive the getaway car or even steal the dynamite, but they won't shoot or light the fuse. They don't have the heart for it. They may be wonderful agents, but they won't do certain things."

I decided it wouldn't hurt to ask. "Are Ted and Joan the shy-violet types, or are they the sort you can ask to do anything?"

He stiffened. "They're the sort who know their jobs and do their duty."

"The same might be said for the inside agent. But he's like most people in his position. He doesn't want to get caught. Especially doing something like this."

"No," said Pomerlieu thoughtfully. "Especially doing something like this."

The bomb squad had succeeded in loading the plastic bag into the cylinder on the back of the truck, and the truck was now moving away up the driveway.

"Now what?" I asked. "Shall Karen and Debby go away with you?"

He looked around at the gathering darkness, then shook his head. "There is no *away*, Mr. Jackson. It's always the lady and the tiger. No, let them stay here tonight, at least. I'll fill the forest with agents."

While he arranged that, I went looking for Joan Lonergan. I found her out in my corral, taking yet another look around. She did not smile when I came to her, and I decided to get right to the point.

"Somebody came down here from Felix Neck while you were on duty up there this afternoon. Did you see him?"

"Who said I had the duty?"

"Walt Pomerlieu. Did you see anybody while you were up there?"

"I don't report to you. You ask Walt all the questions you want to, but don't ask me."

She walked away into the falling night, leaving me staring after her.

When I had my anger under control, I went inside and started straightening up the house. Karen helped, but Debby stayed curled on the couch with her phone, talking, presumably, with Allen. Young love? By the time the place looked fit again, Pomerlieu and his crew were gone.

I went out into the yard and looked up at the indifferent stars. The earth seemed without form and void, and darkness was on the face of the deep.

16

I got a flashlight out of the Land Cruiser and went into the woods, circling the thread and retying the break to the south of the house, where the deer had gone on its way. The rest of the thread was intact. When I came back to the porch, I found Karen there.

She pointed at the living room door. "She's still on the phone."

"I understand it's a teenage specialty," I said. "You look a little weary."

She shrugged. "It's been a long day." She pushed her hair back from her forehead. She not only looked tired, she looked very young as well.

"It's martini time," I said. "Care to join me?"

"I'd better not," she said. Then she hesitated. "But I think I will. Not too strong."

"Vodka or gin?"

"Either."

I mixed her a three-to-one gin martini and added a couple of green olives stuffed with hot red peppers. For myself I poured a tall vodka on the rocks and added two more olives, black ones, from Zee's private stock.

"Up on the balcony," I said, carrying both drinks.

I went up and she followed me. I put the drinks on the table between our chairs, and we sat and looked across the dark waters of Nantucket Sound. To the right, the Cape Pogue lighthouse flashed at us. Straight across and to the left, the lights of Cape Cod were clearly visible. A couple of moving lights showed boats out on the sound. Above it all the August stars were beginning to fill the sky. The wind moved softly through the trees.

I sipped my drink. It was cold and smooth as ice. I sipped again.

"It's lovely," said Karen.

"We think so."

"How long have you been married?"

"A little over a year."

"Your wife is very beautiful."

"Smart, too. And famous for having excellent taste in men."

She was silent. The darkness hid her face. Then she said, "I'm sorry if I seemed to be coming on to you this afternoon. I apologize. It won't happen again."

"Forget it," I said. "I knew you didn't mean it. You have somebody back in Washington?"

"Washington is a long way off. It's frustrating. I've heard all about husbands whose jobs take them away from their wives. How they find girls in foreign towns and all that. But I never thought it would happen to me."

"A little flirting isn't bad, but you have to keep it light, so nobody takes it seriously."

She put some brightness into her voice. "Well, it's only a few more days. We'll be going back on Monday. I'll see him then."

"I'm luckier," I said. "Zee will be home just after midnight."

"Tell me about the bomb," she said.

I told her what I knew. When I was through, she said, "I don't think Cricket needs to know about this." Then she said what I'd been thinking. "The bomb was there. Why didn't he set it off?"

"I don't know. It doesn't make sense. But a lot about this whole business doesn't make sense. Maybe it's our lack of organization that's keeping us alive. We haven't made any long-range plans except for Sunday's clambake. Everything else we've done has been sort of spontaneous. We've gone off here and there without any warning, so Shadow hasn't been able to depend on us being anywhere in particular at any particular time."

She thought awhile. "But if I was Shadow, by now I'd be catching on to all this spontaneity and planning to take advantage of it. I'd lie outside your driveway and keep track of who came and went until I knew that Debby was in a particular place, and then I'd go after her, if that's what I wanted to do. Right now, for example, if I was out there, I'd know that just the three of us were down here."

"Except for your fellow Secret Service agents

out there in the trees."

"Yeah. Except for them."

"Of course if they weren't there, and unless Shadow figures we're a couple of idiots, he'd know that we'd know that he'd know there were just the three of us down here."

She managed a real laugh. "I really hate these I-know-that-you-know-that-I-know-that-you-know things. It makes us sound a lot smarter than we are."

True. "Well," I said, "if there really are agents all around us, I guess we're about as secure as we can get. On the other hand, if you think Shadow can get to us in spite of all those guardians out there, there are three or four things we can do. We can sneak off through the trees and hide out somewhere else for the night. Or we can get into a car and drive out past Shadow with you and Debby hunkered down on the floor so he can't see you, and then hide out someplace else. Or I can drive out alone and try to make him think that you're hunkered down on the floor, so he'll follow me and you'll be safe here. Or we can just stay here and take turns standing watch while Debby sleeps."

"I think we can stay," she replied. "Nobody is going to get through the net that's around us tonight."

I looked out at the lights on the far Cape Cod shore and thought about the bomb.

"Hey," said Debby's voice from the bottom of the stairs. "Where is everybody?"

"Karen and I are up here having martinis," I said. "Everybody else is gone."

"Martinis, eh? I'll fix one for myself and be right up!"

"Only if you have your own booze supply," I said. "I'm not going to share mine with a young whippersnapper like you. I'll loan you a can of cola, though. You can pay me back later."

"First no beer, now no martini," said Debby. "What kind of a place is this, anyway?"

Her footsteps went away.

"I don't want to worry her with all this," said Karen.

"She's not naive," I said. "She knows something's going on."

"She doesn't need to know everything."

I wasn't sure Karen was right about that. If somebody was trying to mutilate me, I'd want to know everything.

The footsteps came back, then climbed the stairs, following the beam of a flashlight. The beam fell on us, then on an empty chair. Debby sat down in the chair and turned off the light. Our eyes readjusted to the darkness and the stars glowed down at us.

"Oh, excellent," said Debby.

We sat and looked at the stars and the lights.

"Allen's coming," said Debby in a happy voice.

"Good," I said. "If he comes early, he can help open quahogs."

"I'll tell him. We can open them together!"

Spoken with the enthusiasm of one who has

never tried to open hard-shell clams. The famous phrase *clamming up* is based on their well-known capacity to stay shut when they want to. I decided not to lecture on the subject. "By the time you get back to Virginia," I said, "you'll be a master of island lore."

"Yes."

I wondered if anyone was watching us through those night-vision scopes I'd read about, or if I was just being paranoid. Of course, even if I was being paranoid, it didn't mean nobody was out there watching us. I was very tired of not knowing what was going on. I finished my drink and got up. "I'm going out for a while. I'll be back before midnight."

"Where are you going?" asked Karen's voice.

"To see a man."

Debby yawned quite clearly. "Apparently we ladies need our beauty rest," said Karen. "Time for us to hit the hay."

I thought that Debby might indeed get some beauty rest, but I doubted that Karen would. I thought that she and her pistol would be keeping watch while I was gone, even though Walt Pomerlieu's people out there in the woods supposedly provided all the security the house would need.

We went down from the dark balcony, following Debby's flashlight, to the porch. Karen took my glass at the living room door, and I went out to the Land Cruiser.

At the head of my driveway, there were two

men and two cars, one of which was blocking the entrance. I rolled down my window as they played a light on me. I told them I'd be out for a while, but back before midnight. They moved the car and I drove out and turned right toward Vineyard Haven. There might have been a car parked back from the highway beside the Felix Neck driveway, but I couldn't be sure.

I drove up to the blinker, looking in the rear-view mirror at the headlights coming along behind me from the direction of Edgartown, then took a left. One set of lights followed me. In West Tisbury I took another right. This time the headlights went the other way. I wondered if there was a second Shadow in a second car, but saw no such car behind me, so took a left onto Panhandle Road. Then I took Middle Road to Chilmark and went on to Gay Head. It was late, but I hoped that Joe Begay was still up.

He was.

"J.W.," he said, coming out of the house to see who had arrived.

"Is Toni asleep?"

"She's eating and sleeping for two these days, so she's in bed, at least. I'm about to join her." He cocked a brow. "Or am I?"

"I need some help. Maybe you can give it to me."

"This have to do with your Virginia cousin?"

"It does. I need to know things I don't know."

"And I know those things?"

"Maybe." I told him what had happened since

last we'd talked, and what my thoughts were. He listened without saying a word. When I was through, he said, "A bomb, eh? He's getting serious. What do you want from me?"

"Anything you can tell me."

He got out his makings and rolled a cigarette. I had rolled a few joints of my own long ago, but it was a skill I no longer practiced. He filled his paper with Prince Albert, I noticed, not grass, and lit up with an old-fashioned Zippo, the world's champion lighter even though the modern Bic throwaways have replaced it in public fancy.

"Well, there is one thing," he said. "About that bug we found on Zee's car. I've seen that kind before. They're used in special ops by one or two agencies I've worked with. But not too many outfits used them, and they're not the sort of thing you can find in *Soldier of Fortune* or any of those other mags that sell stuff to would-be paramilitary types. You can buy all kinds of stuff from those mags, but you can't buy that bug. It's pretty much unavailable to anybody outside certain agencies."

"What agencies?"

He puffed on his cigarette. The ember glowed hot, then only warm. I inhaled the smoke and waited.

"Well, there's the CIA. Some of their operations people liked these. And then there's the IRS."

I wondered if I'd heard right. It sounded so

weird that it might actually be true. "The Internal Revenue Service? You're kidding me!"

"Not that IRS, although I wouldn't put it past them." He allowed himself a laugh. "I mean the International Research Service."

I ran all the federal acronyms I could think of through my head, but I'm not good at such things in the best of circumstances, so I wasn't surprised that I'd never heard of the International Research Service. I said as much to Joe Begay.

His cigarette flared and faded. "If you read the annual budget reports, you'll see it right there, sort of buried between other agencies having to do with foreign activities. It doesn't have much of a budget of its own, so it doesn't attract much attention, but it gets a lot of money from some big-budget outfits that don't like to tell Congress or anybody else just where all the money goes."

"How does it manage that?"

"IRS gets contracts from those agencies to perform certain services. In turn, the IRS contracts with private businesses for them to do some of the work."

"What kind of work?"

"Like helping our friends and undercutting our enemies. Finagling with currencies, maybe. Spreading information or disinformation. Buying people in powerful positions. Maybe an occasional unsociable act. All in the name of research, of course. All IRS agents are researchers."

"What kind of unsociable acts?"

Joe Begay dropped his cigarette butt and

ground it out under his foot. "Like helping a friendly political faction win an election with the help of high explosives."

An image came uninvited into my mind. "The little girl with no face."

"The very same. The bomb under your house is an echo of that other explosion, wouldn't you say? Poetic justice, as it were?"

Ye gods! "And these bugs we've found on the cars. They're the sort the IRS uses?"

"Indeed." He hesitated.

"What?"

"Remember me mentioning that some people call this island Spook Haven? Well, they do. Because of all the retired intelligence types who live here or summer here. There are a lot of them. Rich old guys from the OSS days and the early days of the CIA, and some younger rich and occasionally not so rich guys, lots of them married into families playing the same games, and all of them from those alphabet outfits down Washington way that do some work they'd just as soon not talk about in public. Black ops and gray ops, and like that. They do white ops, too, of course, though they probably don't count in this case. It's the black and gray operatives who might interest you."

"Yeah?"

"Could be. Some of them are IRS people, and some of them are pretty pissed off by the way that operation turned out. They don't blame the guy in charge when the operation was planned, but they do blame the new guy. They figure it's his fault things got fucked up and they got a black eye. Some of them are really, and I mean really, mad."

The new guy was the president of the United States, now vacationing on Martha's Vineyard. His daughter was my cousin Debby.

I stared through the darkness at Joe Begay's dim figure. "Do you mean to tell me that it's some pissed-off IRS guy right here on Martha's Vineyard who's out to get Cricket Callahan?"

His voice was touched with irony. "You don't sound surprised. Does that mean there aren't more things in heaven and earth, Horatio, than are dreamt of in your philosophy?"

Actually there probably were. But my dreams of Martha's Vineyard didn't exclude vipers. Every Eden has its snakes, after all.

"Tell me more," I said.

17

Two of the rolled heads from the IRS have places here on the island," said Begay. "One of them was the deputy director of operations when the girl lost her face. Name of Kenneth Eppers. An old-timer with fingers in a lot of pies. Known as 'Horrors' to the troops because of some of the stuff he orchestrated. Lives in a big place in Chilmark. They say he can see both sides of the island from there.

"The other one was Horrors's favorite up-and-comer in operations. The very one who planned the operation that went wrong, in fact. A tough cookie who did a lot of good work overseas, then came in out of the cold to work in the head office. Woman named Barbara Miller."

"Never heard of either one of them."

"I don't think you travel in the same circles. Barbara's husband is an international banker and isn't quite as rich as Croesus, but almost. She used to travel with him or for him and that gave her the cover she needed. His name's Ben, by the way, in case you ever want to introduce him to anybody."

"Ben and Barbara. Sound like good names

for a couple of dolls."

"They've got a house off Lambert's Cove Road, up on a hill with a view of the sound. They've got a few other houses, too, but that's the one they like during the summer."

"You're a well of information. Where do you get it?"

"I'm a Native American. We're full of inherent wisdom."

"Or something else."

"Our little chat this morning whetted my curiosity, so after you left I made some more phone calls to Washington and a couple of other places."

The wind rustled through the trees and bushes on either side of Joe's house, and I wished, not for the first time, that I had eyes like a cat, in case there was something in the darkness that had such eyes and was watching me when I couldn't watch back. Another desire from my childhood that had never gone away when I grew up. Or maybe I hadn't really grown up.

I thanked Joe for his information.

"What are you going to do with it?" he asked.

"I don't know, but I'm glad to have it."

"If you need anything else, let me know."

"I will."

I climbed into the Land Cruiser and drove home, full of thoughts.

By the time I turned into my driveway, I realized that I felt better than I had been feeling lately, because I was finally going to do something instead of just having things done to me.

The feeling was quickly modified.

The agents guarding the end of my driveway ID'd me; then, as one moved his car so I could drive down to the house, the other leaned over my window and said, "A guy came by looking for you. Mad as a hornet. Said something about you and his wife. Burned rubber getting out of here when we wouldn't let him in." He looked at me without expression, and I knew what he was thinking.

"It's all a mistake," I said. "You've seen my wife. Do you think I'm actually after somebody else's woman?"

He shrugged and stood back. In his line of work he'd probably met a lot of fools. He'd also probably met men who'd left gorgeous women for plain ones. For that matter, so had I, so it was no wonder that my protest might have sounded hollow to him.

I drove down and parked in the yard. There, I dug the flashlight out from under the seat and checked out my thread. No easy task in the starlit night, but worth it when I found no breaks. Back at the house, I found Karen on the darkened porch. She'd been watching my light dance around through the woods. I found a chair and sat down.

"Any breaks in your defensive perimeter?" she asked.

"No. Any sign of visitors?"

"No, but you got a call from some guy who left a message."

I had a sinking feeling. "What was it?"

"It was about giving you a good beating so you'd stay away from other men's wives. He didn't leave his name." Karen was more sympathetic than her colleague at the end of the driveway had been.

"Mike Qasim. He was up at the end of the drive, too. The agents wouldn't let him in."

"You'd better keep an eye open for him. Sometimes these guys do foolish things. On Monday, you can tell him the truth, but you'd better be careful till then."

Sometimes these guys do foolish things. The words sent facts flipping through my brain. The letters were from somebody mad at the president because of the girl without a face. The bomb that had ruined her had gone off in the Middle East. "Mike" Mahmud ibn Qasim's people were from over there somewhere in the five-seas area, and Mike was a hothead who was quick to seek out his enemies.

Maybe there were others like him on the island.

I touched a hand to my forehead, as Zee tells me I do when I'm thinking. Why do I do that? I said, "Do you know if your people checked Mike out before the president came down?"

"I can find out. Why?"

I told her my thoughts.

After a moment, she said, "You're not just mad at him because of this wife thing, are you?"

"I don't think so."

After another moment, she nodded. "All right.

213

In the morning I'll find out if he's on our list or ought to be."

"It'll be interesting if he is." If he was, it was just one more reason for carrying out the plan I'd worked out. "Is Debby asleep?"

"Yes."

"She a light sleeper?"

"Not a bit. Once she gets settled in, she's down for the count."

"Good. She'll need to be rested."

"Why?"

"In the early morning, I'm going to move her out of here."

I could feel Karen's frown through the darkness. "What do you mean?"

"I mean there's too much going on that I don't know about, and I want Debby to be safe, so I want to move her away from here. I'll need your help."

Karen's voice was firm. "She's as safe as she'll ever be. We're surrounded by security people. Besides, she can't just go off to who knows where. She's in my charge, remember?"

"I've got a stake in this, too," I said. "Zee and I live in this house, and if Shadow makes another play, Zee could get hurt, along with Debby. I don't want that."

"We have agents all around this place. Nobody is going to get through them."

"You have a lot of confidence in your colleagues. Did you know that some of your fellow agents guarding the compound at night are keeping themselves awake by watching one of those little plug-into-the-cigarette-lighter TVs that they borrowed from one of the local cops? How much talent would it take to sneak past some guy watching the late-night show?"

"If that's how you feel," she said, "I'll take her back to the compound right now."

My eyes were getting used to the darkness, and I could see her stand up, a moving shadow against the starlight beyond the porch screens. She seemed to be looking out into the night.

"I can't keep you from doing that," I said, "but that doesn't strike me as the world's best idea. I think Debby's here because Walt Pomerlieu doesn't want her there. I think he thinks here is safer than there, and he wants her here while he tracks down the mole who's there. The trouble is that here isn't safe anymore, either. We've got to take her somewhere else for a couple of days."

"Like where?"

"How's your night vision?" I asked.

I thought she turned toward me. "Not as good as I wish it was. Why?"

"Can you see this pistol in my hand?"
She froze.

"I can see you against the starlight," I said. "Don't move. Do you see this pistol?"

"What's going on?" Her voice was hard.

"Answer the question, Agent Lea. Do you see this pistol?"

"No. What are you doing?" Her hands began to shift position.

"Don't move," I said, remembering how fast she could be.

The hands stopped. "Be careful," she said in a soothing voice. "Don't do anything foolish. Remember, she's the president's daughter, and if you do anything to her, you'll never get away with it."

I didn't think I had much time before she made her play, even though she thought I had the drop; but I didn't need more time. "Don't worry about Debby," I said. "And don't worry about the pistol, either, because I don't have one with me. But I might have had. In fact, you thought I did."

"Bastard!" The word came like a knife through the darkness.

"The point is that you and I don't really know each other," I said. "None of us know one another. I don't know anything about you or Walt Pomerlieu or any of the other agents I've met, and none of them know about Zee and me, other than what they've been able to check out in the last couple of days."

"We know more about you than you realize!" There was a tremor in her voice, as the need for controlling her fear had passed.

"You didn't know enough to doubt the gun in my hand."

She was furious. "You could have gotten yourself killed! That was stupid! Your pistol may have been make-believe, but mine is real! In another minute I might have used it!"

"Yeah, I think you might have, even though

you thought I had you cold and that I'd probably kill you before you could clear leather or nylon or whatever it is you use for holsters these days. I think I told the truth just in time."

"You're a fool! I can't believe you did that!"

She wasn't the first person to think me a fool, nor, probably, would she be the last.

My throat was very dry. "I'm going to have a beer," I said. "Do you want one?"

"No!"

I went into the dark house, found the fridge by Braille and got a Sam Adams, and came back out onto the porch. The Sam Adams tasted cool and rich, as usual. Manna from heaven. It occurred to me that God might be a brewer, among other things.

I found my chair and sat down. "My problem," I said, "is that I need to trust somebody, but I didn't know who that could be. Now, I'm pretty sure it's you."

"Why? Because you think I was about to shoot you? What does that prove? What kind of person are you? My God!" I could see her turn and stare back out into the night.

"It's not just because you thought about shooting me, it's why you might have done it. You never mentioned any danger to yourself; you only mentioned danger to Debby."

"Jesus, is that why you pulled that stunt? To find out that I'd die to protect Debby? It's my job to protect her, for God's sake! It's what I do! It's what the Secret Service does. It's what we all do. We protect the president and his family!"

"Not all of you," I said. "Somebody in your outfit is working for Shadow."

Silence hung between us for a time. Then she said coldly, "You can't be sure of that."

"I'm sure enough," I said. "And so are you."

More silence. I broke it. "And because I'm sure, I didn't know who to trust."

"You can trust Walt Pomerlieu!"

"You trust him. I don't know him. As a matter of fact, I don't know if you should trust him, either. That's why we have to move Debby out of here. We don't know who to trust."

"Psychiatrists probably have a term for people like you!"

"Probably. And you're probably right about trusting Walt Pomerlieu, but I don't know him, so I'm taking him with a grain of salt. The same goes for Ted Harris and Joan Lonergan. Where did they come from, by the way?"

"What do you mean?"

"I mean they were working for some other agency before they came to the Secret Service. What was it?"

"I'm sure I don't know. What difference does it make?"

"They wouldn't be old IRS people, would they?"

She made a snorting noise that was almost a laugh. "Internal Revenue people? I doubt it. They don't seem to be the type to collect taxes."

She obviously had never had her returns

218

audited, but I decided not to point that out.

"How about the International Research Service?"

She turned from the screen and looked toward my voice. "The what?"

"You never heard of the International Research Service?"

"No. What is it?"

"I don't know much about it. Can you find out where they worked before they joined your outfit?"

"Why?"

I hesitated. Good grief, I was getting as secretive as the very people I criticized for being overly secretive. Was I actually a closet only-if-you-need-to-know guy? To prove I wasn't, I told her almost everything I'd been thinking. But not everything. I rarely tell anybody absolutely everything.

When I was done, she was silent for a while, then said, "So Ted Harris and Joan Lonergan know their way around the woods, and you want to know why."

"Yeah."

"Because the IRS screwed up the operation that cost that poor little girl her face, and because if they worked for that outfit, maybe there's a tie-in between them and the threat to Cricket."

"Debby is her name. Yeah, I think that's possible."

"And if that's the case, then having Ted and Joan out there in the woods guarding this place may be like having the fox guard the chicken house."

"Yeah."

"But if it's not Ted or Joan or both of them, it's somebody else on the inside."

"Yeah. Or at least maybe."

"But you don't know who."

"No. The only one I'm pretty sure about is you."

She made another of those sounds that was almost a laugh. "Because I might have killed you. Thanks a lot."

"So I think it's time to get Debby out of here."

"And you don't want anybody to know where she goes. I'm afraid I can't go along with that. I have to stay with her, and I have to let Walt Pomerlieu know where she is, too. If I don't, I'll not only lose my job, I might be lucky to stay out of jail."

I finished my beer. Delish, as always. The God-as-a-brewer idea seemed likelier than ever. Did that mean that heaven was a pub? I'd read less likely descriptions.

"I've been thinking about that," I said, "and I may know how to keep everybody happy, more or less."

"Start with me," she said skeptically.

"All right, here's the plan. Early in the morning, we all set out together to give Debby two days of island fun, doing one thing after another. When we're away from the house, and a guy I know is up and about, I'll borrow his car, which is a four-by-four with beach stickers. I'll also borrow a couple of portable telephones and make arrangements for us to stay at a safe house for the next night or so. We keep one of the phones in the borrowed car and take the other one with us when we're not in the car. You can keep in touch with Walt Pomerlieu by phone, and he can always get in touch with you the same way, any time he wants to. But even though you two can communicate to your hearts' content, he'll never really know exactly where you are unless you tell him. Okay so far?"

"Go on."

"Okay. While you're reassuring him that everything's fine, you won't actually tell him your location. Instead, you'll tell him stuff like, for instance, I'm taking you and Debby on a tour of the island, or I'm taking you for a nature walk up-island, in the Menemsha hills, maybe, or I'm taking you out on a fishing boat, or off to do some surf casting, or some such thing as that. But since you don't know exactly where we'll be, you can't tell him that."

"He won't buy it!"

"Maybe not. But if he's worried about little Debby, I'll have her talk to him or to her folks whenever he wants. In fact, I think it's a good idea to have her talk with Mom and Dad every day, so they don't fret about her. She can tell Walt and her folks what she's been doing and that she's fine and having fun, and that they don't need to be anxious. Of course we have to try to make sure that she is actually fine and having fun. I don't need any grumpy Cricket Callahans on my hands."

She didn't like it very much. "The portable phones let us stay in touch without being located. And by using a borrowed car, we can move around without being spotted. And as long as nobody knows where we are, nobody can hurt Debby. Right?"

"You're a fast thinker for a government employee. Debby can have a good time and be safe from Shadow while she's doing it; Mom and Dad will be in touch with her whenever they want; you and your boss can talk whenever you want to, so he won't have any reason to throw you in jail; and the good guys will have a couple of days to lay their hands on Shadow. It's a perfect scheme."

Well, not quite perfect, maybe. But, as they say, life is what happens when you plan something else.

18

About half past midnight, a car came down the driveway. As its lights came into the yard, I saw Karen outlined against them. Her hand was on her hip, under the tail of her shirt.

"It's Zee," I said, having recognized the sound of her little Jeep's engine.

The car stopped, its headlights went out, and darkness flowed back into the yard. It occurred to me that although it was Zee's car, it might not be Zee. Moreover, after looking at the headlights, I was now blinded by the night. I felt foolish and angry.

But it was Zee. She came up onto the porch, and I said, "Hi."

She found me in the darkness and put her arms around me. I felt the old electricity from her touch. "How come the guards at the gates?" she asked. "And how come no lights?"

"I guess we can have lights," I said, and put them on. "How are things in the hospital biz?"

"They were fine when I left, and now they're somebody else's responsibility, because I'm taking a few days off to prepare for the presidential visit." Zee gave me a kiss, then looked at Karen, then back at me. "How come those guys are up at the head of the driveway?"

I told her about the bugs and the bomb, and her eyes got huge.

"A bomb? Under our house?"

"It's gone now. Everything is all right."

"All right? What do you mean, all right? It doesn't sound all right to me!"

"Anyway, maybe it wasn't really a bomb. In any case, it's gone and so are all the bugs."

Zee lifted her eyes to mine. "A Secret Service guy came into the ER and told me he'd looked for a bug on my Jeep but didn't find one. Do you know about that?"

"I had him go up there. He didn't find one, you say?"

"No." Zee studied me. "You have that look on your face. What's up?"

"What look?"

"That look. The one that says you think you know something or that you've decided to do something. What is it you think you know or you've decided to do?"

"Are you telling me I should abandon my hopes for a career as a poker player?"

"Not if I get to play against you. Talk."

So I told her about my plans for tomorrow.

"I think that's a good idea," she said, when I was done. "You're not the only one who's getting a little tired of bombs and other people messing around with our lives whether we like it or not. Tell you what: You find an ORV for us to use,

224

and I'll get the portable phones we need. I know some people I can borrow them from. I'll get them in the morning after I go shooting. I also know a place where we can stay for a couple of nights."

"You're shooting with Manny tomorrow?"

"At eight o'clock. We'll be done by nine, so Manny can get back to the shop."

I ran times through my head.

"Okay. I want the rest of us to get out of here about five. Shadow might be asleep by then, but even if he isn't, it'll be hard for him to follow us without being spotted."

"Where'll you go at five o'clock in the morning?"

"Out toward Wasque. I'll take a couple of rods so it'll look like we're going fishing, just in case anybody's looking. Shadow will need a four-by-four to follow us."

"And what if he has a four-by-four?"

"I'll lose him on Chappy. I know the place and he doesn't. If he stays on the beach to keep us from getting past him, we'll come home on the ferry. If he covers the ferry, we'll come home on the beach."

"And if there's two of him?"

"You know Acey Doucette."

"What about him?"

"He doesn't know it yet, but Acey is going to loan me that Land Rover he's been trying to sell me for the past year. He'll be glad to let me test-drive it for a couple of days so I'll know how wonderful it is compared to my old Land Cruiser. When we come off of Chappy, it'll be in the Land Rover, and Shadow won't even know it's us. He'll be looking for the Land Cruiser, if he's there at all."

"All he'll have to do to see you is look in through the windows."

"He might try, but Acey Doucette's snappy Land Rover has those dark, tinted windows that let you look out but don't let people look in. Very fashionable in some circles, and just what we need."

Zee nodded. "Okay." She looked at Karen. "You agree to all this?"

Karen nodded reluctantly. "For the time being, at least. If it doesn't work, we can change our minds."

Pragmatic Zee nodded back. "You'd better pack up whatever you and Debby will need for a couple of days, then. The same goes for us, Jeff."

I gave her a kiss. "I'll take one last look around, then see you inside," I said.

Outside, the sounds of night seemed normal: the sigh of the wind, the distant barking of a dog, the cry of a night bird. I walked fifty yards up the driveway and back, listening, then circled the yard, moving, then pausing to listen some more, then moved again. I saw and heard nothing unusual. Walt Pomerlieu's agents were not showing themselves.

Our bedroom light was on, but the curtains were drawn and I could see nothing inside. I stood beneath the big birch tree for a while longer, then went into the house. Zee was already in bed. She watched me undress and set the alarm, then held up her arms and pulled me down.

"I'll be glad when we're alone again," she whispered. "I miss making the loud noises."

"Me, too. But I'll bet we can do this in mime. What do you think?"

She flicked off the light. The last thing I saw were her dark, burning eyes. Then she came to me.

The alarm went off at four, and by five I had rods and quahog rakes on the Land Cruiser's roof rack, and our other fishing and personal gear packed inside. While I worked, I thought about Joe Begay's advice and decided to take my old police .38, so I stuck it under the front seat. Just in case.

Since Zee didn't have to be anywhere until eight, she was cook, and produced the full-bloat breakfast: bacon and eggs, toast, juice, and coffee. Classic high-cholesterol morning cuisine. Whoever first thought of the combination should be enshrined in the chefs' hall of fame.

"I'll meet you in front of Manny Fonseca's shop," said Zee.

"Make sure you lose anybody who's following you."

"I will. Be careful."

Wide-awake Karen, sleepy Debby, and I got into the old Land Cruiser and pulled out through

227

the brightening, predawn morning. It had not been many days before, on such a morning, that I'd first seen Debby coming along South Beach, bent on escape from what she deemed excessive constraints on her liberty. And look at us now: fleeing both Shadow and the Secret Service. So much for the classic choice between freedom and security; we had both and neither.

At the end of our driveway, the two agents peered into the truck.

"We're going fishing," I said. "Last two hours of the falling tide."

The men frowned.

"It's okay," said Karen, flashing her ID. "I'm going along, too."

"I'll call in and let them know," said one of the men. "Where are you going?"

"South shore," I said.

"Well, okay." He stepped back and his partner moved their car aside.

We pulled out and turned toward Edgartown.

Karen actually laughed. "South shore, eh? I thought you only used that one during derby time."

"What do you mean?" asked Debby.

"They say that you hear it all the time during the bass and bluefish derby," said Karen, smiling. "Somebody comes in with a giant fish and everybody wants to know where he got it, so he says 'south shore' or 'north shore,' which means absolutely nothing because each of them is about twenty miles long."

About a half-mile down the road a car pulled out of a driveway and began following us. Shadow or the Secret Service? I drove steadily, slowing but not stopping at the stop sign at the V where the Oak Bluffs and Vineyard Haven roads meet, and going on into town past the empty A & P parking lot.

Karen looked back at the car, then at me. "What are you going to do about that?"

"I'm going to stay ahead of him."

"I think that's one of our cars."

"I'm still going to stay ahead of him."

I took the right fork at Cannonball Park and followed Cooke Street to Pease's Point Way, slowing but not stopping, as the law requires, at the corner of West Tisbury Road. The following car didn't stop, either. Another outlaw. Where were the cops when you needed one?

At the police station on Pease's Point Way, probably. I thought of stopping there, but figured that the car would just drive on by and thus get between me and where I wanted to go, so I went on, ignoring yet another stop sign when I got to Clevelandtown Road and heading on to Katama.

We went by the white rail fence that marks the estate of the only man in Edgartown with cannons on his front lawn, set, apparently, to repel an attack from the harbor. I stepped on the gas and the old Land Cruiser gained speed. But the car behind us lost no ground at all. In fact, it got closer.

"If that's a Secret Service car, why are you

trying to stay ahead of it?" asked Debby.

"Never mind that, dear," said Karen. "It isn't important. We can talk about it later, if you want."

Debby was silent for a while. But then she spoke in a voice that started low and cool and then rose in both volume and heat. "I'm sixteen years old. My dad is president of the United States. I live in the White House. I go to one of the best schools in the country. I've been to five continents. If I lived in some of the places I've seen, I'd probably be a married woman by now. I'd probably have babies and a house to take care of! But you're both keeping things from me, just like I was a little kid who'll have nightmares or something if I know the truth! I'm tired of being treated this way! You tell me what's going on or you can stop right here and let me out of this damned car!"

"Now, Cricket . . . ," said Karen soothingly.

"Don't 'Now, Cricket' me!" cried Debby. "Stop the car, J.W.! Stop it right now."

"I'm not going to stop the car," I said.

"If you don't stop the car, it's kidnapping!"

"See those lights ahead?" I asked. "Those are condominiums. South Beach is just the other side of them. When we get there, we'll lose the car behind us, because we can drive on the sand and they can't. We'll go down the beach a way and then we'll talk. And if you still want to get out of the car, I'll take you back to the compound and leave you there. Meanwhile, be quiet and let

230

Karen try to keep you alive!"

"Keep me alive? What are you talking about?"

The car behind us was getting closer, and it was clear that the old Land Cruiser wasn't up to maintaining any kind of lead. I tried an ancient ploy.

"Hang on," I said. I slowed imperceptibly, then, as the following car got very close, slammed on the brakes. The Land Cruiser slued and skidded, and behind us the car did the same, braking and sliding to avoid ramming us astern. As it slithered sideways, its nose toward the bike path that paralleled the pavement, I accelerated away. The car recovered and came after us, but I had gained just enough of a lead for us to fetch the Katama entrance to the Norton Point Beach, shift into four-wheel drive, and head east over the sands toward Chappaquiddick, leaving our pursuers behind on the pavement.

A half-mile down the beach, I stopped. To our left, Katama Bay shimmered under the brightening sky. Beyond its northern end, on the far side of the narrows, the white buildings of Edgartown could be seen. To our right, the waves of the Atlantic Ocean slapped against the beach. Beyond them, the sea reached to the south. I guessed that you could sail two thousand miles in that direction before reaching the nearest landfall. To the southeast I could see the buoy lights that marked Muskeget Channel, and immediately north of them the sky was glowing where the sun hovered just under the horizon.

I turned off the engine and the headlights.

"Time to talk," I said.

"Past time," said Debby.

"You're probably right," I said.

"I'm not sure about this," said Karen.

"I want to know everything," said Debby. "I'm not a child."

She was and she wasn't. But I nodded. "We don't know everything. A lot of it's just suspicion."

"Tell me all of it. What you think and what you suspect. And what you're not sure of, too, while you're at it."

I remembered just a little of what it was like to be a kid who couldn't get grown-ups to take me seriously. The memory was pretty distant, but it was still there.

"I really don't know if this is a good idea." Karen's voice was filled with discontent.

"You're insulting me," said Debby. "Do you realize that?"

"I'm not trying to insult you," said Karen.

"She's trying to protect you," I said. "She doesn't want you to worry over things you can't do anything about. She's just being a big sister."

"I don't need that kind of protection! I need to be told the truth."

"You're right," I said. "From the beginning?"

"Yes. From the beginning. Everything."

I nodded. "Okay, cousin."

As I talked, the sun peeked over the sea, then rose, bright and life-giving, into the sky, tinting the clouds on the horizon with brilliant color, and dancing on the lips of the waves. I talked for a long time and told her everything.

Well, almost everything.

When I was done, I said, "That's it, kid. Now it's up to you. You can go on over to Chappy with me, or I'll take you back to the compound. Maybe your folks would rather have you there with them, even if Walt Pomerlieu wouldn't."

She thought about that for a while, then said, "It makes a difference, but I think I'll stay with you."

"You're sure?"

"I'm sure."

I doubted that either Karen or I was quite so sure, but I started the engine anyway, and we drove into the rising sun.

19

Acey Doucette lived down toward Pocha Pond, off the dirt road that goes that way after Chappaquiddick's lone paved road ends. I'd originally met him fishing at Wasque Point, and had made the mistake of admiring his then almost brand-new Land Rover. Later, remembering my flattering remarks (mostly devoted to the aluminum body of his truck, which, unlike the metal of my own rusty Land Cruiser, would not corrode), he had begun a campaign to sell the truck to me.

This campaign, I learned from mutual fishing friends and acquaintances, was due to Acey's need for money as the result of his divorce from Nina, the wealthy woman who had, in fact, bought him the Land Rover as a wedding present. Acey, it seemed, was not only an English teacher at the high school, but also an aspiring novelist whose lifestyle, living alone in a large old house on Chappaquiddick while he typed away at his book, had struck his wife-to-be as incredibly romantic. He had done nothing to dissuade her of this view, probably since he held it himself, as his penchant for wearing a beret and a literary air indicated. The consequence was a marriage that lasted a few years and ended when Nina finally realized that Acey was probably never actually going to finish his book.

"Acey is a good guy," George Martin had told me, "but he reminds me of that character Grand in *The Plague*. You ever read that book?"

"Yeah. Grand was the guy who spent his whole life trying to write a sentence so perfect that people would tip their hats to him. Or something like that."

"That's Grand, all right. He never gave up working on that sentence, but he never got it right, either, and somewhere along the line his wife left him. Acey is like that. The way I hear it, he's been working on chapter one for years, trying to get it perfect before he goes on to chapter two. I guess that Nina finally got tired of being a writer's wife and took off."

"Another idyllic vision down the tubes."

"So Acey needs to sell the Land Rover so he can keep on eating until he finishes chapter one."

We pulled into Acey's yard, parked beside the Land Rover, and met Acey at the door.

"You're up and around pretty early," said Acey.

"Worm hunting," I said, and introduced my cousins from Virginia.

Acey was a good-looking guy with soft eyes and a ready smile. Although he was about my age, there was something eternally youthful about him, as though he had managed a Dorian Gray deal of some sort in his mid-twenties that kept him from growing any older. He had the look of someone who should be living in the Latin Quarter in Paris, in a loft, probably, with canvases stacked everywhere and a girl to look after him. His face was without guile and had a kind of passionate yet innocent sensitivity to it that, according to Zee, made him almost irresistible to women.

"Including you?" I'd asked.

"I have eyes for only you," she'd replied, looking up at me and fluttering her lashes.

Sure. Zee and I were married to each other, but neither one of us was blind.

Now, I noticed that Karen was immediately interested in Acey. He and she shook hands a bit longer than was necessary, and seemed momentarily to forget Debby and me.

"We've come to take a test spin in the Land Rover," I reminded him.

"Ah, yes," he said, reluctantly turning away from Karen.

"I'll leave the Toyota as hostage."

"Fine. Maybe I'll take it into town later."

"How's the book coming along?"

He ran a hand through his thick hair and grinned boyishly. "Well, you know. I'm working on it."

"Acey is a writer," I said to Karen, who seemed to perk up at the news.

"Really?"

He gave her a private smile and a modest

shrug. "Well, I'm trying."

I began to transfer our gear into the Land Rover. Debby helped. Acey and Karen talked. When the transfer was completed, my cousins and I climbed into the newer truck.

"A couple of days," I said to Acey. "I'll take this machine out on the beach, and I'll drive it around the island. Give it a workout. Okay?"

"Fair enough," said Acey. "Afterwards, maybe we can make a deal."

"Maybe so."

I drove away, wondering how long it would be before Acey realized that the Toyota's keys were missing. "Forgotten" in my pocket, as a matter of fact. I didn't want Acey to drive the Toyota anywhere. Too many people knew it belonged to me, and some of them might ask Acey why he was driving it and learn that I was now driving his Land Rover, which was exactly what I didn't want either Shadow or anyone else to know. It was better that Acey stayed at home with his novel and lived the lonely artist's life for a while.

We hadn't gotten too far when Debby suddenly said, "Stop!" I pulled over. "Look," she said, pointing. There was a mailbox at the end of a driveway. On it was the name Freeman. "This must be where Allen lives!"

Serendipity. A revised plan for the day sprang from my head, like Athena from the forehead of Zeus. Maybe . . .

But I was cautious. "Allen's probably still in

bed," I said. "Anyway, he's got to go to work, most likely."

"No," said Debby. "It's his day off. He told me so when I called him on the phone."

Maybe there was a God, after all. I sat for a moment and thought things through again. Well, why not? If this worked, my own day would be a lot simpler. Of course, Karen and Debby would have to agree to it. I broached my plan.

"Yes!" said Debby.

"I don't know," said Karen.

"You might have a good time," I said. "It's a perfect day for it."

"Well . . . ," said Karen.

"We'll need a phone," I said. "There's one back at Acey's house."

"Well . . . ," said Karen.

"Let's do it!" said Debby.

I turned the Land Rover around and drove back to Acey's house. He came outside and brightened at the sight of Karen, who seemed to brighten back.

"Acey," I said. "I need a favor. Now, just say no if you can't do it."

He looked at Karen, then back at me. "Okay. Name it."

"My cousins here don't get to the seashore much. I was going to take them to the bathing beach at Wasque today, but something's come up. I wonder if you can take time off from your writing to take them in my place. If you can, Debby wants to use your phone to call a friend

238

of hers, to see if he can come along. Kid named Allen Freeman. Lives right up the road. You know him?"

"The Freemans? Sure, I know them. I know Allen. A day at the beach, eh?" He looked at Karen and smiled his boyish smile. "You like the beach, eh?"

"We don't get there much," said Karen, almost smiling back.

"The phone's right inside," Acey said to Debby. "Sure, J.W., I'll take your cousins to the beach. I could use a break from the typewriter."

There was no hint of sarcasm or insincerity in his voice. He really did think he could use a break from his writing. Part of his charm, I guessed, was his earnestness.

Debby went into the house and came back out, smiling. "Allen can come, and he's got a truck! He says I should come over and help him pack the two of us a lunch. He wants me to meet his parents!"

"And you can stay here and help me pack the two of us a lunch," said Acey to Karen.

Karen wavered.

"I'll take Debby over to the Freeman place," I said, "and she and Allen will pick you two up as soon as they get their act together. Then the four of you can head off for the day. It'll be all right."

"Well . . ."

"Good," said Acey. "That's settled, then.

239

Come on in, Karen. Let's toss some sandwiches together."

"Yeah!" said Debby. "But first, let's get our beach gear out of the truck."

She and Karen did that. I waited while they changed into their bathing suits and beach robes, then I drove Debby, still wearing her big glasses and floppy hat, to the Freemans' house.

Allen Freeman, looking happy, met us at the door and introduced us to his parents, who seemed a bit surprised at having such early visitors and who looked curiously at Debby, as if they were trying to place where they might have seen her before.

"I'll pick you and Karen up about fiveish," I said to Debby. "That should give you enough time in the sun. Don't get burned."

"I won't," she said, exchanging glances with Allen.

I drove back to the beach and went west to the pavement at Katama. There, I looked for the car that had followed me earlier in the morning, but didn't see it. It was a curious feeling to be looking out through windows that people couldn't see into, but it was one I liked, under the circumstances. I drove into town and across to Fuller Street, where Manny Fonseca had his woodworking shop. I parked in front and went inside. The place was rich with the scents of wood, oils, lacquers, and paint. Zee and Manny were there.

"How'd the practice go?" I asked.

"Annie Oakley," said Manny. "In a couple of

years, she'll be giving me lessons."

"That'll be the day." Zee smiled. "See you later, coach." She picked up a bag, gave me a kiss, and led me out the door. When we were inside the Land Rover, she said, "There are two phones in this sack. Where are your cousins?"

I told her.

"They'll be all right?"

"I think so. I'd rather have them there than with me right now. As a matter of fact, I'd rather have you there than with me right now."

She got her worried look. "Why? What are you up to?"

"I plan to visit some people, and I don't know how well I'll be received."

"Who? What people?"

"You ever hear of Kenneth Eppers, also known as Horrors?"

" 'Horrors'? Like in 'House of'?"

"The very same."

"No. Who's Horrors Eppers?"

"Just another off-islander like ourselves, now trying to live the good life on this blessed isle." I told her what Joe Begay had told me about Kenneth Eppers. Then I told her what he'd told me about Barbara Miller and her husband, Ben, the international banker whose work had given Barbara her IRS cover.

Zee nodded. "I get it. You think Horrors or Barbara or maybe even both of them might be Shadow and his gang, if he has a gang."

"You get it, all right," I said. "And then there's

Mike Qasim. He's another possibility." I told her my thoughts about Mike Mahmud ibn Qasim's possible Middle East connections and possible anger about the girl with no face.

Zee shook her head. "No. Not Mike Qasim. He's not the type."

"He's the type to blow his stack about Dora coming to our house. If he gets hot over that, he may get really hot over something like that explosion. Suppose he and the girl were related."

"You don't have any reason to think they are!"

"You're right. But it's a possibility."

"No, it's not. Mike isn't the type, I tell you."

"I think you're probably right," I said. But I didn't take Mike off my list.

"And another thing," said Zee. "I suppose it's occurred to you that if Joe Begay knows about Barbara and Horrors, and if you know about them, and if even I know about them now, the Secret Service and the FBI and probably every other kind of cop knows about them, too."

"Indeed, it did cross my mind."

"So what do you think you can find out that they can't?"

"I don't know, but I think I'll ask. I do have one advantage."

"What advantage?"

"Those other guys all have to obey the law. I don't."

"Yes, you do!"

"Now you know why I wish you were on the beach instead of here with me. You function on too high a moral level for this kind of work."

"I can't be functioning on too high a moral level. I'm married to you, after all."

"A point well taken. But I may have to, how shall I say, pretend a little bit when I talk with Horrors and Barbara."

"I can do that, too. Wives have to pretend more than you might think."

I looked at her. "You aren't talking about that old notion that women fake orgasms because men fake foreplay, are you?"

She lifted her nose a bit. "Maybe." I let go of the steering wheel and grabbed at her. "Get away!" She laughed, pushing at my arms and sliding away across the seat.

"If I need foreplay practice, I think I should get right at it," I said, leering.

Zee slapped at my busy hands and laughed again. "You're too old to do this in a car anymore. I think we'd better go see Horrors and Barbara before you hurt yourself! Wheeee! Stop that!"

"This is only a temporary cease-fire," I said, sitting back. "It only lasts until sundown."

"A deal." She grinned and straightened her clothes, and we drove out of town.

20

First, we drove back down to South Beach. It was only mid-morning, but already the August people were beginning to park, unpack their two-wheel-drive cars, and spread their beach gear and themselves out on the sand. Teenagers were playing in the gentle surf, and parents were keeping a sharp eye on little ones while they wrestled with umbrellas, canvas bags, and beach chairs. Some fathers were already working on their kites or getting out their footballs. Another Vineyard day was getting under way.

We drove to Chappy and went through the dunes until we came to the wooden walk that led from the parking lot to the bathing beach. There, we pulled off the main track and stopped. Zee stayed with the Land Rover, so she could move it in case some overzealous Trustees of Reservations employee came by and was affronted by its presence, and I took one of the phones and walked to the beach. There, on the still not too crowded sand, I found my southern cousins and their men. Karen wore a fairly sedate one-piece suit, but Debby, in addition to her big glasses and floppy hat, was sporting a two-piece outfit not much bigger than a couple of postage stamps. I thought they both looked quite smashing, which was clearly what Acey and Allen thought, too.

I took Karen aside and gave her the telephone, along with the number for the phone we were keeping in the truck.

"Call me anytime," I said, "and I'll call you if I need to. If you report to Walt Pomerlieu —"

"*When* I report to Walt Pomerlieu."

"*When* you report to Walt Pomerlieu, it'll be better if you use your radio. I don't want him to know you've got a phone. I also don't want him to know where you are, so tell him you're on South Beach, if you have to, but don't tell him the exact spot."

"I won't lie to him."

"Don't lie. Just don't tell the whole truth."

"I could lose my job over this."

"Debby could lose more than that."

She frowned her now familiar frown and put the phone into her huge shoulder bag, where, no doubt, she kept her radio and pistol, along with all the normal equipment that women carry around with them.

"I'll see you this afternoon," I said, and walked away before she could give me any of the good reasons why we should probably be doing something other than I planned.

On the other side of the dunes, the Land Rover was waiting for me.

"When this is over," said Zee, "we should dedicate a couple of days to serious fishing. We'll need a Vineyard vacation."

"Fishing and family planning," I said. "Or at least the fun part of family planning."

"If you ever get by the foreplay practice."

"I do want to get that right."

We threw a U and went back to Katama, meeting other ORVs on their way to fishing and beaching spots that were inaccessible to folk without four-wheel drive. ORV drivers scorn the beaches that can be reached with ordinary cars, and rejoice in the relative seclusion their four-by-fours allow them, ignoring the often plain truth that the ORV beaches are sometimes almost as crowded as the others, thanks to an ever-increasing number of Jeeps on the island.

Illusion, like image, is everything, some say.

According to Joe Begay, Kenneth Eppers's house was somewhere in Chilmark, on top of a hill, with a view of both the north and south shores of the island. That description eliminated a lot of houses, but left a fair number, so as we headed out of Edgartown on West Tisbury Road, I asked Zee to ring Joe for more precise directions to both Eppers's house and Barbara Miller's.

It was the first time I'd ever been in a car where a cellular phone was used, and the experience made me feel that in spite of my many backward ways, I was at least entering the twentieth century before it ended.

Joe Begay was at home. I drove while Zee spoke, listened, scribbled on a notepad, asked how Toni was doing, listened some more, thanked Joe, and hung up.

"Kenneth Eppers lives off Middle Road," she said. "Up toward the far end. There's a white rock at the end of his driveway. How does Joe Begay know these things? He's only been on the island for a year or two."

"Joe likes to be informed," I said. "It's a hold-over from the work he used to do."

"Was he in the same business as Eppers and Barbara Miller?"

"I think they may have had mutual acquaintances and interests."

She stared out the window, then said, "Joe doesn't seem the type."

"You don't think Mike Qasim is the type, either. I think the ones who don't seem the type are the best types for certain lines of work."

She looked at me, then back at the road. We took a left at West Tisbury, passing by Alley's Store on the right, and Tom Maley's field of dancing statues on the left, then hooked a right onto Music Street and drove until we could take another left onto Middle Road. It was the same route we'd taken when Shadow had first followed us, but he wasn't there today.

One summer, before I met Zee, I'd taken it upon myself to walk every paved road on Martha's Vineyard. The first morning after this decision, I'd walked to the Edgartown A & P and back. The next morning I'd driven to the A & P, parked the Land Cruiser, and walked up the beach road to the Big Bridge and back. The next morning, I'd parked at the Big Bridge and walked to Oak Bluffs and back. In this fashion, I walked twice, there and back, over all of the island's paved roads, and many of its unpaved ones. Of all the roads I'd walked, Middle Road was one of the loveliest, winding, as it does, between stone walls, past open fields and lovely houses, under trees, and over hills.

When wondering who owned some of the fine houses I'd passed then and since, it hadn't occurred to me that one of the owners might be a government agent so famous for his violent foreign plans that even his own people nicknamed him Horrors, and who now might be planning an attack on the daughter of the president of the United States.

Not all snakes live under rocks.

We passed the field that held the long-horned cattle, which always caught my eye, and went on.

"Do we have a master plan?" asked Zee.

" 'Make sure you're right, then go straight ahead,' as Davy Crockett used to say. Or was that Jim Bowie? Or maybe Fess Parker."

"But are you sure you're right?"

"No, but I might be."

Up toward the Beetlebung Corner end of Middle Road was a driveway adorned on one side by a footstool-size rock painted white and a mailbox with a number on it. No name, Eppers or otherwise, was on the box. The sandy driveway led up through the trees toward a hill. I drove past, found a spot where I could pull

248

off the road and park, and did that.

"Why don't you drive up to his house?" asked Zee, as I got out.

"Because if he is Shadow, he'll learn what car I'm driving. I'll walk up. You stay here, in case."

"No, I'm going with you." But she hesitated. "In case of what?"

"In case some cop stops and wants you to move the truck. In case Eppers chases me with a shotgun and I have to get out of there in a hurry. Why don't you get over behind the wheel?"

"He may not even be home. And what are you going to do up there if he is?"

"I'm going to talk to him, that's all. I won't be long."

"How long?"

I didn't know. "An hour at the most."

"If you're not here by then, I'll call the cops and then drive right up there, looking for you."

"You won't have to do that."

"I love you!"

"I love you, too."

I walked back to the driveway and followed it up through the trees and scrub. The higher I got, the more I could see, until, finally, looking north, I could see the Elizabeth Islands, and looking a bit west of south, I could see Nomans Land lying just off the Gay Head coast. Another turn of the driveway brought me to Kenneth Eppers's house.

It was a classic old New England farmhouse not unlike that belonging to my friend John Skye, who summered on the island and wintered in Weststock, Massachusetts, where he taught things medieval at the college there. Eppers's house was two stories high, partially encircled by a porch, sided with white clapboard, topped with wooden shingles, and sporting a large center chimney, which spoke of many fireplaces.

Beyond it was a neat white outbuilding that struck me as a combined storehouse and garage. A well-trimmed lawn fell away from the house on all sides, and beyond the outbuilding, in the lee of the island's prevailing southwest winds, I could see a vegetable garden. There were flow-ered boxes under the windows of the house, and a flower-bordered walk leading to the front door from the parking area in front of the outbuilding.

Was this the sort of house owned by an ex–IRS director? There wasn't a single barred window or TV camera scanning the grounds, or a guy with dark glasses and a hand under his jacket giving me the once-over.

I walked up to the door and rang the bell.

A woman opened the door. She looked about fifty or so, and was wearing one of those casual, pastel-colored shirt-and-shorts combinations that I call rich-girl clothes. Her hair was gray and neat. She wore a gold wristwatch, a gold bracelet decorated with little bunches of grapes, and a simple gold necklace from which hung a golden image of the Vineyard. A pair of glasses swung from a cord around her neck.

She smiled at me. "Yes?"

"I'm J. W. Jackson," I said. "I'm looking for Kenneth Eppers."

"I'm Jean Eppers. My husband's in the study. Have we met?"

I suspected that she would have remembered if we had. "No," I said, "nor have I met your husband."

She noted that I had no car. "Are you a journalist, Mr. Jackson?"

"No. I'm more or less retired."

"You're rather young to be retired."

"Your husband and I have mutual acquaintances. I'd like to talk with him about some interests we may have in common."

"Ken is retired," she said, emphasizing the *is*. "He's no longer involved with his previous career."

"Yes, I know."

I waited. Her eyes flicked over me.

"Are you living in Washington, Mr. Jackson?"

"No. I live here on the island. In Edgartown. I won't take up much of your husband's time, Mrs. Eppers. I told my wife I wouldn't be gone more than an hour."

"Where's your car, Mr. Jackson?"

"My wife dropped me off and went on to Menemsha to pick up some swordfish and visit a friend. She'll pick me up down on the road on her way home."

Jean Eppers's smile had never gone away. I couldn't tell if it was real or practiced. I imagined that having lived in Washington for many years, she'd mastered hiding her true feelings.

She stepped back from the door. "What a busybody I am, Mr. Jackson. Please come in. The study is right down the hall. I'll get Ken."

She led me into a waiting room furnished with simple, comfortable chairs and small tables. On the polished oak floor was an ornate but worn Oriental rug. Prints of hunting and fishing scenes hung on the walls.

"He might prefer to talk with me in the study," I said.

She held her smile. "Ah. Then I'll tell him you're here. Make yourself comfortable."

How many times in the past, I wondered, had Jean Eppers led unknown people to her husband so that they might speak together about unidentified common interests?

I looked down the hall and watched her come out of a side room and walk, smiling, to me.

"Ken says to come right down, Mr. Jackson." She touched my arm. "And don't let him keep you too long. He's supposed to be writing his memoirs, but he'll do almost anything to get away from his word processor!"

"I won't take up much of his time, Mrs. Eppers. If I'm not down at the road when my wife comes by, I may have to walk home."

She gave me a chuckle that almost sounded real, and waved me down the hall.

I walked along an Oriental hall carpet and turned into the study.

The walls were lined ceiling high with bookshelves filled with books that actually looked as though they had been read. Between bookcases on three walls were alcoves containing shelves of miscellany: statuary, photographs, folk art from several continents — objects collected over a lifetime. Above the shelves were portraits of people I presumed were ancestors. On the fourth wall, the shelves were interrupted by large windows looking north toward Vineyard Sound. In front of one of them was a large, worn desk topped by stacks of papers and a computer. Behind the desk sat a man who rose as I came in.

He didn't look like anyone you'd nickname Horrors, but then, Buckingham probably thought John Felton looked pretty innocent, too.

21

Kenneth Eppers was a slight, balding man who at first glance looked like a part-time clerk in a ma-and-pa grocery store. He had rimless glasses set on a thin nose and was wearing an open white short-sleeve shirt over chinos. Only the slippers on his feet and the Rolex on his wrist belied his otherwise clerkish image.

Until I looked at his eyes.

They were watery blue and surrounded by fine lines, but they were not the eyes of a grocery clerk.

"Mr. Jackson." He came around the desk and shook my big hand within his smallish one. "I'm Ken Eppers." He gestured to a leather chair and took one himself. "My wife tells me that you believe we have some interests in common. What can I do for you?"

I saw no reason to make an elliptical approach to the issue.

"I'm hoping that you can tell me something useful about the letters threatening Cricket Callahan."

The watery eyes became ice, but his voice was unchanged. "My wife told me that you claim to

254

have no connection with any government agencies, Mr. Jackson. Did you deceive her?"

"No. I don't work for anybody, in government or out. My interest is personal. Cricket Callahan and I are cousins of a kind. I don't want to have anything happen to her."

He stared at me. "I'm afraid I can't help you, Mr. Jackson. I don't know what you're talking about." He started to rise. "If you'll excuse me, I really must get back to work."

I stayed where I was. "Yes. Your memoirs. I'll be interested in reading your version of what happened when that girl got her face blown away."

A flicker of emotion touched his face, and he looked at his watch as though to hide his expression. "A most unfortunate incident."

"Particularly since you and Barbara Miller planned the business and lost your jobs as a result."

He stared at me with his arctic eyes, then sat down again. "I was thinking of the girl and the others with her, not of my job."

"You've been with one Washington agency or another for a long time," I said. "You'd made it to deputy director of operations for the IRS. That was the acme of a lifetime in the business. And Barbara Miller was your prize dog, the pick of the litter. The plan that went wrong was her baby, and yours, and was supposed to be a crowning achievement for you both. Who knows, maybe you'd even make director of the agency someday, and Barbara would make deputy. What a powerhouse pair that would be. But instead, both of your heads went rolling. I find it difficult to believe that losing your jobs meant nothing to you, and that Horrors Eppers is only sorry for the girl and the others, and not for himself."

Eppers's mouth twitched. "You seem fairly well informed for someone with no Washington connections, Mr. Jackson. I thought the 'Horrors' title was strictly internal, though I suppose I should have known better."

"I'm told you earned it."

He sank into his chair, then dug into a pants pocket and came up with a battered briar and an ornate Zippo lighter decorated with a seal and glittering stones. He tamped the pipe with a finger I now noticed was tobacco stained and lit up, exhaling small puffs of smoke as he got the pipe going. He looked at me, noted my eyes on the lighter, and passed it across. The seal and the language of what appeared to be an inscription were unfamiliar to me, but the inset gems looked real enough. I passed it back.

"The gift of a grateful and still friendly government, which shall be nameless for the moment," he said, returning the lighter to his pocket.

I said, "I used to smoke a pipe myself, and I had a Zippo, too. But mine wasn't decorated with diamonds or rubies."

"A reward," he replied with irony, "for one of those operations which gave Horrors his name."

256

He gestured at the items that adorned the study. "There are other such items here. I keep them to remind me of the nature of the work I do. Or, I should say, the work I used to do."

I was surprised by a tone I thought I heard in his voice. Not pride, or indifference, or scorn, but a sadness.

"Were you ever in a war?" he asked.

"Briefly."

"Vietnam? Combat?"

"A very short tour."

"I was in the Korean War," he said. "The Police Action, as they called it. After that I went to work in Washington. Having been in combat yourself, perhaps you'll understand me when I say that in many ways the battles have never stopped. Whatever motivates nations and men to fight official wars also motivates them to fight unofficial ones. My jobs have had to do with the unofficial ones. The operation you're interested in was one of my failures." He paused. "Not the first, either."

"But the last."

He puffed his pipe and nodded. "Yes. That last operation was well intended, if there is such a thing as good political intent, which is, I imagine, arguable. The object, in any event, was to ensure a victory for a national faction that was probably more democratic than its principal rivals.

"The purpose of the operation was to weaken the leadership of the most powerful rival faction,

257

but at the last moment things went awry, as can happen. . . ." His voice drifted to a stop as he drew on his pipe.

I could hear the sarcasm in my voice when I said, "And the explosives intended for the rival leadership went off in a public market instead."

"The particulars are in files that will be unavailable to the public for at least fifty years," said Eppers with a thin smile. "People in my business are very reluctant to have the details of their activities and the line of command — responsibility, that is — known to anyone, especially taxpayers and critics in powerful places."

"Always in the national interest, of course."

"Of course. We have secrets that are so secret that even their classifications are secret. You may recall that when the Iron Curtain fell and previously secret Soviet documents began to be made public, a lot of people in Washington got very worried for fear that secrets the Soviets had stolen from us would now become known to our citizens. Bad enough that our enemies should know what we've been up to, but incredibly worse if our own people should. Even the secret keepers are aware of the irony, by the way. Some of them, anyway."

Eppers was, at any rate. I said, "But now we have these letters threatening the president's daughter. The logical suspects are people morally offended by that last failed operation, or people who suffered as a consequence. You're in the latter category: a man whose career was cut off because of it. Do you know anything about the letters?"

Eppers's cold eyes sparkled. "The Secret Service, the FBI, and some other people have asked me the same. I told them no, and I'm telling you the same." He drew on his pipe and blew a puff of smoke. "Are you a wealthy man, Mr. Jackson?"

"No." I wondered if my face somehow showed that I was actually feeling a bit poor of late.

"Well, I am," said Eppers. "I am what is known as old New England money. A lot of people like me have been involved in the intelligence business, going back to World War II and even before that. You might have heard of the OSS, for instance. We're well educated, well connected, influential, and patriotic. And we know other wealthy, connected, influential people much like ourselves in other countries. A lot of us went to the same prep schools and universities. We sometimes married one another's sisters or brothers. We are, in short, volunteers who have the time and talents to do the work because we don't really have to earn a living. We're the old-boy network you've heard so much about, and we've done a lot of good work for our countries, along with the bad that gets publicized sometimes." He looked at me through the smoke of his pipe. "Do you follow me, Mr. Jackson?"

"I think so."

"Then you may understand this, too. We work and we win some and lose some, but eventually quitting time comes. Maybe we just get old, or tired, or bored; or maybe something happens that makes us decide to retire. The last straw, as it were. It might be something big, or it might be something little, but it's the last straw." He contemplated his pipe, then raised his eyes again. "For me the girl's face was the last straw. I submitted my resignation immediately and came here. I feel ten years younger."

I studied his face, trying to penetrate behind those watery eyes that now seemed to have lost their icy sheen.

"Are you saying that you harbor no ill feeling toward the president and his family?"

That little smile flickered across his mouth. It struck me as a disguise for pain. "For what? For okaying an operation that my staff and I designed? The president did not get my vote in the last election, but he's in no way to blame for the failure of the plan. If anyone is responsible, it's myself."

The smile that had flitted across his lips reminded me of Byron's phrase: "And if I laugh at any mortal thing, it is that I may not weep." I was also reminded of why I'd left the Boston PD. After being shot by and then shooting to death the robber I'd met in that alley, I had hung up my badge and come to the Vineyard to retire. Maybe Eppers and I had more in common than might be guessed.

"What about Barbara Miller?" I asked. "I'm told that she was the agent in the field. Does she feel the same way as you?"

"I'm afraid I can't speak for Barbara," replied Eppers.

"Do you think she might be the letter writer?"

His eyes cooled. "I think not."

I looked at my watch and got up. "I have to go. Thanks for your time."

He stood. "I hope I've been helpful."

"I know more than when I came in," I said. Then, somewhat to my own surprise, I added, "I wish you a happy retirement."

"Thank you, Mr. Jackson."

"I look forward to reading your memoirs."

He smiled. "If I ever get them written."

"Your wife will see to it that you do."

"She will certainly try."

We shook hands and I left the house. At the turn of the drive that would lead me out of sight, I turned and waved. Horrors Eppers and his wife were on the porch looking after me. They waved back, and I went on down the driveway.

Zee was glad to see me. "I was almost ready to phone the cops, my dear."

"No need." I slid into the passenger seat and gave her a kiss. Lips sweeter than wine.

"Well?"

"Wind up the machine, and we'll talk while we drive."

"Where away, Captain?"

"Lambert's Cove Road. The Miller residence, if you please, Jeeves."

"Aye, aye, sir." She started the engine and we

drove up to Beetlebung Corner, took a sharp right toward Menemsha, then another right onto North Road. As we headed back down-island, I told her about my conversation with Eppers.

"And do you believe him?" asked Zee, when I was done.

I had been wondering about that myself. "I think I do," I said. "But I've believed liars before."

"Mmmm, me, too. But sometimes you've got to trust your instincts."

"Yes," I said. Sometimes, I thought.

We drove east till we got to the upper end of Lambert's Cove Road, and took the left turn onto that lovely, narrow, wandering lane. Lambert's Cove Road and the Middle Road are two of the Vineyard's prettiest byways, and I wondered if there was some irony involved in Horrors Eppers and Barbara Miller having chosen such lovely sites for their homes. I suspected that there might be some Beauty and the Beast metaphor involved, but couldn't make it out. Did beasts love beauty? Did beauties love beasts? Were beauty and the beast one and the same? I gave up.

There are a lot of houses pretty close to Lambert's Cove Road, but a lot more that are off at the ends of narrow dirt roads fronted by lines of mailboxes. The island's most famous pop singer lived up there somewhere, as did a lot of other celebrity types who liked their privacy. Since I like mine, too, we all got along very well.

"Here we are," said Zee, slowing. "Joe Begay gives good directions. I still wonder how he knows the things he knows."

"He's a manly man, like me. We manly men know all kinds of stuff."

"Save me, Lord!"

We were passing one of the dirt roads, this one fronted by four mailboxes, one of which was adorned with the name Miller.

"Same process as before," I said. "We'll find a place to pull off the road, and I'll walk up to the house."

We found a place to pull off. "Same process as before," said Zee. "If you're not back in an hour, I'm calling the cops, then driving up to find you."

"Make it an hour and a half," I said. "That might be a long dirt road."

"One hour," said Zee.

"Give me a kiss."

She did that, and I got out and trotted back to the driveway. As I did, it occurred to me that some such kisses are the last that partners ever exchange. They casually kiss each other good-bye, and later that day he looks the wrong way and steps in front of a car, or she feels an unexpected chest pain and falls before she can reach a phone.

Such thoughts made me want to forget Barbara Miller and go back to Zee and take her in my arms and never leave her.

But I kept going.

22

About a quarter of a mile up the winding driveway, a little hand-painted sign saying MILLER pointed to a side road. I followed along and soon came to the house.

It was a large wooden building with several wings, about twice as big as Eppers's place, all in all. There was a three-car garage and a small barn, and everything was new in spite of its attempts to look old. I thought it looked just like a summer place for an international banker, although I couldn't remember having seen any bankers' summer places before. Everything was neat and tidy.

There was a flower garden beside the house, and a woman wearing a straw hat and cotton gloves was working in it. She was on her knees, and there was a basket beside her containing hand tools for digging and cultivating. She looked about forty years old. Not far from my own age. The prime of life.

She looked up as I approached.

"My name is J. W. Jackson," I said. "I'm looking for Barbara Miller."

She got to her feet. "I'm Barbara Miller."

Her face was just shy of horsey, but she had the sharp, ironic eyes that homely women sometimes have, indicating that they know perfectly well that they're not beautiful, but have decided that they're going to live busy, active, interesting lives anyway, and do just that.

I liked her immediately, in spite of an instant, simultaneous inner warning not to. I try not to trust my intuitions because even though they're usually pretty dependable, sometimes they're not.

Now she looked at me with those intelligent eyes, and waited.

"Nice flowers," I said. "My main garden is mostly vegetables, but some of it's flowers, and I have flower boxes on the fence and hanging baskets and pots. At the moment I'm trying to get my new hydrangeas just the right shade of blue. I like those orange begonias over there."

She glanced at them and nodded. "Yes, they're lovely. Did you come to talk to me about flowers, Mr. Jackson?"

"No. I want to talk with you about the letters that have been threatening Cricket Callahan. I just came from talking with Kenneth Eppers."

"May I see your identification, please?"

"I don't work for anybody, Mrs. Miller, but here's my driver's license."

She looked at it and handed it back. "I don't think I have anything to say to you, Mr. Jackson."

"I'm sort of a cousin of Cricket's," I said. "This is a personal thing, nothing official."

"I'm afraid I can't help you. So, if you'll excuse me . . ."

"I presume you know about the letters. There have been several of them. They seem to be tied to that last overseas operation that you headed."

"I'm retired from the agency," said Barbara Miller. "I'm forbidden by law from discussing agency activities. So, good-bye, Mr. Jackson."

"You retired abruptly and under duress, Mrs. Miller. You had a promising career and you were very good at your work. And you liked it, too, I'm sure —"

"Did I?" she interrupted. "What makes you think so?"

Intuition spoke. "Because you're not the sort of woman who would devote her life to something she didn't like doing. You spent years at the IRS. You wouldn't have done that if you didn't enjoy it."

"Wouldn't I? There is such a thing as duty to country."

I nodded. "Kenneth Eppers has a strong dose of that in his veins, and maybe you do, too. But you can serve your country in a lot of ways. You chose to work with the IRS. Are you telling me that you didn't enjoy the work?"

Her horsey face momentarily revealed its big teeth. "No, I'm not telling you that."

"And because you're not, it's reasonable to presume that when you lost your job, you'd be mad at the guy who fired you. The president of the United States, in this case."

266

Again the big teeth appeared in her quick, horsey, ironic smile. "I wasn't fired. I resigned."

"Whatever. You have the motive and expertise to write and deliver those letters and probably to make good on the threat. Did you write the letters? And if you didn't, do you know who did?"

She pulled off her gloves and shook her head, still smiling that ironic smile. "If you're giving thought to a career in politics, Mr. Jackson, I believe you should reconsider your plans."

"Though it will probably break dear Grandmother's heart, I'll take your advice. Do you know who wrote those letters?"

"Tell me what Ken told you."

"Did he call you after I left him?"

"Do you always answer questions with questions?"

"Do you always ignore questions?"

"Actually, when I first went to work in Washington, a very good teacher trained me to avoid answering them if they were embarrassing, and to answer them expansively if it was to my benefit to do so. Surely you've observed the evening news bits: the very professional dancing and weaving that takes place during congressional hearings and investigations. Tell me what Ken told you."

"You can phone him and ask him, if he hasn't already phoned you."

"Of course I can. I'm interested in your version right now. I can get his later, if I need it." She gestured toward a bench shaded by a large oak.

"Shall we sit while you talk?"

I could think of no reason not to tell her what she wanted to know. "I think I'm being out-ployed," I said. "But, yes, let's sit while I talk. Afterwards, if I'm lucky, maybe you'll talk."

"Maybe. You first."

Me first. We sat, I talked, and she listened. She was a good listener, which was probably one of the characteristics that had made her compe-tent at her job. When I was through, she thought for a moment, then nodded.

"Yes. That sounds like what Ken would say. He really was ready to retire anyway, I think. If it hadn't been that last operation, it would have been something else."

"But that wasn't the case with you, was it?"

"You are a persistent fellow, Mr. Jackson. But, no, it wasn't the case with me." She glanced at my left hand. "I see that you're married. Do you have children?"

I was caught off-guard. "No." I thought of Zee's expression when she'd looked at Toni Begay's expanding belly. "Not yet, anyway."

"There's no not-yet for me, Mr. Jackson. I can't have children, and I've known it since I was a girl. My husband and I considered adopt-ing, but decided against it. Instead, we've de-voted ourselves to each other and to our work. I cannot imagine anything worse than losing a child, but when I lost this job, after devoting almost half of my life to it, it was something akin to that sort of loss, I think. Or at least to losing a part of myself. It was a very terrible experience for me."

The calm tone of her speech was in direct contrast to its content. Her face, too, was without any particular expression. It was as though she were talking about someone else, perhaps someone in a movie or a novel.

She went on: "Had anyone told me that a woman like myself, a mature woman who had made decisions affecting nations, would suffer such malaise at the loss of a job, I'd not have believed it. I thought my life had ended, and perhaps it would have, except for my husband. Ben saw me through it. I was depressed for months, and Ben stayed with me, putting his own work on hold, or farming it out to people less capable than himself, hiding every pill he could find in the house, suffering with me, taking the suffering onto himself, never letting me be alone with my despair until, finally, I began to be better. Until, later, I really was well, and knew that my work had to be seen as just that, my work. Not as my life."

She smiled her equine smile. "And so you find me now, Mr. Jackson, a woman with neither job nor children, but with a loving husband and a more or less happy life."

"And no impulse for vengeance."

"None. I headed the field operations for that last project. Shall I avenge myself on a president who only okayed it on the advice of his director of intelligence?"

"You say you're more or less happy. What do you mean?"

"Are you perfectly happy?"

"No. Do you know the contents of the letters to Cricket Callahan?"

She nodded. "Yes. I know about the letters because I've been interviewed by the Secret Service and others who harbor suspicions like your own. But to answer your question, you remember the pictures of that poor little girl, don't you? Do you think I can ever be perfectly happy, having seen that face and knowing that I was in part responsible for it? I think I've gotten over the loss of my work, but I don't ever expect to get over the picture of that little face."

I sat there and looked at the lovely flower garden and thought that, as usual, old Will was right: Life's a walking shadow. For some of us, at least.

I said, "Time will help you," hoping that it would.

"Thank you."

We sat a while longer. Then I said, "If it's not you and it's not Kenneth Eppers, who is it?"

Barbara Miller shook her head. "I don't know. Someone who's very angry. Very angry indeed."

I thought about that, then looked at my watch and stood up. "My wife is waiting for me, and your husband is probably wondering what we're talking about. You can assure him I haven't succeeded in selling you another vacuum cleaner."

"My husband is in Cairo, Mr. Jackson. He flew over two days ago and won't be back until tomorrow. His business keeps him on the go." She put out her hand, and I shook it. "Well, goodbye, Mr. Jackson."

As I was turning toward the driveway, I heard the sound of an automobile engine and saw a Volvo station wagon come into the yard. It stopped, and a woman got out. Her smile was filled with large teeth.

She looked not unlike an older Barbara Miller, which turned out not to be surprising.

"I thought I heard voices." Her smile was filled with large teeth.

Barbara Miller said, "Mr. Jackson, this is my sister, Margaret. She's keeping me company while Ben is abroad. Margaret, this is Mr. Jackson."

"How do you do, Mr. Jackson."

We shook hands.

"You're not driving me away," I said. "But I do have to leave."

As I walked down to the road, I ran things through my mind. They ran out the other side without pausing, as often happens to me. I wondered why Margaret's face was familiar to me.

Zee was waiting impatiently.

"Well?"

I told her what had passed between Barbara

271

Miller and me. When I was done, Zee put a hand on my knee. "The whole thing's as fuzzy as ever to me."

"Me, too."

"Now what?"

"Now you take me to the safe house you've found, so I can use my wonderful powers of investigation to check it out before we stay there for the night."

"Oh, you won't have to do that," said Zee. "You've been there before."

"I have?"

"Sure. You know Bill Vanderbeck. It's his place, up in Gay Head. He's gone off-island for a few days with Angela Marcus, so his house is empty. Toni Begay arranged it for me."

"Ah."

Bill Vanderbeck was an uncle of Toni Begay, and Angela Marcus was a very wealthy widow. Both lived in Gay Head and had parlayed a shared love of gardening into something more after the death of her husband. So now they were going off-island together, eh? More evidence that romance doesn't end when your hair turns gray. I liked both Bill and Angela, and was pleased that they were hitting it off. Particularly at the moment, because Bill's house was just what we needed: a pleasant, secluded house with plenty of room for all of us. Close to the Gay Head beaches, too. Debby and Karen might want to relax on the colored sands at the foot of the famous cliffs, a place where they were quite unlikely to encounter Shadow or his friends.

"Well," said Zee, "since you don't have to use your famous skills to approve the safe house, that seems to leave us with some time of our very own, for the first time since Debby arrived. I think we should use it judiciously. What do you suggest we do?"

I leered.

"Not right here on Lambert's Cove Road in broad daylight," said Zee. "How about heading for East Beach? We've got the fishing gear we need, so we can try for some Spanish mackerel or bonito at The Jetties."

"Sounds good. You drive and I'll stimulate your primary and secondary erotic zones while we go. That way, we won't waste a moment."

"You just leave my zones alone, or we'll end up in a ditch instead of at the beach."

Zee started the Land Rover and we drove out the lower end of Lambert's Cove Road and took a left. At the T in Vineyard Haven, the third worst site for traffic backups on the island — trailing only the dread Five Corners down by the Vineyard Haven ferry landing and Edgartown's infamous A & P traffic jam — we took a right and headed for Chappy.

If Shadow was abroad, he didn't seem to be paying any attention to us.

A half hour later, as we passed the Wasque bathing beach, I telephoned Karen and arranged to pick her and Debby up later in the afternoon.

"How are things going with cousin Debby?" I asked in closing.

"I think Debby has a beau. They're both acting a little dopey."

"And how about you and Acey?"

"He has nice eyes."

"Have you told him that?"

"Not yet."

We drove to The Jetties and tried for every kind of fish we thought might be there. We caught nothing. The sun was warm, and the pale August sky curved softly down into the brownish haze on the horizon. The dark blue waters of Nantucket Sound reached eastward toward the sea. Shadow seemed far away. I thought about that, and something glimmered far back in the dark recesses of my mind.

23

The glimmer remained a glimmer, nothing more, but I was encouraged, since it was the only light I'd seen since I'd first become aware of Debby's problems. Both the light and Shadow were dim images, but they might become clearer. Sometimes that sort of thing happened.

A bit before five, we abandoned the fishless sea and drove to Acey Doucette's house. Cousins Karen and Debby were showered and clothed for land activities when we got there, and both seemed on good terms with their respective men. Debby, in fact, seemed a bit moony, as did Allen Freeman.

I walked up behind Debby, put my big hands on her shoulders, and said, "Say good-bye, Debby."

"Good-bye, Debby."

I looked at Allen. "Say good-bye, Allen."

"Good-bye, Allen."

Two semi–wise-guy kids.

"You can see each other later," I said, and directed Debby into the Land Rover.

Meanwhile, Karen and Acey accomplished a less reluctant separation, but not without eyeing each other with interest and making noises of their own about seeing one another again.

When all my crew was aboard, we drove off over the beach to Katama, joining the other ORVs trailing homeward.

"Did you have fun?" asked Zee, looking back from the passenger seat.

"Lots," said Debby. "I want to do it again tomorrow, in the afternoon. Allen gets through work at three and has the rest of the day off."

"I imagine Acey Doucette can get off work anytime," said Zee, flicking her eyes at Karen.

"He's a writer," said Karen. "He can work whenever he wants to."

If that was true, the writer's life seemed like a pretty good one. No wonder people wanted to be novelists. On the other hand, I thought I detected a note of irony in the voices of both women.

Having given some thought to where I could shop with the least possibility of being spotted by either Shadow or the Secret Service, I stopped at Jim's Package Store in Oak Bluffs and got a two-day supply of booze and soft drinks, and at Cronig's Market in Vineyard Haven for food. Then we drove on to Gay Head, where, as the evening sun slanted in from the west, we eventually arrived at Bill Vanderbeck's very ordinary house.

I knew Bill was supposedly on the mainland with his widow friend, but with Bill you could never be sure. I looked around, then led the way into the house through his unlatched door. Bill, like me, didn't believe very much in locks.

"Who lives here?" asked Debby.

Nobody seemed home. "Bill Vanderbeck," I said. "He's a friend. There are bedrooms upstairs. Take your choice."

"Where is he?"

"Wandering in America for a few days."

"What does he do?"

"Some people say he's a shaman."

She gave me a studious look. "A shaman? Isn't a shaman a priest or a medicine man? Is he an Indian?"

"I never heard him say he was a shaman, or an Indian, either, but most people would say he's a Wampanoag, and some of them think he's a shaman."

Karen had been listening. "Isn't a shaman someone who's supposed to be able to influence the spirits? Is that what this man does?"

"I don't know what he does," I said. "All I know about him is that lots of times, people don't see him when he's there. One minute he won't be there, and the next one he will. He says it's just because he's so ordinary that nobody notices him. Anyway, he's not here now, and we have the place to ourselves. Or, at least, I don't think he's here now. Go find yourselves some beds."

"A safe house," said Debby, slinging her bag over her shoulder and looking at the stairs. "Just like in the spy movies."

"Yes," I said. "A safe house. Nobody knows

we're here. Not Shadow and not Walt Pomerlieu. We should be able to get a good night's sleep without worrying about defensive perimeters or any of that sort of thing."

"I have to tell Walt where we are," said Karen.

Debby and Zee stopped what they were doing. The four of us seemed, suddenly, to have become a tableau.

"If you do that," I said, "it'll no longer be a safe house."

"Of course it will be. I have to tell him. I'm responsible for Cricket's . . . for Debby's safety."

"If he knows where we are, other people will know."

"I have to report to him. It's part of my job."

"Look," I said. "When we get unpacked and settled in, we'll take Debby out for a drive, and she can call her folks and let them know she's okay. She can tell them all about her day, and they won't be able to trace the call. Afterwards you can talk with your boss. You can tell him I'm taking the two of you to a friend's house up-island someplace, but you don't know exactly where. That'll be the truth, because you really don't know exactly where you are right now, do you?"

"No, but I know we're at Bill Vanderbeck's house in Gay Head someplace."

"You can tell him everything but the Bill Vanderbeck part."

"I don't like this."

I pointed at Debby. "And I don't like having

Shadow knowing where we are, where Debby is. If Walt Pomerlieu tries to fire you for keeping your mouth shut, I'll tell him I made you do it."

She narrowed her eyes. "Oh, yeah? And how did you manage that?"

"How should I know? I'll think of something. Maybe I tied you to your bed and tickled your feet with a feather until you were completely in my power. Maybe I threatened Debby myself, if you didn't do as I said. Maybe I said I'd kill myself if you told him. . . ."

"I don't think that last one would work," said Zee.

"The point is," I said to Karen, "that you trust Walt Pomerlieu and his people, but I want at least one night when nobody knows where we are. I need a little time when I don't have to worry about Shadow."

"Time? How much time?"

I wasn't sure. "A day. Maybe two."

"To do what?"

"To nail Shadow."

Karen arched a brow. "Nail Shadow? Do you know who Shadow is?"

"There are two hundred and fifty million people in the United States," I said. "I think I've eliminated most of them. In the next day or so, I may get it down to one. But I need to know that Debby's someplace where Shadow won't find her, and the only way I know how to do that is to not tell anybody where she is. I figure we can sleep here, and tomorrow morning, you and

Debby can go conch fishing out of Menemsha. Joe Begay keeps the *Matilda* there, and Jimmy Souza takes her out most mornings. I'll call Joe tonight and see if it's okay. You'll have fun, and you'll be doing something most people never get to do, and you'll be safe as long as nobody knows where you are."

"You can trust Walt Pomerlieu," insisted Karen.

"Probably. But —"

"I'm going up to find my bed," said Debby rather decisively. "Then I want to tell Mom and Dad all about Allen."

"All?" asked Zee.

"Well, almost all," said Debby with a grin, and she headed upstairs. The rest of us exchanged glances and trailed after her. Zee and I found an only slightly saggy double bed in a room not too far from the lone upstairs bathroom and dumped our gear. Then I went down and brought the food and drink into the kitchen. By the time the women came back downstairs, I had a martini going and was wondering if Karen's feet really were ticklish. It was a question that probably would have interested Pushkin.

I drove up to the Gay Head Cliffs, where we actually managed to find a parking place. While Debby called her parents on the car phone, and Karen leaned on a fender, talking into her radio, Zee and I walked up between the souvenir shops and food shops to the observation area and watched the sun go down over the western water.

No green flash occurred.

"Do you really know who Shadow is?" asked Zee.

"Not quite. But I may know how to find out."

"How?"

"If I can keep Debby out of circulation long enough, I'll go back to Edgartown and pick up the film that was in Burt Phillips's camera."

"What do you expect to find?"

"I don't know. A picture of somebody going into our driveway or coming out? Somebody who wasn't supposed to be there at all, but was? Shadow, maybe?"

"The somebody who killed Burt Phillips?"

Nurses work with dead and damaged people all the time, but most of them somehow manage to remain gentle and kind anyway. I don't know how they do it, since I'd think that after a while you'd have to grow a protective shell of some kind, some sort of armor that would keep your emotions guarded from what your brain and hands were dealing with. Now I looked down at Zee, my wife, the professional healer, and wondered again how she could at once be so loving and so pragmatic.

"Yes," I said. "The same someone who killed old Burt in the woods."

We walked back down between the shops to the car. Karen was through with her call, and Debby was finishing hers as we got there.

We drove away, just in case Walt Pomerlieu had some way of zeroing in on our location, and went back to the house. Where Zee got to work on supper while I called Joe Begay.

Yes, said Joe, it would be fine if my Virginia cousins went out with Jimmy Souza in the morning, but they'd have to be on the dock early, because Jimmy wasn't the kind to burn daylight. I told him I'd have them there at the appointed hour. I remembered what Debby had said about Allen getting off work in the middle of the afternoon, and asked when Jimmy usually got back. He said Jimmy liked to leave early and get back early. I said that was just what the doctor ordered.

He asked what else was new, and I told him I'd come by his place for coffee and a chat after dropping the cousins off in Menemsha. He said that would be fine. I told him I'd bring Zee along, and he said that would be even finer.

Supper was frozen pizzas, washed down with beer for the big people and soda for the younger cousin.

"You can have beer at the clambake, if your folks say it's okay," I said, when she again mildly protested being denied access to our bottles of Sam Adams.

"How old were you when you had your first beer?" she challenged.

"My father says I liked it when I was a baby."

"A lot of little kids like beer," said nurse Zee.

"Then why can't I have some?" asked Debby with a fake whine.

"Because you're not a little kid," I said.

"You're not little enough to have it, and you're not big enough to have it. You're in that awkward stage, in between."

"It's not fair."

I leaned forward. "It's just that beer is for human beings, and you aren't one of them yet. You're a teenager, and a teenager is a humanoid who looks like a real human and has been programmed to think she's a real human, but actually isn't. With proper guidance from people like me and Zee and Karen and your parents and your teachers and other real humans, someday you'll be a human, too. And then you can have beer." I sat back. "Do you understand?"

She stared at me with wide, wide eyes and pressed her hands together prayerfully. "A real human being? Me? You mean like happened to Pinocchio?"

"Exactly. On the other hand, you're a cricket yourself."

"Do I get to have a cricket?"

"Naturally."

"What a happy day this is, cousin Jeff. So kind of you to clarify things for me."

"What are cousins for? Go on, now. Have a soda."

The night was a quiet one, as I know since I was up for most of it, just in case Shadow was smarter than I expected. But he didn't show up, and in the early light of dawn, I drove Karen and Debby to Menemsha, where they boarded the *Matilda* and met Jimmy Souza, who had no idea that he was playing host to the president's daughter, but who was obviously charmed by having such lovely feminine company aboard his boat. I watched them as the *Matilda* went out past the yachts into Vineyard Sound, then drove back to Bill Vanderbeck's house, picked up Zee, and went on to Joe Begay's place.

There, over coffee, envious Zee chatted with pregnant Toni, and Joe Begay, who knew how to listen, did that as I talked.

"It sounds like things are coming to a head," he said, when I was done. "Do you need any help?"

"I can always use help," I said. Which turned out to be very true.

24

As Zee and I drove toward Edgartown through the warming August air, the island seemed particularly beautiful to me: Faint mists were rising from Menemsha Pond, the green trees looked ethereal, and even the houses along the roadside were clothed in a special morning light that gave them a fairy-tale appearance. I saw all this beauty, and thought of the people in those innocent houses and of the torturer's horse and of the dogs going on with their doggy lives.

And I thought of what might happen before the day was ended, and I wondered what I wished.

Did I wish that I'd never met Cricket Callahan? Had we never met, I'd not know about the letters or about Shadow, and this morning I'd be at home with Zee, paying no heed to presidential doings, instead of driving down this road, hoping to prove someone a villain by looking at a dead man's photographs.

Or was it okay that Cricket had come down the beach and that Zee and I had become entangled in the webs that encircled her? Troubles had come with Cricket, albeit through no fault of hers, and our quiet lives had become dangerous as a consequence, but given my druthers, would I really have preferred to know nothing of Shadow and his threats?

Zee complicated things. If she was somewhere else, somewhere safe — visiting her parents, for instance, or otherwise far away in America for some reason — I recognized that I would accept the danger in exchange for the knowledge, because the knowledge was leading me to Shadow, and once I had Shadow, Cricket would be safe. Or safer, at least, since public people like her are never completely safe from the other Shadows out there. Safer, then; which, though an imperfect consummation of this case, was nevertheless devoutly to be wished.

But Zee wasn't in America, and wouldn't go if I asked her to. Would be irked, in fact, by the very idea that I thought that she should seek sanctuary that I wouldn't seek myself. Zee did not take to the notion that she needed to be protected by her husband, or by anybody else.

Good old Zee. I glanced at her.

"Why are you smiling?" she asked, smiling.

"Because you're you."

She kissed me. "And you're you."

Futile efforts sometimes have to be made, even though you know they're doomed to failure. I said, "I don't suppose you'd agree to go visit your folks for a couple of days, starting right now?"

"I knew you were going to say something like that sooner or later. No."

"I knew you were going to say that."

"Then why did you ask?" she asked.

"We truly manly men always try to get our womenfolk out of the line of fire."

"If you think I'm going to get out of the line of fire and leave you in it, you've got another think coming!"

"Do you think we're actually in the line of fire?"

"I think Debby's got troubles and that as long as we're near her, we've got them, too."

"Should we step away from her, then?"

"I've been thinking about that."

"And?"

"I guess we could. After all, protecting her is the Secret Service's job, not ours."

"So?"

"The thing is, I like Debby, and I think that we've not only kept Shadow away from her while she's been with us, but that she's had her Roman holiday, too, what with palling around with the twins and Allen Freeman, doing the things a normal girl does on vacation. And if you're right about Burt Phillips's pictures, we may get Shadow before he can find her again, and that makes it even more important to stick with her. Besides, the president of the United States may be coming to our house on Sunday, and I doubt if that'll ever happen again, and it won't happen this time if anything happens to Debby first."

"So we stay in the picture."

"Yes. But we're not going to do anything fool-ish."

"Foolish?" I said, putting a hand on my chest. "Me do something foolish? Redickle-dockle!"

"It's a good thing you're married," said Zee seriously. "You need a wife to look after you."

"But you're probably wrong about one thing," I said. "I'll bet that once Prez comes to our clambake, he'll beg for more invitations in the future. We won't be able to keep him away."

"You really are a very strange man," said Zee, giving me another kiss. "But I love you anyway for some reason."

"Get on your trusty car phone and call Jake Spitz," I said. "See if he can meet us in, say, an hour or two. Someplace private."

She reached for the phone. "What'll I tell him it's all about?"

"Tell him it's about cousin Debby and Shadow. And tell him not to tell the Secret Service guys about the meeting."

She dialed and asked for Spitz, gave her name, listened, waited, said thank you, and hung up, then dialed again, gave her name, listened, put a hand over the speaker, and turned to me.

"It's taking a while, but at least I'm talking to human beings and not to one of those machines that wants you to dial a number on your Touch-Tone phone before you can actually get through." She turned away and took her hand off the speaker. "Yes. Hi, Jake, it's Zee Jackson. Jeff and I would like to meet you in an hour or so, and we'd just as soon not have anybody else know about it. No, it's not supposed to be a rendezvous between you and me, but now that you mention it, maybe I can get rid of Jeff between now and then. How about the Fireside, in Oak Bluffs? I doubt if anybody you know will be there in the morning. Good. See you." She hung up and looked at me. "He didn't ask what it was about. He just said he'd see us there."

"The Fireside, eh? I wouldn't have thought of that."

"You think of a lot of things, but not of everything, Sweets."

"You occupy so much of my mind that there just isn't room for much else in my brain."

"Some people would say there wasn't much room there anyway. But not me. I'd never say that."

We drove down into Edgartown just early enough to find a parking space and just late enough to find the photography shop open. Perfect timing.

"Here you are, Mr. Jackson," said the clerk, bringing me the developed film. "Sorry this wasn't ready yesterday when your friend came by to pick it up, but we'd gotten your film mixed up with someone else's and didn't get things straightened out till last night. Hope you didn't have to make a special trip this morning."

"No problem," I said. "What did my friend look like?"

He arched a brow. "Don't you know?"

"It doesn't make any difference. It's just that it could have been one of several people."

"Ah," said the clerk. "Well, I'm afraid I don't know. I was on my lunch hour when your friend came in."

I put a warm grin on my face. "Male or female?"

He grinned back. "Can't help you, Mr. Jackson." Then he was suddenly serious. "There's no problem, is there? You did authorize your friend to pick up the film?"

"No problem at all," I said, digging out my wallet. "Whoever came by had my okay."

"If you want, I'll talk to the clerk who waited on your friend."

"Thanks. It's not important, but I am curious."

"Be glad to, Mr. Jackson. We want our customers to be happy."

Walking back to the car, Zee said, "Who was it? Shadow?"

"That's my guess."

"But how did he know the film was there?"

"He heard me say I was going to take the film in. We didn't get rid of the bugs in our house until afterwards."

Shadow couldn't stop me from having the film developed, and he didn't know where I took it, but by passing himself off as my friend, sent to pick up the film, he could make the rounds of photography shops until he found the right one, and this being the friendly Vineyard, where bad guys don't try to steal rolls of film, he stood a good chance of getting the film before we did. In fact, it was just luck that he didn't, but that bit of luck, good for me, bad for him, might just be the luck that showed his face to me.

We got into the Land Rover and opened the package of prints.

Burt Phillips's last photographs were of driveways.

I recognized the one leading down to the president's vacation hideaway. Burt had taken several pictures of cars going in and coming out. The license plates were pretty clear on all of the cars. Burt no doubt had a contact somewhere — probably in the Registry of Motor Vehicles — who could tell him who owned or had rented the cars, so that Burt could know who was entering and leaving the compound.

I didn't recognize any other driveways until I was nearly through the prints. Then I saw our own.

The first of a series of shots was of the entrance to the driveway. The second was of our mailbox, with the driveway in the background. Burt had apparently gotten out of his car for that shot. The third picture was of John Skye's Wagoneer coming out of the drive. There was none of it going in. That meant that Burt had either neglected to take a picture of the Wagoneer when it turned into the drive, or that he had arrived between the time the twins arrived and the time they and

Debby left for the beach. Although Debby had been in the Wagoneer when it left, she couldn't really be seen in the photograph because she had apparently been sitting on the far side of the rear seat, with one of the twins (don't ask me which) between her and Burt's camera.

The next picture was of Zee and me in the Land Cruiser, as we headed for the clamming flats. Burt had a pretty good shot of Zee looking right at him.

The next photo was of a Volvo entering the driveway, and the one after that was of the Volvo coming back out and turning toward Vineyard Haven. I could see an elbow sticking out of the driver-side window, but I couldn't see the face that went with the elbow.

The next three were a sequence: the Land Cruiser turning into the driveway; the Land Cruiser stopped, its driver's door open, and me walking toward the camera; and a photo of me getting closer.

That was when Burt had put down his camera and driven away.

The last picture was of Zee's little Jeep coming out of the drive, as she had headed for work at the hospital later that afternoon. Burt had come back in time to take that shot and to be seen by Zee, who had reported him to me. It was the last photograph old Burt ever took.

Zee tapped a finger on the pictures of the Volvo.

"If we can find out who was in that car, we'll

know . . ." She paused. "What'll we know?"

I said, "We'll know who went down to our house while we were gone, at least. Maybe we'll know more."

"Can you find out who owns the car?"

"If I can't, Jake Spitz can. Let's go."

"It didn't have a front license plate. How are we going to ID it?"

"Jake can double-check, but I think I know who owns it."

"Who?"

"I saw it, or one like it, up at Barbara Miller's house. It belongs to her sister, Margaret."

"Barbara Miller's sister went down to our house while we were gone? What for?" Zee put her hand to her mouth. "You mean she may be Shadow?"

"Maybe, but I doubt it."

"Mysteriouser and mysteriouser," said Zee.

Actually, I thought things were clearing up. I was down to two suspects, although I didn't know who the second one was yet.

"Jake should be able to tell us what we need to know," I said.

While I drove, Zee went through the pictures again. "I'd guess Burt Phillips took pictures of the cars that came and went from the president's compound," she said. "Then he traced the cars to find out who was socializing with Joe Callahan. Then he hung around the houses where those people lived and tried to get pictures of them, or maybe even of the Callahans themselves. If nothing else, he got pictures of more cars that presumably contained people who were in the president's social circle. All so he could sell stories and photos to outfits like the *National Planet*."

"Everybody's got to make a living somehow."

"If all he got was pictures of cars, it's quite a stretch to make a story out of them."

"People who read the *National Planet* are used to stretches. They thrive on stretches. 'I was a love child of Elvis and a creature from outer space.' Compared to stuff like that, Burt was a model of scientific method."

In Oak Bluffs, we found a spot to leave the car over by the wonderfully renovated Victorian house on the south side of the park, and walked back past the music grandstand to the Fireside, on Circuit Avenue.

The Fireside is far from being the island's classiest saloon, but it's popular with the young crowd and with a lot of old boozers, too. It's where all of the island's barroom fights used to start before such fracases became popular in Edgartown as well. The whole place smells of spilled beer, cigarettes, grass, and various bodily emissions. My young friend Bonzo, who long ago blew out a perfectly good brain with some bad acid, now works at the Fireside at the end of a broom or clearing tables. Bonzo labors happily and tirelessly to keep things clean, but there's too much Fireside and not enough Bonzo for him to accomplish that aim, so the bar always looks and smells like it could use a good scrubbing.

Two hours before noon, there weren't many people in the Fireside, and we spotted Jake Spitz immediately, where he sat in the farthermost booth and sipped at a cup of coffee. We went to him and sat down.

"You want to hear a funny story?" asked Spitz. "This booth reminds me of it. One time I was sitting in a booth down in D.C., and I could hear this woman and man going at it in the next booth. She was sort of hissing at him and he was apologizing all over the place.

" 'You unfaithful wretch,' she says. 'You promised me you were through with other women, and now you've got yourself another floozy. This is the last straw! I warned you last time, and now I'm leaving you!'

" 'Oh, no,' he begs. 'I'm sorry. I swear it'll never happen again. Give me one more chance!'

" 'That's what you said the last time, you philanderer!'

"And they go on and on like that with her hissing and him swearing he'd be true and groveling and apologizing until all at once she breaks off and says, 'My God! I've got to go. There's my husband.' And she takes off, sort of covering her face with her hand as she heads for the door." Spitz smiled.

"Did you make that up?" asked Zee, grinning.

"Honest to God, no. It really happened. I swear. People are weird."

"Speaking of weird," I said, "take a look at these." I tossed him the envelope of photographs.

"The order is important, so don't mess them up."

He glanced through them, then looked at me with arched brows. "This'll take some time," I said, and I told him the story of what had happened since Cricket Callahan and I had first met on the beach, and what I thought or suspected.

He listened, then looked through the photos again, and went back to those of the Volvo.

"This car, eh?"

Zee nodded. "We'd like to know who it belongs to."

"And you don't want the Secret Service to know anything about this."

"That's right," I said.

"Because you don't know who to trust."

"Except Karen Lea. I trust her. And you."

"You might not be too surprised to know who drives the blue sedan that follows you," he said.

I felt my forehead wrinkle. "You know who drives that car?"

He nodded. "Joan Lonergan."

While I thought about that, Zee said, "But when we were being trailed by that car and Karen radioed in to find out if it was a Secret Service car, nobody knew."

"That's because it isn't a Secret Service car. It's Joan's personal car." He picked up a photo of the Volvo. "Just like this is —"

"Walt Pomerlieu's personal car," I said, ending his sentence for him. "I saw it up at Barbara Miller's place yesterday. How do you happen to

296

know about those cars?"

Jake Spitz looked at me with interest. "You saw the Volvo up at Barbara's place, eh? Well, you seem to have your suspect list narrowed down. Shadow is either Walt Pomerlieu or Joan Lonergan, or maybe both. No wonder you don't trust the Secret Service."

"Yeah," I said. I thought of the bomb underneath my house and felt a chill, as though death had walked through the door and sat down beside me.

"Don't frown so hard," said Spitz with a little smile. "You might break your face. Let me simplify your life for you. Joan Lonergan put the bugs on your cars, but she didn't plant the bomb or the bugs in your house. Someone else did that."

"How do you know that?"

"Because Joan and Ted Harris don't really work for the Secret Service, they work for the FBI. They work for me."

25

So that leaves Walt Pomerlieu," said Zee, a bit wide-eyed. "Walt Pomerlieu. I guess you weren't just being paranoid, after all, Jeff."

"Maybe I was," I said, "but you know the joke: Just because you're a hypochondriac doesn't mean you're not sick."

"Well, we know Walt owns the Volvo, at least," said Spitz. "It's the one his wife drives. They brought it up so she'd have wheels while she visited her sister during Walt's stint here with the president. We've got to check out his schedule before we'll know if he had the Volvo when Burt Phillips took these pictures. If he did, he could have planted the bugs in the house and the bomb. That shouldn't be too hard to find out, but even if we have that information, it might not be enough to convince a jury. How come you don't look as surprised as I feel about this?"

"Probably for the same reason you don't look as surprised as you say you feel. Because from the first, there was something odd about this whole business.

"It wasn't the fact that the letters tied the threat to Cricket to that botched IRS operation that ruined that poor little girl's face, because revenge is always a popular excuse for killing and mutilating people.

"And it wasn't the fact that the letters had followed Cricket around wherever she went, both here and overseas. That was interesting only because it showed that whoever was sending them knew the presidential schedule well enough to make sure the letters got there when Cricket did.

"One interesting thing was that the letters started coming only after the president and his family vacationed here on the Vineyard the first time, but the botched operation had happened almost a year before that. Why the delay? Italians may prefer their vengeance cold, but most people like it right away.

"Another thing was the fact that even though the letters kept coming, nobody actually attacked Cricket or even tried to. How come? How come, for example, Shadow didn't at least do something like send her a letter bomb? But he didn't do that." I looked at Spitz. "Did he?"

"No."

"So what we've got is threatening letters following Cricket around for a year, obviously being sent by somebody with inside information about her itinerary, but, until this week, when Cricket came to visit Zee and me, with no overt acts that might be called violent or sinister. Since Cricket came to us, though, there's been a lot of that sort of thing, particularly the murder of Burt Phillips."

"I'm still not sure why he had to murder Burt," said Zee. "All poor old Burt had was a picture of the Volvo. He didn't know who owned it."

"Two reasons," said Spitz. "First, because Burt could trace the car just like we did, and second because Burt saw Shadow's face."

"But the driver's face doesn't show in the film," said Zee.

I found Burt's photo of the Volvo coming out of the driveway and put it in front of her. "You don't see a face, but you do see an elbow sticking out of the driver-side window, and the car's turning toward Vineyard Haven, toward Burt's camera. When the car went by Burt, the window was down and Burt could see the driver plain as day."

"And the driver could see Burt seeing him," said Zee, nodding. "And since he couldn't stop right there on the highway and do Burt in, what with traffic and walkers and bicyclists and all, he pulled into the next drive up the way, which happened to lead down to Felix Neck, and waited, right?"

"Right."

"For Burt to go home, so Walt Pomerlieu . . . right?"

"Maybe," said Spitz.

"So Walt, or whoever, could follow him there, where there might be more privacy." She shivered. "I really don't understand people like that. I know they're there, but I don't understand them."

Spitz's voice was gentle, almost soothing. "They say the stock market is motivated by fear and greed. Killers aren't much different. In this case, it was fear of being found out. Burt knew too much."

I said, "I imagine Burt almost faked him out of his shoes when he pretended to drive away that first time, then turned right around and came back. One irony is that Burt actually didn't know anything at all. He didn't know who he'd photographed, or that he had any reason to fear him. That's why he was such an easy victim. Being the nosy guy Burt was professionally, I imagine that when he met Shadow there, he probably tried to find out who he was and whether he had any interest in Cricket Callahan. I don't know what Shadow told him, but when Burt turned his back on him, it certainly never occurred to him that Shadow was going to kill him. . . ."

I had a sudden attack of remorse, and stopped talking. Zee looked at me and saw something in my face. She put her hand on my arm. "What's the matter?"

Guilt has some odd characteristics. You can feel guilty even though you know you really aren't. If anyone else admitted feeling guilt over the same thing, you'd tell them it was nothing to feel guilty about. But even if they believe you, they keep right on feeling guilty. And the same goes for you. It doesn't do any good to know that you're not really guilty, because you feel that way anyhow. I am very wary of guilt for these and other reasons, but sometimes it catches up with me just the same. It passes with time, usually, but while it's there, it's bad.

I made myself speak, but couldn't keep the bitterness out of my voice. "It's ironic that the driver didn't have to follow Burt home, after all; Burt came to him. He walked right into his arms, there in the trees beside the Felix Neck driveway. And I was the one who sent him there. Burt was afraid of me, so he went someplace he figured was safe to make his phone call to the garage, and he got himself killed because he did that. It happened because of me."

"It didn't happen because of you," said Spitz, in that same soothing voice he'd used before. "It just happened. You didn't know Shadow was in there any more than Burt knew that Shadow had planted that bomb."

Ignorant armies clashing by night.

I knew he was right, that what we sometimes think of as cause and effect is actually only the fell clutch of circumstance, but I also knew I was going to feel bad for a time.

"Oh, Jeff," said Zee, my wife, the nurse, the healer. She put her arms around me, and held herself against me. Sweet, strong Zee.

And after a while, I could kiss the top of her head and say, "I'm okay." And I was. As close as I expected to be for a while, at least.

"It's not your fault," she said, keeping her hands on my arm, looking into my soul with her great, dark eyes. "Jake is right. It just happened."

"I know." I gave her the most authentic-looking smile I could manage and took a deep breath. "Where were we?"

"Sinister acts as soon as Cricket Callahan came to stay at your place," said Spitz. "People coming through the woods to your house, people bugging your house and your cars, people putting bombs under your bedrooms, people following you in a blue sedan. Stuff like that."

"Yeah, until I finally took Debby and Karen out of there yesterday. The point is that one reason for letting Debby come to us in the first place, aside from the Roman holiday part of it, seemed to be that she'd be safer at our place, where nobody but Mom and Dad and a few of the Secret Service people knew she was, than she would be at the compound or traveling around the island with her folks.

"The plan sort of made sense, but in fact Shadow wasn't fooled for a minute. He had never made any threatening moves during the past year, but he made a lot as soon as Debby was here, exactly where he wasn't supposed to know she was."

"I'm with you so far," said Spitz. "Great minds must run in common gutters."

"So things were out of whack," I said. "It began to make more sense if I figured Debby was with us just so Shadow could get to her easier. Now, I'm sure that was the plan. Here's what I think. I think that revenge was the motive for the

303

letters, and I think that the letters didn't start coming until Joe Callahan visited the Vineyard, because during the first year after the botched operation the writer was too occupied with other things to take revenge, even though he was filled with vengeful thoughts. Sort of like the convict who'd love to kill the judge who sent him to jail, but can't because he's still there.

"But by the time Prez came to the island a year ago, the writer was, as it were, out of jail. He finally had time and opportunity to get even, and I think he felt like the president's visit to his island was the last straw, the final insult, the last twist of the knife. Prez was here having a wonderful time right where the writer had been having a terrible one. It was like salt in his wounds."

"So he started sending a stream of letters threatening to make Cricket's face look like that other poor girl's," said Zee. "Knowing that even if Cricket never learned about them, her father would be told."

"Yeah. Psychological warfare. The same letter, over and over. I imagine that presidents get pretty used to the idea that there are crazies out there who'd like to kill them, because that goes with their job. But a threat to a daughter is something else. I doubt if a father ever gets used to that, and I think that the writer knows it. I think he knows it because he saw someone he loves suffering long, and because he suffered himself as a result. Pain like that can transform some people into monsters."

"Who is he?" asked Zee.

I looked at her. "I can't prove it yet, but I think it's Ben Miller."

Across the table, Jake Spitz arched a brow and did not look surprised, but said nothing. I wondered if he knew anything I didn't know, and guessed that he did. I babbled on.

"Ben Miller has motive and he's had opportunity. When Barbara lost her job after the bungled operation overseas, it was like losing her life. She says she might actually have died, in fact, but Ben put his business interests aside and cared for her during the year it took her to get herself glued back together. She's the great love of his life, and he almost lost her, so he hated the man who almost killed her. And just last year, when that man, Joe Callahan, came to the Vineyard to have a good time, Barbara was finally over her crisis and Ben was able to go back to his work and find time for revenge. He began sending the letters."

"Which did the job, all right. So we've got motive. What about opportunity?"

"Ben is an international banker who travels all the time and has business contacts everywhere. He also knows people Barbara worked with when she was with the IRS. Wherever Cricket Callahan travels, Ben knows people who'll mail letters for him. No problem, then, having the letters follow Cricket around. The people who mail them probably don't even know what's in the envelopes. All they know is that Ben is a bigwig with good connections, so they're not surprised that he's corresponding with Prez and his family. And since the people who mail the letters really are innocent agents, the Secret Service has no reason to think they're involved, and probably won't ever catch up with them."

"Don't be too sure of that," said Spitz.

"I'm not too sure of any of this," I said.

"Neither am I," said Zee. "Ben Miller may have sent the letters, but we know he's not Shadow. Walt Pomerlieu owns the Volvo, so he's probably the driver in Burt Phillips's pictures, and the guy who planted the bugs and bombs and who killed Burt. But what's the tie-in between Walt Pomerlieu and Ben Miller?"

"The tie-in is that Walt and Ben are brothers-in-law. They married sisters. The first day I met him, Walt Pomerlieu told me that his wife's name is Maggie. He even showed me a picture of her and the kids. I didn't think much of it at the time. Just a picture of a plain-looking woman with big teeth. But when I was up at Barbara Miller's place I was introduced to her sister, Margaret, who's staying with her while Ben is overseas tending to his banks, or whatever it is that he does. Margaret looked like her sister, and I thought I'd seen her before. But the Maggie-is-Margaret idea didn't come to me until we knew that the Volvo and Walt Pomerlieu went together. As soon as I saw the picture Burt took of the Volvo, and remembered the one in Barbara's yard, I remembered the family photo that

Walt had showed us, and a lot of things fell into place."

"Let me see if I've got this right," said Zee. "When Barbara lost her job and fell apart, Maggie and Walt were as worried about her and as mad at the president as Ben was. Being a head Secret Service guy, Walt knew all about the president's travel plans, and made sure Ben knew them, too, so the letters would always get through. Walt was also in the perfect position to keep the investigation of the letter-writer a little out of focus, just enough to keep Ben safe."

"Right," said Spitz. "But things unravel over the long haul. People make mistakes, or investigators get lucky, or somebody starts taking a new slant on things. The FBI and the Secret Service may be rivals, but they have common interests, too, including protecting the president and his family, and it wasn't too long into this letter-writing campaign that some people began to think the same thing J.W., here, thought: that maybe somebody in the Secret Service itself couldn't be trusted."

"Spook types are professionally suspicious," I said to Zee. "They automatically don't believe you. They don't disbelieve you, necessarily, but they don't believe you, either."

"Are you like that, Jake?" asked Zee.

"No comment," said Jake.

"Did you know that Maggie Pomerlieu and Barbara Miller are sisters?" she asked.

He nodded. "Yes, we noticed that. And we've

noticed other things, too. For instance, we noticed that Ben Miller made business trips to countries a week or two before the president and Cricket got there, and it occurred to us that it might mean something, considering the hard time Barbara had after she left the IRS. Like maybe he left the letters with people to be mailed later to the president. And we knew that Ben Miller and Walt Pomerlieu have been close since they were kids together in prep school, even before they married sisters. The old-boy Yankee network rearing its famous head. The Intelligence-International Finance Society and Marching Band we know so well. Old, rich, honorable, patriotic families and all that." He paused. "So that's why we filtered Joan and Ted into the Secret Service. We needed somebody to check things out from the inside. Since then we've had a lot of theories, but up till now we couldn't prove anything."

"And now you can?" asked Zee.

"I'm not sure," said Spitz.

I thought of old New England money and of my own relative poverty, and a vision of extortion appeared in my brain. I examined it for a while, and the more I looked at it, the more I liked it. There were dangers for sure, but the rewards justified chancing them. All I needed to do was be careful.

26

It was just before noon when I called Walt Pomerlieu from our house. There was a nip in his voice when he got on the phone.

"Mr. Jackson, I'm glad you called. Where is your young charge? We haven't heard from her or Karen since yesterday, and her parents are getting worried."

"They're fine," I said. "They've gone fishing. I'll be picking them up later."

"Where are they fishing? I need to know where they are at all times, as I'm sure you can understand."

I was sure I could. "They're absolutely safe," I said. "They can radio in if they have any problems. I'd like to see you privately about another matter. I'm alone at home. Can you come by?"

"What's it about, Mr. Jackson?"

"This line may be secure at your end, but I'm not sure about my end. When you hear what I have to say, I think you'll agree it was best not to discuss it by phone. In fact, I think you'll agree that it's best not to discuss it with anyone but ourselves."

"That sounds very mysterious, Mr. Jackson."

"It has to do with the death of Burt Phillips," I prodded.

He hesitated. Then, "All right. At your house, you say? I'm on my way."

I was on the porch having the first beer of the day and reading *Field and Stream* when he came down the driveway in one of the Secret Service's fleet of vehicles. He parked beside Zee's little Jeep, stepped out and looked around, then came up and rapped on the screen door. I told him to come in, and he did.

I put the magazine down on the table beside the chair, set my mug on the magazine, and got up to shake hands. "Care for a beer?" I asked. "Sam Adams. America's finest bottled brew."

"Sure."

I went into the kitchen and came out with a bottle and mug. He took them and filled the mug.

"Where are Cricket and Karen?"

I sat down again and waved him into another chair. "Fishing, like I told you. They're fine. Before we have our little talk, are you sure that your people found all of the bugs in this house? I don't think we'll want our conversation recorded anywhere."

He sipped his beer and frowned. "The house is clean. What's this all about?"

"Photographs."

They were in an envelope under the copy of *Field and Stream*. I handed them to him. "I've numbered them in sequence. They're most interesting if you look at them in the order they were taken."

He looked through the first of them. "What are these?"

"They were in Burt Phillips's camera. He took them the day that he died."

He flipped through the rest of the pictures, pausing so imperceptibly at the ones of himself that had I not been watching for the hesitation, I'd not have seen it. "Where did you get these? I personally checked out the film in Burt Phillips's camera. It was blank. He'd never used it."

"I'll bet you checked it out personally. But you found unused film because I put a new roll in after I took this one out of Burt's camera. While he was down the road to Felix Neck, where he got himself killed."

His eyes were hard. "You're in trouble," he said. "You've interfered with a murder investigation."

"I don't think I'm in trouble," I said. "I think you're in trouble. You killed Burt Phillips."

He glared. "You're mad."

"I'm not even upset. What I am is poor. I just got married, and I'm going to need more income than I needed when I was single. I did a little research on you, Walt, and I know that you, being the rich guy you are, can afford to supplement my income a little. Don't worry, I'm not greedy. You can keep that set of pictures, by the way. I have the negatives."

"What are you talking about?"

"I'm talking about you being off duty when we were all away from the house and Burt got your picture coming out of our driveway in your classic Volvo. You drove in not knowing whether anybody'd be here or not. If we were here, you were just checking up, but if we weren't you finally had your chance to do in Cricket and get away with it. You knew which bed she'd be sleeping in, and you planted your trusty radio-detonated bomb right under it. Then you planted the bugs to be double sure you'd always know what was going on. But when you came out, there was poor old Burt, and he could ID you, so you had to get rid of him. How am I doing so far?"

He glared. "You're crazy."

"Maybe. The plan was to kill Debby that night, after she was asleep. You told us to expect a late call from you, and you phoned on schedule. You expected to have me verify that Debby was in bed and you planned to detonate the bomb while we were talking. It would give you and Ben Miller perfect alibis. When the bomb went off, Ben would be in Egypt and you would be on the phone, probably with witnesses, other agents who weren't in on your plans.

"But Debby wasn't home. She was spending the night at John Skye's house. So the plan went awry, and the next day, because Joan Lonergan took the call from my house and told you there was a problem with bugs, you had no choice but to have your agents sweep this place, and of course one of them found the bomb. Am I boring you? I hope not."

I went on, and when I was done, he continued to glare, as if in amazement. "How many people have heard these incredible accusations? This is slander! You think you're poor now, but when my lawyers are through with you, you'll have nothing! Nothing!"

"Don't worry," I said. "So far, this is just between you and me. That's why I waited to talk to you until after my wife went to work, and why I sent Debby and Karen off fishing. I don't think anybody else needs to know about this." I paused, then added, "Yet."

His eyes left me and looked out through the screen at the yard. His head turned and then came back, and his eyes returned to mine. "Yet? I warn you, Mr. Jackson, that I will tolerate no such scandalous allegations as yours to be attached to my name."

I made a casual gesture. "If it really is slander, I imagine you and your lawyers will have me in jail or the poorhouse when you get done with me. Serve me right, too. People shouldn't go around saying nasty, untrue things about other people." I drank more of my beer. "On the other hand, I'm pretty sure of myself. I guess the only way to check it out is for me to take my photos and my ideas to, say, the FBI or the state police and have them look into things. If I'm as full of shit as you say I am, they'll give you a clean bill of health and I'll be dead meat for your lawyers. What do you think? Shall I do that?"

He thought for a while, studying me as he did. Then he said, "I don't think you realize how damaging your accusations will be, even when they're proven false, as they certainly will be. My reputation will be forever compromised, my honor smudged. Are you so immoral a person as to ruin an innocent man? I took you for something better."

I gave him an admiring glance. "You're good. I'd probably be beginning to feel a little doubtful about myself right now if I hadn't gotten a description of you an hour or so ago from the guy who waited on you down at the photo shop yesterday, when you tried to pick up my film. It was you, all right, which means that you're the guy who bugged this house in the first place. You're half of the letter-writing team, Walt, and your brother-in-law is the other half."

He got up. "Do you mind if I look through your house? I know you said we'd be meeting in private, but you'll forgive me for not trusting you completely. I'm alone, and I'd like to be sure you are, too."

I waved toward the living room door. "Take a look. I'll be right here."

He went into the house, and I waited until he came out again. Hands in his pockets, he leaned a shoulder against the door frame.

"It seems we are indeed by ourselves," he said.

"So. How much will it cost me to buy your silence in this matter? I don't care to risk an official investigation that would inevitably harm my career and my family's reputation, even though in the end I'd be found innocent of any wrongdoing. What's your price, Mr. Jackson?"

"I had an annual salary supplement in mind, not a lump sum."

"And that supplement would be what?"

I told him, and he gave a faint smile.

"That could add up over the years, Mr. Jackson."

"As I told you, I've done a little research about your family and its finances. You can afford me. I'm not being greedy."

"But what's to prevent you from becoming so in the future, Mr. Jackson?"

"Call me J.W. All my friends do, and I think we should consider each other friends, don't you, Walt?"

"All right, J.W. What's to keep you from becoming greedy in the future?"

"You have my word, Walt. I'm not interested in being rich. I like the sort of life I lead right now."

He stood away from the door and picked up his mug of beer. "Look at it my way, J.W. You'll have your story and the negatives to back it up, and you'll be able to hand them to the FBI or whoever any time you want to. And what's to stop you?"

"The annual supplement. If I talk, the money

stops. Believe me, that's ample motive for keeping what I know to myself." I smiled.

"And will your wife feel the same way? Or will she want more? I recall the old saying that men cannot resist beauty and women cannot resist money."

"My wife knows nothing about any of this, and I don't plan on telling her. Zee is a sweetheart, but women can't keep their mouths shut about such things. If we can work this deal out, she'll never know about it."

He finished his beer and set the mug down on the table. "Where are the negatives, then? What if she finds them? Or are they somewhere where she won't find them?"

I finished my own beer. Delish, as always. "Don't worry. I'm the only one who knows where they are, so you're perfectly safe. Well, I suppose that it's possible somebody might find them here someday, but even if they did they wouldn't know what they were looking at, would they?"

His ears almost physically perked up. "Here? Are they here somewhere?"

I felt a little rush of emotion. "Somewhere, maybe. But I'd be a fool to tell you where, and you'd never be able to find them by yourself."

He looked at me thoughtfully. And then he brought his left hand out of his pocket, and there was a small pistol in it.

"You're a fool anyway, Mr. Jackson," he said. "I don't need to find them. All I need to do is burn down these buildings of yours, and I'll burn the negatives, too. Don't you agree?"

My throat felt like the Gobi Desert, and my voice was a croak. "Is that gun loaded?"

"Very loaded, Mr. Jackson. I know that when they find you in the rubble, they'll discover that you were shot. But they won't know who did it, because nobody knows I'm here."

"Now, be careful," I said, in a voice that sounded like tin. "Don't shoot. If you shoot, it'll be murder. Look, I'll give you the negatives. Is that what you want? I'll give them to you and I'll never say anything to anybody. Okay? Just point that gun someplace else."

"You and Burt Phillips are just the same," said Pomerlieu. "You're both full of threats. He was going to write a story about me, and you want my money. He was willing to ruin my family's name, and so are you."

"No. I'd never do anything like that. Look, you take the negatives. Just don't shoot." My tinny voice had become a whine. I could feel sweat on my forehead.

"Where are they?"

"Out in my shed. I'll get them. Just don't shoot."

"Go get them."

We went through the house and out the back door. He walked behind me. We got to the shed.

"They're inside," I said, "in a bundle of old tax forms in a box."

"Get them."

"Don't shoot." I stood to one side of the door and opened it.

Jake Spitz stood there, using a two-handed grip on a .45 automatic that was pointed at Pomerlieu.

"Put down the gun, Walt," he said.

Pomerlieu's gun was pointed at me. He hesitated.

"Put it down, Mr. Pomerlieu," said Zee, stepping out from behind the shed, well off to Pomerlieu's right. She held her Beretta 380, and she, too, was using the two-handed grip.

Ted and Joan drifted into view from the trees to his left, pistols in hand. "Put down the gun, Walt," said Ted.

Still, he hesitated.

"We have agents all around us, and they're closing in right now," said Spitz in the gentle voice I'd heard earlier in the Fireside. "You can't get away. And even if you managed it, we've got everything on tape. You're not the only one who can plant a bug, you know. Now put the gun down."

Instead, Pomerlieu raised it and put the muzzle in his mouth.

"Don't," said my voice. "Think of Maggie."

He looked at me.

My voice went on. It sounded something like Spitz's. "Do you want Maggie to see you after you pull that trigger? Do you? Don't you love her? And another thing: You're innocent until they prove you guilty in court. So far, all they have is a taped talk and guesswork. They don't have any proof. Maybe they'll never have it. Think of that. Think of Maggie. Think of your boys."

He stared at me. Then, keeping his eyes on me, he took the pistol out of his mouth and dropped it on the ground.

27

"I imagine that a suicide in the backyard would have put the kibosh on the big clambake," said Joe Begay. "The ambiance of the setting wouldn't make for happy times."

"I guess not," said Toni, opening a last little-neck and placing it in its half shell on the platter with the others. She dropped the other half of the shell into the bucket at her feet.

The bucket was half filled with half shells, and there were now three platters of littlenecks awaiting the arrival of the afternoon guests. I got up and put the platter in the fridge along with the other two, and we turned our attention to preparing clams Casino. Earlier that morning I'd taken all of the shellfish out of the freezer, and now they were beginning to thaw, which made them easy to open. They would also taste just as good as if they were fresh from the pond.

It was Sunday, and we were sitting on the back steps, outside the kitchen door. It was about noon, and Joe and I had bottles of Rolling Rock beside us. Pregnant Toni was having iced tea. The August sky was pale and blue, and the wind was hushing through the trees. I let my eyes survey the yard. I'd mowed the lawn that morning, and things looked pretty good.

Zee stuck her head out of the door behind us. "Let's get it on, here. The garlic butter is ready to go and the bacon's been cut. I need clams."

So we opened cherrystones on the half shell and put them on cookie sheets. Zee topped each clam with a bit of garlic butter, a little square of bacon, and just enough seasoned bread crumbs to sop up any stray juice, and put the cookie sheets into the fridge, which was getting pretty crowded. Besides the littlenecks and the Casinos, there were trays of stuffed clams and bags of mussels and steamers. To get all the shellfish in, I'd had to take a lot of other stuff out. Principally bread and veggies, which were now spread out on the kitchen table. I had plenty of food, and later I'd put beer, wine, and soft drinks into coolers of ice.

"You guys should join us," I said to Toni. "John and Mattie Skye and the girls will be here, and a kid named Allen Freeman from over on Chappy, and I think Acey Doucette might be coming."

"Acey Doucette? I didn't know you and Acey were close."

"I left that invitation up to Karen Lea. If she wants to invite him, I told her he'd be welcome."

"I hear you might be buying his Land Rover."

"That's what Acey thinks, and if I had more money, maybe I would. But I don't have more money, so I'm keeping the old Land Cruiser for a few more years. I invited the chief, too, but I don't think he'll come. He says he sees all the VIPs he needs to, and after a while one looks a lot like the next one. Besides, I think he's already met Joe Callahan. In the line of duty, as they say."

"Well, I haven't," said Toni, "and I'd like to."

"Join the party, then."

She looked at Joe. "Okay?"

"I'm not your boss," he said, "I'm your husband. If you want to do it, we'll do it."

"Don't you want to?"

"Why not?" asked Joe. "I've met a couple presidents. It won't hurt to meet one more."

She raised a brow. "When did you meet a couple presidents? I don't think you ever mentioned that before."

"I'll tell you all about it later," he said.

She got up. "Well, like I say, I haven't met any presidents, and I'm not going to meet this one all soaked with clam juice. I'm going to go home and change. You can tell me about your presidents on the way."

"Informality is the dress code," I said. "Personally, I only plan on changing into clean shorts and another T-shirt."

They got into their car and drove up the driveway. They hadn't been gone long when two Secret Service cars came down the sandy lane. Ted and Joan and two other agents got out of the first one.

"Where are your cousins?" asked Joan immediately.

"Over on Chappy with the Skye twins and various male companions," I said. "Having a last Vineyard fling before they have to go home."

"I don't like it," said Ted, frowning.

"You're not the liking type," I said. "Stop worrying. They're fine. Ben Miller is in custody overseas, and Walt Pomerlieu is in the Dukes County jail, where you wanted to put me the first time we met, so the cousins are in no danger from anybody."

"There are always scumbags and crazies out there," said Ted, as the second car disgorged other agents.

"Nobody knows where the kids are, and they're coming back in a couple of hours," I said. "Why didn't you tell me it was Joan who came down to my house through the woods? Why shouldn't I know she was checking things out to make sure the bad guys weren't there?"

"Why should I tell you anything?" asked ever-friendly Ted.

Joan stood in front of the other agents and made a broad gesture that took in most of western civilization. "All right, let's secure the place. Check everything out."

The agents began to move.

"Give me the guest list," said Ted. He took it and frowned some more. "You know these people?" When I said yes, he didn't seem to believe me. Once again I was glad I wasn't a Secret

Service agent. What suspicious lives they led.

"Before the girls get back and use up all the hot water," said Zee, "I am taking a shower and washing my hair."

I decided not to repeat my sage maxim that the reason women don't run the world is because they don't have time to do that and wash their hair, too.

Later, when John Skye's Wagoneer came down the drive, whichever twin was driving was wide-eyed.

"Cricket told us who she was while we were out there on the beach! You'd think we would have guessed, but . . . And now there's a couple of Secret Service guys and an Edgartown cop up there at the end of your driveway! They stopped us and checked our names on a list before we could come on down! Wow!"

"It's like those security checks on airplanes," I said. "They may be inconvenient, but we should be glad they're there."

"I guess!"

"And are your twin noses out of joint because we've all been fibbing about my cousins?"

"No! We think it's great! Wait till we tell our friends! Besides, Cricket's still our friend, anyway, even if she isn't Debby anymore!"

To verify this, there were hugs inside the Wagoneer. Then Karen and Debby climbed out and there were good-byes and see-you-laters before the Wagoneer headed for home so the twins could change into their clambake clothes.

"How were things at the beach?" I asked my sandy-haired, salty-skinned cousins.

They'd been great.

And was Acey Doucette coming to the afternoon shindig?

He was. Karen might have someone back in Washington, but a beau in the hand was . . . etc.

Well, I thought, maybe being in the presidential presence would infuse Acey with greater literary energies; enough, perhaps, so that he might even finish a chapter and start another. Who knew what good might come of this encounter?

While Karen and Debby took turns in the shower, Zee was in our bedroom, busy doing whatever it is that women do with themselves to make themselves feel presentable. Some women, I was sure, probably had to do a lot of that, but I couldn't see that Zee needed to. Whenever I mentioned this, however, she would smile patiently, pat me on the cheek, and say I just didn't understand, but that it wasn't my fault, because it was a testosterone thing, a kind of blindness caused by hormones.

The tables and chairs in the yard and up on the balcony would seat everybody who was coming, so I didn't have to tend to that. Out by the beech tree I set up the table I use to hold food and utensils when we have clambakes, and put the gas grill nearby with its big cooking pot. I put some water in the bottom of the pot and emptied the bags of steamer clams on top of it, so they'd have time to thaw a bit more before cooking time. Then I went in and got to work peeling potatoes, carrots, and onions. When they were ready, I put them to boil on the stove, and cut kielbasa and linguiça into short lengths, to go along with the hot dogs I'd also be cooking. When that was done, I fixed garlic bread and wrapped it in tinfoil for future warming, then melted enough additional butter to go along with the steamers and mussels, and set that pot at the back of the stove. Then I got ice out of the freezer and put it in my big cooler, along with a case of Sam Adams, soft drinks, and three bottles of sauvignon blanc, the house white.

I put the cooler in the shade out by the food table and set a garbage can for rubbish beside the entrance to the outdoor shower, and I'd done as much preparing as I could do for the moment. Later, just before people were scheduled to show up, I'd put out the paper napkins, plastic glasses, heavy paper plates, and the plastic knives and forks. Plastic and paper. Two more of the handy materials of modern times. Tacky, maybe, but very utile.

Not unlike myself, perhaps.

I was showered, shaved, and togged in clean shorts and a T-shirt that said YOU CAN'T KILL A DEAD DOG when the first cars began coming down the drive. By the time the presidential caravan arrived, late, as the Great Man had a habit of being, or so I'd been told, everybody else was already there, including Jake Spitz, who, when Walt Pomerlieu's name came up, refrained

326

from gloating over the fact that Pomerlieu was Secret Service, not FBI.

The presidential caravan was shorter than usual, consisting of only three cars: the armored Suburban that conveyed the Callahans; one car full of casually dressed agents, who immediately made themselves as inconspicuous as possible; and a third, which contained, among other people, photographers who seemed intent upon recording everything for posterity.

President Joe Callahan turned out to be a tall man with a thick head of hair and a pair of sharp eyes. He and his wife were cordiality itself, greeting Zee and me with apparently unaffected pleasure, kissing their shining daughter, shaking the hands of deferential Karen and the other guests, and, in general, making everyone feel at ease. They were born politicians, I thought, as the cameras clicked.

I handed the president a beer and poured white wine for his wife, then pointed to the cooler. "That's the bar. The host gets you the first one. After that, you're on your own."

They laughed. "Fair enough."

Cricket was right there with Allen Freeman. "Daddy, can I have a beer? J.W. wouldn't give me any, but he says that today if it's okay with you, it's okay with him."

"Well, I don't know," said her mother.

"Mom! I'm sixteen! It's only one beer. You let me have wine and champagne sometimes!"

"Just a little. And only sometimes."

"Daddy? Just one beer?"

"It's illegal."

"Just one?"

He smiled. "Just one."

"All right!"

"Now that you've got it," I said to her, "I hope you appreciate it. That's Sam Adams, America's finest bottled beer, and you shouldn't waste a drop."

"How about Allen? Can he have one, too?"

"I'm going over to get the grill started," I said. "I'm not going to be watching the cooler."

"I think I'll settle for a soda," said diplomatic Allen, as I walked away. He still seemed a bit stunned by his discovery that Debby was really Cricket Callahan.

There was food for all.

The first course was littlenecks on the half shell, accompanied by seafood sauce. Next came clams Casino, a dish so good that it's gobbled up even by people who don't think they like clams, including those who wouldn't think of eating a littleneck. Then came mussels steamed in white wine and served with garlic butter. Yum, as always.

Next came stuffed quahogs, hot and spicy from the oven. I use a bastardized version of Euell Gibbons's recipe from *Stalking the Blue-Eyed Scallop*, one of the finest of the natural food cookbooks. What an irony that old Euell, who developed so many excellent recipes for wild foods, should have died of stomach ulcers. Either there's no justice, or God has a wicked sense of humor.

Finally came the steamers, accompanied by boiled potatoes, carrots, and onions, and by steamed kielbasa, linguiça, and hot dogs, and by garlic bread.

There was watermelon for dessert.

Delish, from soup to nuts. When we were through, the garbage barrel was stuffed with rubbish, and the humans were stuffed with food.

The cameras had clicked steadily and, as near as I could tell, everyone had had a good time. Now, the Secret Service people began to assemble.

Joe Callahan was sitting with me on our balcony, looking out over the garden, Sengekontacket Pond, and the barrier beach beyond to the waters of Nantucket Sound, where sailboats were motoring home in the windless evening. "Terrific place you've got. I see why Cricket loves it here. I wish we could live like this."

"But you can't," I said. "You've chosen another kind of life."

He looked at me, then nodded. "Yes. Of course you're right."

A Secret Service agent stood looking up at us. "Mr. President, you have another engagement this evening."

Callahan stood up. "A lot of this job is going places you don't necessarily want to go and seeing people you don't necessarily want to see."

He put out his hand. "Thank you for everything. Let us know if you ever get to Washington. We'd like to see you. Cricket, especially. She's become very fond of you."

"If we get there, I'll let you know."

By the time we got downstairs, someone had arranged our friends into a sort of waiting line, and the president and his wife and daughter passed along it, shaking hands and saying good-byes, on their way to the caravan of cars that was lined up in preparation for departure. There, Zee and I got final handshakes, and a quick kiss for each of us from Cricket.

"Good-bye," she said. "I had a wonderful time. You're good cousins. I got to go to the beach, and to go clamming, and to pull in a bluefish, and to go conching, and shooting, and to meet people I never would have met!"

"Come back," I said. "You have what it takes to be an islander."

"I will!"

Then the caravan was gone.

"Well," said Zee, "they were nice."

"I wouldn't want his job," I said.

"No."

"I think there's enough beer for one more round," said John Skye, heading for the cooler.

"Not for me," said Zee, her hand on her stomach. She turned toward me and hooked her other hand around my neck and pulled me down for a kiss. "I love you."

"Even though I don't have a steady job?"

"And because you don't own a suit, either."

We'd barely finished breakfast the next morning when a car came down the driveway.

"Somebody forgot something," said Zee.

But nobody had forgotten anything. The car stopped and Mike Qasim got out.

Good grief. I went out onto the lawn to meet him. He didn't seem to have his Persian dagger, but I didn't know if that was a good sign.

"Put up your hands and defend yourself, you wife thief! I'm going to teach you not to seduce my Dora!" Mike raised his fists and set his feet.

He was only as tall as my armpit and I outweighed him by fifty pounds, but he was a terrier.

"I never even tried to seduce your wife," I said. "We asked her to come here so she could fix Cricket Callahan's hair. To change the way she looked, so she could go places and not be recognized. You know who Cricket Callahan is. She's the daughter of the president of the United States."

"Oh, ho, what a liar you are! Cricket Callahan here? You must think me a fool! But you are the fool, as well as a wife thief! Put up your fists!" He tucked his chin into his shoulder and shuffled around on the grass, throwing short jabs in my direction.

I studied his style. "It wouldn't be a fair fight," I said. "I'm a lot bigger than you are."

"Oh, you coward! Don't worry about me. I am going to beat you until you can't stand! Defend yourself, I say!" Mike's face was red and he threw a right cross through the air.

"I'm not worried about you," I said. "I'm worried about me. There's twice as much of me for you to hit as there is of you for me to hit. It isn't fair."

He paused. "What are you saying? You are afraid to fight? Oh, you coward!" He shuffled toward me, throwing that jab through the air.

I held up my hands to stop him. "All right," I said. "I'll fight you. But it's got to be fair." I turned and called to Zee. "Bring out a piece of chalk, please."

"Chalk?" asked Mike, lowering his hands.

Zee came out of the porch with a piece of chalk and looked at me with raised brows.

"Now, here's what we'll do," I said. "Mike, you come over here and stand right in front of me, and Zee will mark the outlines of your body on my clothes. Okay? Then, when we fight, you can only hit me inside the chalk marks. That will make it a fair fight, because we'll both have the same target area. All right?"

Mike frowned.

"You have to do it," I said. "I'm an innocent man, as my wife or your wife will tell you, if you ask them, so if I have to fight you, I don't want to be at a disadvantage. So come on over here and we'll mark off your target area."

Mike lifted his fists and let them drop. He frowned at me some more, then he looked at Zee. "Is it true what he says about Cricket Callahan? And that you were here all the time my wife was here?"

She nodded gravely. "It's true. It was a top-secret operation, so no one, not even you, could know about it. But now the president has gone back to Washington and the story can be told." She waved a finger at him. "You must learn to trust your wife, Mike. She loves you and would never betray you."

His eyes narrowed, then widened. "You are right, madame! It was an act of patriotism, then! How excellent! Wait until I tell my friends and customers!" He came forward and shook my hand, then went and shook Zee's. "My apologies, sir. Oh, what a glorious day!"

He got back into his car and drove away.

Zee looked at me and shook her head. "Where did you come up with that chalk bit?"

"Knowledge from a misspent youth. When I was a kid, I read that Abe Lincoln pulled that trick on somebody and got away with it. Anyway, I'm glad it helped defuse Mike."

"Me, too. What a manly man you are."

"Virility is its own reward, my sweet."

Early in September, we got a package containing an inscribed photograph of the Callahans and the Jacksons together on our front lawn. We hung it in the living room, beside the one of Zee and her forty-two-pound bass (seven pounds bigger than any I'd ever caught).

A week later, smiling a radiant smile I'd not seen before, Zee handed me an envelope. I opened it and found myself looking at a Father's Day card. It was months until Father's Day, and it took me several heartbeats to know what it meant. Then I felt a rush of excitement.

Three recipes used in
A Deadly Vineyard Holiday

(All delish, of course)

STUFFED BLUEFISH
(Page 69)

Catch or buy a bluefish.
Scale it and fillet it.
Use as much of it as you think you'll need.
Place one fillet, skin-side down, in a greased
  roasting pan.
Cover the fillet with the stuffing of your
  choice. (I use store-bought mixes, then
  doctor them up with various spices and
  other stuff that I like, including some hot
  sauce.)
Place the second fillet, skin-side up, on top.
Bake, uncovered, in a 400-degree oven until
  done (about 20 minutes, depending on the
  size of the fish).

RITZ SCALLOPS
(Page 92)

1 pound of scallops
1 cup crushed Ritz cracker crumbs
1/2 cup of butter

Mix scallops and crumbs together in a buttered baking dish, pour the butter over the top, bake for 25 minutes at 375 degrees. (Note: J.W. doubles this recipe in this book.)

CLAMS CASINO
(Page 321)

Open as many hard-shell clams (quahogs) as you think you'll need.
Loosen the meat from each clam and place it in a half shell.
To each half shell, add a bit of garlic butter, maybe some bread crumbs, some spices you think you might like, and top the whole thing with a square of bacon. If you don't eat bacon, use turkey bacon. If you don't eat turkey bacon, don't use that either.
Put the clams on a cookie sheet and broil until the bacon is crisp.